"REAL CHANGE IN SOCIETY MUST START FROM INDIVIDUAL INITIATIVE."
THE DALAI LAMA

WRITTEN BY: KONN LAVERY
EDITED BY: WILL GABRIEL

reveal
BOOKS

EBOOK ISBN-13: 978-0-9958938-7-0
PAPERBACK ISBN-13: 978-0-9958938-6-3

PUBLISHED IN CANADA BY REVEAL BOOKS.
BOOK ARTWORK AND DESIGN BY KONN LAVERY OF REVEAL DESIGN.
PHOTO CREDIT: NASTASSJA BRINKER.
PRINTED IN THE UNITED STATES OF AMERICA.
FIRST EDITION 2018.

FIND OUT MORE AT:
KONNLAVERY.COM

THANK YOU

THAT'S RIGHT, I MEAN YOU. THE PERSON THAT IS HOLDING THIS BOOK RIGHT NOW. THANK YOU FOR TAKING THE TIME TO READ THROUGH THIS NOVEL. WRITING IS A JOURNEY AND THIS MARKS THE END OF A CHAPTER (PUN INTENDED) OF AN ERA IN MY LIFE. I BELIEVE THAT FICTION IS THE BEST WAY TO MASK TRUTHS, EDUCATE AND INSPIRE PEOPLE. THIS IS WHY I WRITE. SO READ INTO THIS BOOK AS MUCH OR AS LITTLE AS YOU'D LIKE.

I'D ALSO LIKE TO GIVE SPECIAL ACKNOWLEDGMENT TO THE PEOPLE WHO HELPED BRING THIS NOVEL TO LIFE: KYLE LAVERY, LEE "GOD DAMN" NIELSEN (BFA), LINDSEY MOLYNEAUX, LISA MOLYNEAUX, NICK MCQUADE, SAMANTHA GARNETT EYFORD, SUZIE HESS AND WILL GABRIEL.

I'D ALSO LIKE TO THANK MY MOTHER, BRENDA LAVERY FOR HER COUNTLESS YEARS OF SUPPORT IN MY CREATIVE OUTLETS. MY FATHER, TERRY LAVERY, MY SISTER, KIRRA LAVERY, NASTASSJA BRINKER, THE CITY OF EDMONTON AND SPANK.

ALSO A HUGE THANK YOU TO MY FRIENDS, FAMILY AND FANS WHO SUPPORT MY PASSION OF STORYTELLING.

IN THE DARKEST STREETS OF EDMONTON, CRIME IS AROUND EVERY CORNER. THE POLICE HAVE EXHAUSTED THEIR RESOURCES. CITIZENS ARE IN A CONSTANT STATE OF FEAR. THE CITY IS IN DIRE NEED OF JUSTICE. SOMEONE NEEDS TO GIVE THE FELONS WHAT THEY DESERVE – SKIP THE COURTS AND DELIVER THEIR VERDICT WITH A FIST FULL OF FURY!

AT LEAST THAT IS WHAT MICHAEL BRADFORD TELLS HIMSELF. HE STRUGGLES WITH VIOLENT TENDENCIES WHILE PERSONALLY INVESTIGATING THE CRYSTAL MOTHS, EDMONTON'S MOST NOTORIOUS GANG. HIS VIGILANTE METHODS GET CAUGHT ON FILM AND ARE UPLOADED TO THE WEB WITH THE HASHTAG YEGMAN. THESE VIDEOS CATCH THE ATTENTION OF A REBELLIOUS JOURNALISM STUDENT WHOSE ASPIRES TO COVER THE DEVELOPING STORY ON THE CITY'S UNDERGROUND HERO.

YEGMAN BY KONN LAVERY

It Goes Like This...

CHAPTER 1
BANG BANG

S team seeped from the black liquid that filled the paper cup. Coffee: a staple of the working man. The fuel that amplifies productivity. It also has the flavour of dirt. Like the majority of the working class, I need it to stay vigilant. Its taste is something that I simply got used to—kind of like my frequent use of cigarettes. I guess the two go hand in hand when you're in a high-stress environment day in, day out.

Wake up, I thought. I adjusted the utility belt of my dark-blue uniform then brushed the crumbs from my torso. Some of them rested between the crevasses of my work shirt and the gunmetal name tag by my chest reading *Michael Bradford*.

Another day on the force was about to start. Like the beginning of any workday, I had my pre-shift meal of caffeine and a muffin. If you could call that a meal. The combo isn't a glorious start to a day, but it's all I ever have time for. My focus is on the work. Despite its difficulty, the job is more rewarding than good eating habits. The challenges are why I have to mentally prepare myself every day. You never know when you could get stabbed.

I placed my paper coffee cup on my desk, next to the silver-framed photo of an elderly woman with curly grey hair.

Mom. I recalled how she humoured my interest in the law when I was growing up. Bonnie is her name, and I owe her a lot from my youth. That's why I want to make sure I take care of her in her old age.

Having her son become a cop wasn't easy on her. I'm sure she would prefer if I was strapped to a desk. If only she knew half of the chaos that goes on during the job. Unfortunately for Mom, it was the best option for me. Politics was never my specialty and being a lawyer was too technical. There just isn't anything else that gives the same rush as starting a day on patrol. No other craft has made me this excited. Computers? Art? Engineering? Come on, it's not even close. I guess I can be one of those cops who stays on the force for fifty years—or until they get shot. Hopefully, that will happen after Mom is gone.

Footsteps echoed down the hall, getting louder as another officer marched toward my desk. He brushed his slicked-back hair while looking over at me with his emerald eyes.

"Evening, sunshine," he said. It was Ace, my partner.

I swung my legs off my desk and looked up at him. It was basically like looking in the mirror. We have the same height and same build. If it wasn't for his hair, we'd look indistinguishable.

He stared at my cup. "Drink up. It's time to hit the road."

I took a sip of my coffee. "Just getting mentally ready. I'm still not used to doing beat work again."

"Yeah, it's the last week for this volunteer crap. We'll be back on patrol next week, hopefully in Three Delta," Ace replied.

"Wouldn't that be nice? These night shifts are killer." I snatched the remainder of my blueberry muffin from on top of the desk and devoured it before getting up, wiping my face.

"I heard a new club is having its grand opening night," Ace said, grabbing a notebook from his desk and putting it into his pocket.

"Really?" I downed the remainder of my coffee before tossing the cup into the garbage can that separated our desks. "Not sure how I missed that. Looks like we're going to have a hectic Friday."

"Yeah, well, it's better than responding to those Snapper calls."

"True, club kids are easier than that shit," I said, thinking of the infamous Snapper—a name that brings chills to many Edmontonian folk.

Ace shook his head. "What kind of coward preys on junkies?"

"Serial killers and drug dealers," I said with a smirk. My partner was right, though. The Snapper is selective with his victims. When he finds one, the first thing he'll do is beat their faces into a pulp. After he's done making them bleed, he breaks their necks.

"I hope we can catch the son-of-a-bitch," Ace said.

"One can hope. Major Crimes hasn't got a clue about it." I folded my arms. "So what's this new club?"

"It's called The Glowing Monkey. From what I know, it's one of those electronic dance clubs that are popping up all over the place."

"Oh great," I sighed. "As if we didn't have enough."

"It's rather close to Y Afterhours, so we're going to have to keep close tabs on some of the street urchins."

Street urchins: the inside name that Ace and I gave drug dealers that hustle on the streets. They're the bottom of the barrel—sometimes I'd argue they're below that—of the drug dealing distribution chain.

I rubbed my brow. "Street urchins aside, it's probably going to attract the Crystal Moths."

"Every club attracts that gang," Ace replied.

"Like a moth to the light."

Ace chuckled. "Nice one. That explanation makes more sense than their ridiculous dress code. Have you ever seen one not in white?"

"Nah, every single one dresses like that. It's like they're in a boy band."

"It makes them easy to spot. Maybe we'll see some tonight." Ace pulled out a ring of keys from his side pocket. "Let's roll."

I nodded and the two of us left our desks. We marched side by side down the fluorescent-lit halls toward the front entrance. Our exit led us to the lobby where about half a dozen civilians were lined up, waiting to chat with the police manning the front desk.

"I don't know where he is! That's why I am here!" came a raspy voice from a stick-thin, wrinkly lady in dirty jeans and a torn windbreaker. She leaned against the counter, speaking to the officer on the other side of the glass.

Another man sat in a chair at one of the lower stations beside the door Ace and I entered from. He was large and had grease stains on his shirt. He gripped a cane, breathing heavily. "I just don't want him coming near me anymore. He makes me feel unsafe."

I held my breath as my partner and I walked by the man, trying to avoid his unbearable odour. Either he didn't care about his intense scent of sweat and must or he couldn't smell it.

Ace and I exited through the front entrance, pushing the door aside and embracing the cool downtown scenery of skyscrapers and the darkening sky. We're assigned to the main station in the heart of the city.

"I never liked doing front-desk work," I muttered as we walked down the concrete staircase.

"You and me both," Ace said.

Only once was I assigned to work the front desk. I wanted to give it a try to see if I could help people in a way that didn't involve street action. I thought it might put Mom's mind at ease and I could learn to enjoy sitting still. That didn't work out. Now I avoid it as much as possible. You need a special level of patience to deal with the public while restrained to a desk. It's like working at a call centre, but you can never hang up the phone.

"You know, Ace, I'd really like to be able to do something more," I said.

"Do more?" he asked.

"Yeah. This beat work for the past week has got me thinking: I'd like to get involved with solving cases." We stepped down the last set of stairs.

"Cases? You mean like being a detective?"

"Yeah, I think we'd be able to get more results than we can just doing patrol. We could go after the street urchins' higher-ups."

"What's this we? That's way too much paperwork. Leave that stuff to guys like Glenn Hayes. He's good at his job and we're good at our job." He pointed at me. "You of all people would get frustrated without the constant stimulation of the streets. You *just said* you didn't like the front desk."

"Yeah, you're right about that. Just pondering the idea. It'd be nice to start seeing some results first-hand, you know?"

"Look at you, Mr. Do-Gooder," Ace said with a smirk as we approached our squad car. He unlocked the unit with his remote starter and headed to the driver's side. "I'll drive this time," he said, opening the door and ducking into the vehicle.

"I guess I'm saying I'd like to do more," I stepped in and buckled my seat belt as Ace started the engine, causing the patrol unit to roar to life.

Ace shifted the car into reverse. "As you always do. You know what I think?"

"Besides getting a girlfriend?" I replied, knowing how he brought the topic up any time he felt I got too preachy about anything.

"I think you need more of a life outside of work."

"Not a lot interests me. Sometimes I wonder if I am going to be one of those people who does the same job for the rest of his life."

"I get that fear too, but do you really want to get into all of that extra typing? Personally, I like what we do and how we do it."

"So do I. But sometimes it's discouraging."

"How so?"

"We have to be incredibly cautious. One mistake and it's a big internal investigation."

"Well, that's a part of the job, Michael. You knew that when signing up." Ace shifted back into drive and turned out of the station toward to the main drag of downtown: Jasper Ave.

After four blocks, we came up to a red light then turned off to the main road. I broke the silence: "It'd be nice to appreciate the city again."

"You're full of deep thoughts today," Ace said, spinning the wheel.

I eyed the bright lights of the oncoming traffic and licked my lips. "It's this beat work. Think about it. We spend all our time out here making sure the streets are safe—seeing the darker sides of the city. Where's the good side?"

Ace let out a laugh. "Good? Come on, Michael, that's all a matter of perspective."

I raised my eyebrow. "You don't believe in good or evil?"

"No, I don't. I think we're all just people. Some put themselves in difficult situations that conflict with the majority. Their stance is, more often than not, the law. Someone breaks the law, and we bust them. It's that simple."

"Humour me: with that logic, do you think a killer is okay?"

Ace shook his head. "What? No. Of course not."

"Is it wrong?" I asked.

"Sure," Ace said.

"So, something wrong is evil—not good. The two aren't a matter of perspective, Ace."

"Evil is. A serial killer doesn't see what they're doing as wrong. Like the Snapper, for example. They're mentally sick."

I shook my head. "He's not sick. He's a monster, and that makes him evil."

"Whatever. Doesn't really matter what you call it. I enjoy helping people, and this is the best way for me to do that."

"Same here. It's not like I'm good at negotiating with people."

"Which is another reason why detective work isn't for you," Ace said. "Also, why a girlfriend would do you some 'good.'"

I rolled my eyes. "Yeah." I sighed, eyeing the busy sidewalks across the street.

It was shortly after nine, and we were on One Delta, the shift that goes from nine to eight in the morning. The bars already had people lining up outside of their doors. The bouncers at the front were checking IDs before they let people in. I couldn't help but wonder how many of those were fake IDs. Or how many bouncers let someone in for an under-the-table offer— of any kind. And who was smuggling in drugs or weapons.

The next alley we drove by had four guys and a girl walking from the main drag, laughing and lighting up a cigarette—or was it a joint? The one girl had a chrome flask. She tried to conceal drinking from it with her coat. Her drunken movements made it all too easy to spot.

I'd love to stop and fine them, I thought. Realistically, it wasn't worth our effort. Besides, this is the last week we're volunteering to do beat work, and this wasn't our area.

What we would do is get to our section, park the unit, and cover a one-to-three-block radius before returning to the vehicle. Then we'd move the unit and repeat the cycle. The normal beat routine.

Ace glanced over at me. "Hey, let's take a drive around to The Glowing Monkey before we park. See what we have to look forward to later this evening." He pressed on the gas to pass the just-turned yellow light, speeding through the intersection.

"What street is it on?" I asked.

"Just up this block."

Ace turned the vehicle away from Jasper Ave and into a darker street leading north. Up ahead, we could see bright neon lights on the left side of the road coming from a two-floor building. The rest of the street was pretty dull. A number of construction signs blocked the road where potholes would be filled, reducing the road into two lanes from the regular four. Only the one narrow, black building was lit up. Swarms of people cluttered the sidewalk and trickled out onto the closed-off lanes.

"This is it: The Glowing Monkey," Ace said.

Our car passed the club slowly, letting us take a good look at what was in store for us later. The club goers wore a range of attire including furry cat-eared hats, baggy pants, beads, and glow sticks. Some guys wore clean dress shirts and the ladies were in skimpy skirts. It was typical wear for a dance club.

Directly above the front door of the club was a green neon sign in bubbly text. "What a stupid name," I said. The sign was complete with yellow lights in the shape of a monkey. The rest of the building was a black matte. The main floor had no windows—only the one door. The second floor did, showing purple lights on the ceiling inside.

"We never used to have so many of these electronic clubs in the city," I stated. "What happened to kids being into rock and roll?"

Ace shrugged. "No idea. It probably doesn't help that the Crystal Moths started popping up in the past year. It really changed the place."

"Yeah, they put a spin on the whole nightlife. I'm still baffled at how they managed to grow so quickly."

"We had a pretty good handle on the gangs, but these guys are crafty. Now they have everyone craving their crack and MDMA."

"Everything that a party kid wants." I sighed. "This city is in need of a massive cleanup."

"Tell that to the mayor." Ace raised his eyebrow. "Maybe he can pull some magical funds out of his ass or something. Oh wait. No. He'll just have us go on speeding ticket raids."

"That's not the problem."

Ace shook his head. "I was joking. We need more officers. Until then, we do what we can."

Do what we can? I thought. Don't get me wrong, I have major respect for my partner, but sometimes he says the dumbest things. We only do what we can within the constraints of the justice system. The advantage criminals have is that they don't obey any protocols. Crafty pricks can murder, rape, and steal while we chase their tracks. By the time one transgression is handled, a couple more slip under the radar. My partner doesn't get that, and sometimes it isn't worth arguing with him. He prefers to shrug things off.

"Let's get started. We should be on foot," I said.

"All right. Let's go a little further west. We'll make our way back to The Glowing Monkey once it's closer to midnight. Things will get a little busier then."

"Good plan."

Ace drove back down to Jasper Ave, heading for 109th Street. The drive was a bit mundane. From the car, we could only observe all the activity. I stared out the window like a dog, just waiting for the right opportunity to get out onto the street. Waiting to sink my teeth into the first fool that did something wrong. It was that unmatched rush I got at the start of a shift kicking in.

"You know, I've been thinking." Ace scratched his neck. "You ever look at one of those robot vacuums?"

I squinted and looked over at my partner. "What?"

"It'd be nice to not have to vacuum on your own, you know?"

"I guess." I looked back at the sidewalks as we passed an alley, eyeing the sea of clubbers entering and leaving the various bars.

"I just find it such a chore, and the girlfriend gets annoyed when I don't do it. A robot would solve our problem. I think . . ."

I lost track of Ace's comments as we passed an alley where a group of three men dressed in white suits walked in a single row. *White suits*, I thought. My eyes widened. *Crystal Moths*. "Hey, Ace. Check out those three in the alley."

Ace quickly glanced over then brought his eyes back to the road. "So? Let's park and start the beat."

"They're in white. Pull down the alley so we can profile them."

Ace sighed. "Fine. Then, we park." He changed into the left lane and quickly pulled a U-ie, backtracking to the alleyway.

The high beams from our unit lit up the alleyway as we rolled onto the crooked road. The lights shined directly onto the backs of the three men.

The one to the right turned around. He had slicked-back hair and a goatee. He patted the back of the shorter, bald man in the middle. All three of them moved over to the right side, including the tall, slim man on the left.

Ace pressed the radio button on the dashboard and spoke. "Control from One Delta Two Three. We have potential Crystal Moths on 107th Street and 102nd Ave." Ace decelerated the vehicle as we passed the three.

I held my breath, not blinking, and eyed the three men. They glared at our unit as the hood moved passed them.

"One is Caucasian, one African American, the other Asian. All dressed in white suits. The Caucasian: slim with dark, gelled hair. Asian: bald, slightly shorter, and built. African American: tallest, ponytail." Ace stated.

I took note of their hands, pants pockets, and belts. None of them appeared to be concealing weapons. They were clean. There was nothing we could work with, despite the obvious fact that they were Crystal Moth members.

The voice of a female came through the radio, distorted. It was Stacey. She generally worked the evenings. "One Delta Two Three from Control, noted."

The three men moved over to the side of the alley as Ace pressed on the acceleration. "I will admit, they are out for trouble."

I wiped my face. "If only there was another form of identification for the Crystal Moths."

"Supposedly there is," Ace said.

"That's all speculation," I said. "Any Crystal Moth we've brought in hasn't had scarification."

Ace turned the car back onto the street. "Yet here you are getting worked up on profiling these guys based on speculation."

"Well, yeah. That's not the point."

"You're too ambitious. That's what gets you into trouble with the sergeant."

I folded my arms and stared out the window. I've gotten into heat with the sergeant for some of my more direct approaches. He got pissed off any time I tried to do what was right if it differed from the procedural course of action. I suppose keeping his squad in line is his job, though.

"We'll keep an eye on those guys," Ace said. "Come on. Let's start strolling."

He brought the unit a block over, parking by a meter near one of the major intersections on Jasper Ave and 109th Street. This section has a bar on all four corners and a plaza with restaurants, cafés, and a liquor store, making it a popular attraction for the downtown lifestyle.

Ace unbuckled his seat belt and put on his deep-blue officer's hat complete with a central badge and a red horizontal stripe wrapped just above the beak. "Shall we?"

I got out of the vehicle and put on my own hat, slamming the door shut before placing both hands on my buckle and eyeing the busy streets. The two of us began walking side by side toward Jasper Ave. Considering it was the weekend, the beat work would most likely consist of ticketing people for public indecency, open bottles, and drunken fights.

"So what are your thoughts on that vacuum?" Ace asked as we crossed the street onto Jasper Ave.

"I don't know, I don't think it's that huge of an issue to vacuum the place on your own. Let's just stay focused."

"Are you taking Britney's side?" Ace asked jokingly.

A group of what looked like college kids stepped aside so Ace and I could walk by. Two of them were boys and the other three were girls wearing light coats and shivering from the cool air.

"Good evening." Ace tipped his hat at them.

"Howdy, officers!" One of the boys, blond, waved at us with a slanted smile.

Kind of a doofus, I thought while giving the group a cold stare. *Would have they stepped aside for another group of pedestrians who weren't wearing the uniform?*

The further we walked, the more compacted the sidewalks were with people. They stumbled and ran up and down the streets. Some talked loudly while others weaved in and out of the crowds to get further ahead. The large groups of people that stood still on the sidewalks were directly outside of bars, smoking, talking, and laughing.

We were about to pass our first bar. It used to be one of the city's most popular locations: Oil City. It was where the city's hockey team would go and party at after a game. Now, I've lost track of what the bar's called. They change their names so quickly. Ace and I still call it Oil City.

"You fucking asshole!" came the nasally voice of a blonde girl in a short, tight black dress. She stomped in high heels like a newborn calf, storming up to a man with jacked arms and no neck, wearing a tight black shirt and jeans that made his ass poke out.

"Baby girl," the man said, reaching out to grab her hips.

"Don't you fucking touch me!" She snarled and spat at his face. The saliva launched from her mouth onto his nose with a splatter. "I know what you and Jessica did last night."

The man's eyes widened as if they were about to pop out of his face. His veins rose from his neck.

"Looks like we got a roid-rager," Ace muttered.

Roid-rager: an inside term we use to describe testosterone-filled men who are short-tempered, well-built, and find any reason to start a fight. Basically, the male version of a drama queen. These stereotypes often *juice* to gain better performance during their workout routines, which complements their short tempers.

"You bitch. You trying to give me AIDS or something?" He wiped the saliva from his face and snatched the girl's arm. "What's your problem?"

"Hey, man. Keep it cool," came another man's voice from the crowd. He stepped out, slightly thinner and fashioning a well-trimmed beard.

"Stay out of it, prick." The roid-rager turned to face the man, pulling the girl with him.

"Let go of me!" she cried.

The scenario was intensifying rapidly. Thankfully, we were close enough to de-escalate the situation before anyone got hurt—as long as the roid-rager didn't overreact.

I stepped in front of Ace and picked up momentum, moving through the crowd that blocked our way to the three. People were quick to move aside. The ones that didn't were guided by their friends.

Ace was right behind me. We had dealt with this sort of thing before. More often than not, our presence is enough to bring the conflict to a sudden stop.

I exited the sea of people with my arm behind my back and my hand just above my gun holster, stopping with one side shifted forward about two metres from the roid-rager. "Is there a problem?" my voice boomed. I stared directly into his brown eyes.

The roid-rager turned toward me. He stared, not letting go of the girl's arm. "No, officer. We're just having a chat."

I nodded, pressing my tongue against my bottom jaw. *I'd love for him chat with my fist.* My patience for those types of smartasses is thin. I don't enjoy dealing with sly remarks. Plus, his inflated sense of masculinity was aggravating.

Stay calm. Follow procedure, I thought.

"He was hurting me!" the girl whined. She was probably overacting. Seeing the way she dressed, it was safe to profile her as a girl that craved attention from those around her.

"Why don't you let go of the girl?" I stepped closer to the man. One metre away.

The roid-rager released her and raised his hands. "*All right*. Nice to see the law take the side of an AIDS-spitting whore."

I stepped closer to the roid-rager until we were about a foot apart. I knew Ace was close behind me, though I was probably pushing it more than Ace would prefer. It was difficult for me to let people get the last remark in. Can't people just accept defeat?

"Look, officer," came the voice of the bearded man. He came up beside the roid-rager and me. "We're just having a few drinks. It isn't anything to be alarmed of. My friends here are just having a bad night."

"Is that so?" I raised an eyebrow, scanning him, the roid-rager, the blonde, and back to Ace who was off to my left. My partner kept his hands on his back hip where his holster was. He kept his eye locked on the roid-rager.

I smiled at the bearded man. "Fair enough. We all have our rough days, don't we?"

The bearded man smiled back. "That we do."

Sometimes, that involves spitting on people, I thought.

Ace and I stepped back into the crowd, leaving the three drunken fools to continue with their evening.

"Good call." Ace wiped his nose. "I really did not want to get involved with that."

"Nor did I. But that roid-rager was beginning to annoy me. It took a lot of discipline not to do anything."

"I know. Remember how you used to be? I'm proud of you," Ace said.

"Yeah, but those scumbags got what they deserved," I said, recalling the several sticky scenarios that I've been involved in. The media called them "police brutality"—which gets more views than "officer uses reasonable force." The sergeant also tore me a new one and suspended me for a good four months. Since then, I've worked on my behaviour to avoid that headache.

Ace pointed at me. "You're lucky the sergeant didn't have you hand in your gun for good, right there and then."

"The first time or the last time?" I smirked.

"Every time! You've got to take those warnings more seriously."

"It's hard to remember them, honestly. All of the faces and scenarios start to blur after a while." *One giant cesspool of crime.*

"I clearly remember how miserable you were while you were suspended. Look, let's save this chat for a drink."

Ace was right. We were on patrol. Chatting about how I would step beyond my boundaries was not the best idea. What if a civilian heard us?

The two of us continued our patrol for what seemed to be only minutes, when in fact, several hours had gone by. Once you're on duty, time is a blur—unless you get into a fight. Then, a moment lasts forever.

We marched for a couple of blocks before returning to our unit. Then we drove several blocks, parked, and patrolled again. Walk, drive, park, repeat. Most of our patrols are simply to provide a presence to the public so nothing escalates.

Our radios went off several times with Control and other officers keeping in communication about the area or identifying potential suspects. No one had mentioned the three men we saw earlier in the evening. So far, the night was proving to be just another weekend downtown.

Finally, our beat brought us up to the same block as The Glowing Monkey. Ace parked the vehicle right on Jasper Ave before we started to walk up to the club. A part of me wanted to stand outside of The Glowing Monkey all night. That would be bad for business, wouldn't it? A good person would have nothing to worry about if they saw a cop standing outside a club—but that's the funny part: a *good* person. They didn't exist here. Everyone was up to something.

Our radio fuzzed again, and Stacey's voice came in from the station. "One Delta from Control. We have a call about the new club on 105th Street, The Glowing Monkey. Any units in the area?"

Ace stopped walking, pressing on his com. "Control from One Delta Two Three. Status?"

"A girl called about an assault."

"We're on our way. Only a block from the location," Ace said.

"One Delta Two Three from Control, confirmed," Stacey replied. "The girl said her name was Becky. She has black-and-red dreadlocks. She says she is by the front entrance. Currently three men—early to mid twenties—got into an argument and it escalated into a fist fight."

I nodded at Ace and spoke into my intercom. "All right. We're on the block."

Another officer spoke through the shared channel. "Control from One Delta Three Five, we're three blocks from the location. On pursuit." The voice was younger—one of the other units that patrolled downtown. Considering that a fight was breaking out, we'd need to have a number of officers on standby. If it escalated from fists to weapons, we'd swarm the scene.

I felt my heart race. This was the moment Ace and I were waiting for all evening. Well, at least I know *I'd* been waiting for it. Ace is hard to read. Some days he wants action, and other days he wants an easy shift. Regardless, this was time to act.

"I guess we get some action after all," Ace said.

"Good," I replied.

"Honestly, I thought it was going to be at least two before we heard anything."

"That's how things used to be. Come on."

Ace and I said nothing more. We rushed up the dark block toward the bright glowing club. It was easy for us to spot the fight. Three men were on the road, two throwing punches and another on the ground.

"Cops are here!" shouted the crackly voice of a man in the crowd on the sidewalk.

The crowd observing the fight had spread well beyond the closed-off lanes and into oncoming traffic. The drivers had to carefully maneuver around them. There was a dreadlocked girl out by the entrance, on her phone—presumably Becky. We'd have to get her witness statement when this was over.

I was about twenty paces from the three brawling men, clearly able to see the details of the scene. One of the three was wearing a white rag tied around his arm. He held another guy—had to be about 18—by the front collar of his shirt. He slammed his fist into the kid's face several times. Blood splattered from his now-cracked nose and oozed down into his mouth. The third guy wore glow sticks and was on the floor trying to get up. His movement was wobbly.

Obscure place for a rag. Especially a white one, I thought as I ran.

"Break it up!" Ace shouted, pulling out his baton.

The guy with the glow sticks got to his feet and charged into the group, knocking the white-rag-tied man off the kid.

Ace and I rushed into the brawl. I went to grab hold of the man with the white rag by the arms, but he drew switchblade from his pocket and swung at me.

The crowd screamed at the sight of the knife and backed away.

I instinctively pulled out my gun and pointed it at him. "Drop it!" I shouted.

The man eyed me and then Ace who stood off to his side. He was now separated from the other two he was fighting. The man dropped his knife, raised his arms, and took a deep breath. It was difficult to see his face through the sweaty, dark bangs that covered his eyes. His jaw clenched with frustration.

"Wrists together," I ordered.

Ace walked closer to man while sheathing his baton back into his belt. He then reached for his cuffs, causing them to jingle.

A gunshot fired and the man with the white rag jerked. Blood sprayed from the side of his head. The red liquid splattered onto Ace's face and against my hands.

Screams erupted from the crowd and they began to scatter in all directions.

"Everyone on the ground!" I ordered, stepping back as the man in front of me tumbled to the ground.

Ace squeezed the *talk* button on his radio. "Code One! Control from One Delta Two Three. A shot has been fired. Code One!"

Some of the people dropped to the floor as I scanned the crowd to see if I could spot where the shot came from. It was tough to locate—there were too many people buzzing around. *He jerked toward the club. It came from the other side.* I turned to eye the opposite side of the street. It was empty. An alleyway divided two brick buildings.

Ace pulled out his gun, moving toward me, and spoke into his radio. "We need all available units to The Glowing Monkey."

We kept our guns aimed low, standing back to back.

The crowd kept running down the street despite Ace's order. I scanned the swarm of people, mostly kids no older than twenty. Some got down on their knees. They kept low as their bodies shook in fear.

One man with slicked-back hair, dressed in a white suit, fled from the road and into the alleyway on the other side of the street.

"Ace! Alley!" I shouted. *White suit. The man from before?* "Freeze!"

The man glanced back at me and Ace with a smug smile as he reached into his blazer pocket.

No, I thought, watching as the man began to remove his hand from his jacket. I aimed at the man and pulled on the trigger, feeling the pressure build until the trigger pulled completely. The bullet roared from the chamber, whizzing through the air and straight toward the man.

The bullet ripped through his shoulder, throwing him against the concrete wall. He slid down, collapsing to the ground. His wounded shoulder hit the road as he clenched his jaw, squinting in pain. His hands fell out of his blazer, dropping a cellphone.

A cellphone? I thought. "Fuck." My gut tightened.

A second gunshot went off through the alleyway. Ace and I hastily moved against the closest building. I pressed on the radio. "We have a second shot. Code one!"

A goddamn cellphone. No time to ponder—I neutralized him. I knew I would be paying for it later with a ton of unnecessary reports and the sergeant lecturing me about the use of firearms in the street. That smiling prick may have just had a cellphone, but I knew he was involved in this. Why would he run? Why would he be in white if he wasn't one of the Crystal Moths?

He was in the alley earlier. I know that was him. Unfortunately, it wasn't the time to think about it. It was time to act.

Blue and red lights began to highlight the scene as the sound of sirens blasted up from the other side of the street. Reinforcements.

I glanced further north to see that a couple of officers were rushing toward us—One Delta Three Five.

Stacey's voice came through the radio. "Copy that, we have—"

Another shot echoed through the alleyway, drowning out the sound from the radio. Some brick from the corner of the building shattered—the bullet's impact missing us by inches.

Quite frankly, I couldn't care less about what the radio was saying. The adrenaline was coursing through my system and I was focused on the gunman in the alley.

I gotta make this right, I thought. "Can you see him?" I asked, glancing back at the crowd of people to see that most of them had cleared the area. A few were still on the ground.

"I think he's behind the dumpster. I saw him slide down there," Ace replied.

The reinforcement unit parked in the middle of the street and two more officers came out of the vehicle with their guns drawn. More sirens echoed as red-and-blue lights were spotted on the opposite end of the alleyway. We had the gunman trapped.

I crept down on my knees. "Keep an eye out."

"We've got another unit boxing him in from the other side. Wait," Ace said.

I ignored his order and peeked around the corner carefully, low enough that I could see a pair of black dress shoes standing on the other side of the wheeled dumpster—exactly what I was looking for. Pressing the radio button, I said, "Suspect behind the dumpster." Carefully, I got down onto my chest and extended my arm with the gun pointed directly at the man's ankles.

"I got a clear shot, Ace."

"Michael, we have him boxed. He'll surrender. Stand down."

The feet moved forward. He was about to step out. His feet were still aligned with my gun. I could end this.

I pulled the trigger, and another bullet roared from the chamber and down the alleyway. The sound bounced off the walls, amplifying the noise. It was followed by a cry as the bullet shredded through one of the shoes, tearing open the flesh of his foot. The man collapsed to the ground, dropping his handgun. His arm stuck out from the dumpster—a white blazer.

"Now!" I shouted.

Ace pressed his radio. "Suspect down!" He moved first into the alley as I got to my feet and followed behind him. We kept our weapons pointed at the suspect. We rushed past the previous man I shot and around the dumpster toward the man on the ground. He wore a full white suit, was tall, slim and had a ponytail.

What a coincidence, I thought.

"Don't move!" Ace's voice boomed. He quickly kicked the gun from the man's reach. It slid against the uneven pavement until it hit the wall of the far building.

I holstered my gun and went for my cuffs as the officers from the other end of the alley caught up to us.

"You know we're going to be in a lot of shit for this," Ace said with a deep sigh. "You idiot."

"As you keep saying," I replied. "Look, though. These are the guys from earlier!" I argued.

"It isn't that simple! We're going to have a lot of explaining to do." Ace shook his head and took a step away, looking back at The Glowing Monkey.

Ace was right. I didn't fully think it through in the heat of the moment. I got trigger happy and wanted to neutralize the situation.

Ace will forgive me. We've been through this, I thought. *I know they're both Crystal Moths. That will be enough to justify my actions.*

I grabbed the man's arms and cuffed his wrists together from behind, keeping pressure on his head with my hand, my knee on his back. He exhaled heavily, clearly trying to ignore the pain in his foot. Chances were, he wasn't going to run. He was wounded. I just wanted to remind him that he lost. You don't shoot freely at someone. No. It doesn't work that way. Not with me.

ACE

YEGman

Chapter 2
OVER THE EDGE

The sound of rapid tapping on the plastic keyboard filled the office space. My fingers pressed forcefully with each letter I typed, filling out my report on the evening's event. That's the least rewarding part of the job—paperwork. The technicalities get on my nerves.

It's like writing a novel, I thought.

With my free hand, I grabbed my cup of caffeine and chugged the last bit of it before stacking the paper cup inside three empty ones. The coffee, the report—all of this could have been avoided if I didn't stupidly fire a gun and critically injure someone.

It was the right thing to do, I thought while punching the keys on the keyboard harder. Filling out the report revealed my oversight. How did I get so caught off guard? If I had waited for a split second, I would have seen that damned cellphone. I suppose I do get overeager when I see an opportunity to do what's right.

He's a Crystal Moth. He's guilty of something, I thought.

I finished typing a line of my statement and leaned away from the keyboard and took a deep sigh. I pressed my fingers against my forehead. There was still a great deal of work to do, leaving me exhausted and discouraged.

I should be asleep, I thought, looking up at the clock. It was four in the morning. *Damn beat work.*

"Don't stop now," Ace said in a monotone voice.

I leaned in my chair to see my partner at his desk, also typing away at his report.

"I know." I hunched back over my desk and started typing again.

We got to the station shortly after we cleared the scene and the forensics team arrived to investigate the shootings. It was only a matter of time before the sergeant arrived at the office to ream me out for using my gun.

"I don't get why you can't just keep your cool in scenarios like that," Ace said.

I exhaled through my nostrils. "I know. I messed up."

"I mean, why did you fire the gun twice? At an innocent bystander, at that."

"He resisted an order and ran! Look, let's not get into this now. Let's just get through this paperwork and we'll chat it over with the sergeant."

Ace raised his eyebrows. "All right, if you say so."

I could tell he was pissed. He's normally pretty cheery. Not this time. I don't blame him. It was me who didn't follow procedure and got him roped into this mess.

The two of us worked in silence, hammering away at our reports, awaiting our impending doom with the sergeant. The sergeant is split in many directions all the time: pressure from his superiors, his officers, and the politics. Hell, I swear the only times we get to see him are when something goes wrong.

Loud speech began to pick up down the hall. It echoed off the walls due to the emptiness of the station at this time in the morning. It was too early for Delta Three to be here and most of the Delta Two officers had gone home for the day.

The words were in a single voice. It was raspy, speaking abruptly into what I assumed to be a cellphone.

"No, we don't want to offer the press an inside story of the incident right now." The man's voice shot. It was unmistakably Robert Cliffman's voice—the sergeant. He always sounded aggressive because of how suddenly he ended sentences. Plus, his voice was amplified in the hall. I doubt he wanted to be up at this time in the morning to deal with some trigger-happy cop.

"He's pissed," I mumbled.

"As am I," Ace said.

"Are they still at the scene? Keep them behind the tape." The sound of dress shoes clicking against tile floor grew louder. Before we had a chance to get up, the sergeant was behind us, staring at us with his piercing blue eyes. He lowered his phone from his ginger-bearded mouth and spoke. "All right, Bradford and Borne." He eyed us both for a second before scratching his broad jaw. "My office." The sergeant stormed from our desks and brought the phone back up to his face, expecting us to follow. "Have them clear the street until the forensics team does what they need to do."

Ace and I exchanged glances and got up from our seats.

"He's going to tear us a new asshole." Ace shook his head. "Thanks."

My nostrils flared as I took the lead. Ace followed behind, keeping his hands in his pockets. I truly felt I took the right course of action with the knowledge I had at the time. I would just explain my side of the story to the sergeant. Simple as that.

He'll see why I did what I did. I had clear sight of the gunman and took aim. The other guy fled in the gunman's direction. They're both Crystal Moths, I thought. Then again, I had a gut-wrenching feeling that the sergeant was not going to agree with me. He would say I was careless in action.

At the other end of the station, we saw the sergeant in his office, standing behind his desk and still chatting on the phone. We entered the office and put our hands behind our backs, standing tall and waiting for the sergeant to get off his phone.

"Yeah." The sergeant said while pointing to the door.

Ace swung it shut and then stepped over to the blinds, twisting the handle to close the steel blades, providing privacy.

"Okay. Look, I've got to go, we'll catch up shortly." The sergeant took the phone from his ear and tossed it on his desk. It collided with a small stack of business cards. Some of the cards slid off the edge and onto the floor.

He looked at the cards and shook his head. "All right, what the fuck were you two doing out there?" He stared at us, brows slanted inward.

Ace ground his teeth and shifted his stance slightly. "We responded to a call about a fight outside of The Glowing Monkey."

"Yeah, I get that. Afterward." The sergeant walked to the other side of the desk, waving his hand. "I know it will be in the report, but I want to hear it first-hand from you. Paperwork bullshit aside." He raised four of his fingers. "Four gunshots were made, one man dead, and two severely injured. We have dozens of witnesses too."

I swallowed heavily while staring down at the stack of fallen business cards. *Michelle Houston. I've talked to that reporter before*, I thought, eyeing the card with the lady's name. It had the city's news logo on it.

I was trying to distract myself so I didn't speak up out of emotional frustration. I wanted nothing more than to explain why I had to take the course of action that I did. I could tell that the sergeant would not have any of it, though. Acting impulsively was a foolish behaviour. That's not what cops do. I was out of my role. The meeting with the sergeant was going to be a bitch-fest where we nod and say *yes*. Then it would be over.

Just take it, I thought, staring at a dark-blue business card of a Dr. Lang.

The sergeant shouted, "We are not here to shoot wildly at the first thing that scares us. Do you realize what this will look like on the news? That club attracts a younger crowd who probably took video of the event. That fiasco is going to be up online! How is that going to make us look then?" The sergeant exhaled slowly and stroked his beard. "We have a hard enough time keeping the media at bay with this social media craze. It isn't doing us or the city any favours."

I can't keep spacing out at these cards. The sergeant is ripping into Ace. I couldn't let him go down in flames with me. I tightened my fists and spoke. "Ace did everything by the book, sir."

"Excuse me?" the sergeant said.

I looked up at the sergeant. "Ace was following orders. I fired at a suspect who fled the scene."

"The guy you pegged in the shoulder? We're going to hear about that from the media when he gets out of the hospital."

"He was a suspect and he attempted to flee the scene," I repeated.

"The gunman's location was already identified!" The sergeant raised his arms.

"Why did he run toward him, then?"

"Christ, Bradford! We've been through this scenario before. You don't need to take down anyone who acts abnormally."

"He was in all white, like the gunman."

"You always have a justification too. Somehow you talk yourself into believing you did right. It's insane. If you weren't a good cop, you would have been kicked off the force years ago." He placed his extended fingers on opposite ends of his desk. "But I don't know how much longer I can protect you."

I swallowed heavily. At the back of my mind, I knew he was on my side, but he had to answer to the higher-ups. That's what worried me.

Ace stepped forward. "Sergeant, note though that Michael had right to his action." He glanced at me before continuing. "The man he shot first was with two other men, also in all white, earlier in the evening. We profiled them."

The sergeant shrugged. "So?"

Ace swallowed heavily. "The Crystal Moths all dress in white. Plus, the kid who was shot had a white rag around his arm."

The sergeant stood up and folded his arms. "That may be so, but again, that is speculation. You can't act on hunches like that. Major Crimes will look into it and I'll chat with detective Hayes about these details."

I cleared my throat before speaking. "The man I shot—we have his cellphone now. Prior to that, he was smiling at the whole fight scene. Who would smile at that unless they were involved?"

"That's a hunch, Bradford! If I didn't like you, this would be much easier." The sergeant shook his head. "But you're a real pain in the ass when it comes to the legalities of all of this." He pointed at the desk assertively several times. "You can't act based on intuition like that. He smiled and tried to run. Maybe he was a lowlife who enjoyed violence. Maybe he was on ecstasy—who knows?"

"So it'd be better to let him escape? We have his cellphone and tha—"

The sergeant cut me off. "And what if we can't find anything on it, huh? What then? Just make a public apology to the media, his family, and to him saying 'Oops, we shot you based on a hunch. Our bad.'" The sergeant shook his head. "No, we can't do that. You should know this."

I looked to the ground and clenched my hands tighter, my fingernails digging into the skin. The sergeant was a good man, but he was too tied down by legalities.

He's limited by the procedures. We all are. I straightened my posture and said, "I assure you, sergeant, he was involved."

"Why are you still arguing about this with me? You had the gunman trapped. He was the primary suspect." The sergeant stared at me without blinking.

Several moments of silence passed with none of us saying a word. The only sound came from the ticking of the clock on top of the wall, mounted behind Ace and me. We had all worked with each other for years and have been in scenarios like this. Ace would back me up when he could, even if there wasn't much else to say. When the sergeant stared in silence, it meant that was his final stance on the situation.

The sergeant scratched the back of his head and sighed. "It pains me to do this, but I need you to hand over your gun."

I blinked twice, my eyebrows slanted. "Sorry, sir?" I glanced over at Ace whose jaw dropped.

"You heard me, Bradford." He pointed at the desk, avoiding eye contact. "Drop it there."

"Are you suspending me?"

"Yes, I am. I don't want it to go this way, but there's no other option. Think about your impulsive behaviour." He cleared his throat. "What I am doing now is damage control. You are suspended until we have all the facts. We'll read your statement. This will look better to the news, better with the higher-ups, and to be honest"—he shook his head slowly and stared at me—"you need the break."

I bit my lip, trying to hold in the surge of energy I felt channel within my veins. It was a spark of rage that coursed throughout my body. I looked toward the wall where the sergeant kept his awards. I had to distract myself from eye contact. It was too much.

His trophies for being a cop—a good cop that followed the rules, I thought. The sergeant knew how to hold himself back, something that I'm clearly incapable of doing. Is that how he got to be a sergeant? Simply not acting when he knew something had to be done?

I know that smug Crystal Moth prick was involved, I thought, inhaling heavily through my nostrils.

"When was the last time you took a holiday?" the sergeant asked.

I shook my head. "I don't know, sir."

"Think of it as that. We just need to clear this shit up. Hand it over." The sergeant waved his open palm at me.

I unbuckled my utility belt and unharnessed my gun holster, placing it on the desk carelessly.

"Thank you," the sergeant said.

With a quick bow, I exhaled once more through my nose, trying to extract all of the boiling anger that engulfed my body. My arms felt ultra-charged, ready to hit the desk. My throat itched to roar out all of my frustrations. Frustration from the legalities, the documents, and the shaming I got for not taking the procedural action and choosing to do what was needed.

Without waiting to be dismissed, I stormed out of the sergeant's office. With my hands clenched into fists, I marched back to my desk to grab some of the belongings that I wanted to take home.

Just my notepad, my phone . . . Damn it, I still have to fill out the rest of that report. Ah, fuck the report, I thought.

"Michael!" came Ace's voice from behind me.

"Not now." I slowed my breathing, trying to keep myself civil. *Stay cool.*

"Michael." My head stayed down, but I could hear his footsteps to my left. "Look, we're going to get all of this sorted out. It's only temporary."

"Temporary?" I turned to look at my partner, his face painted with concern. "Who knows how long this suspension will last. Remember last time? The facts are pretty solidly against me. Maybe if this was my first fuck up. But no, it's not, Ace." I kept walking until I made it to my desk, hastily grabbing a tray filled with papers.

Ace walked up and folded his arms. "It's tough not to take this personally, I know."

I dumped the papers out and started filling the tray with my notepad, my phone charger, the photo of Mom, and several other necessities. "No, you wouldn't. Your record has always been spotless. The only times you have had shit happen is because of me." I grabbed the tray and double-checked my pocket for my car keys.

"Just go home and get some rest. Seriously." Ace scratched his neck as I passed him. "I've got to finish my report."

"I know," I said, walking away. Ace has a good heart—one of the few people in the world that I'm willing to trust. He's always had my back, and I know he worries about me. As do I. Suspension isn't easy to handle. I've seen cops go into spiralling depressions over it. It's like having a piece of you torn out. The thing you strive for in life is suddenly missing. This shit that the station is pulling is the tipping point. Why do I bother putting in so much effort if it results in this?

I can't handle this again. I pressed my lips tightly and stormed down the hall leading to the locker room where I had a change of clothes. I'd have to put them on and sorrowfully hand over the uniform.

The unfortunate thing is that nothing else quite interests me like policing does. Now that it's taken away from me—again—what the hell do I do? Just sit at home all day and watch the tube or read the papers like every other civilian—every other passive observer of the city in chaos? Simply wait and wish for things to get better?

After surrendering my uniform, I hurried out of the station and into the parking lot. There were only a handful of cars and a couple of officer units parked. The air was crisp, and the sky was a dark haze of blue that lit up in the east—it had to be around 6 a.m. now. Ace and I were at the office for far longer than I thought. That doesn't matter, though, because all I have to look forward to is pacing around and waiting until I hear back from the sergeant about the verdict of my career.

I guess I'll just sit at home with my dick in my hand, I thought, pulling my keys from my pocket and pressing the ignition button. The running lights lit up with the start of the engine, and the doors unlocked.

I opened the door to my black Range Rover and placed the tray on the passenger seat. I buckled in and shifted into reverse. Blind to my frustration, I slammed the acceleration, reversing hastily. I shifted the vehicle into drive and spun the wheel, steering to the exit of the parking lot.

"Off I go to sit and wait," I mumbled to myself. What else is there for me to do?

Chapter 3

Always Something To Do

D im yellow lights reflected off my small whisky glass. It rested on a coaster on top of a dark wooden counter that was covered in scratches and chips. The chipped varnish reflected images of the brick walls and black open ceiling. I grabbed hold of the glass, swirling it side to side, balancing it on the edge of its base. The glass was filled with a cheap whisky—J&B, I believe it was. To be honest, I wasn't sure anymore. All I knew was that this was the fourth glass of the evening. I've never been much of a drinker, so it's easy for me to get pie-eyed. Drinking seems like such a waste of time. It costs too much, and you feel like shit after.

That doesn't mean I can't enjoy a glass of wine or beer here and there, but drinking for the sake of getting stupid is beyond my understanding. Perhaps the mindset comes from being on the force for all these years. Dealing with bewildering drunks turned me off of embracing consumption. Now, being suspended, I found myself staring down at a glass, my forearm resting on the bar, sulking in my own misery. Drinking should be a social thing if I recall. What does it mean that I was drinking alone?

Spiralling, I thought, taking another sip from the glass. It was strong, bitter, and made me flinch a little. I don't have a tolerance for liquor, let alone whisky. It did give me something to feel, though, besides frustration, anger, and sorrow. Despite all the drinking, I found it tough to keep my mind from wandering back to last night's events.

What was I thinking?

If only I'd been more reserved, kept to my training, and ignored that smug prick, I'd be back at the station finishing off my report and Ace and I could have called it a day. Instead, I got to go home, lay down in my bed, and wait for the closest bar to open so I could drown in self-pity.

How long do I have to wait until the investigation is concluded? I thought. *Months? A year?* I made a mistake that I can't take back. One of those typical *only time will tell* situations.

"Reckless gunfire brought chaos to the streets of downtown," came the voice of the anchorwoman on the flat-screen television mounted behind the bar.

I leaned up and eyed the television to see the newscaster speaking over the early moments of a cellphone recording—obvious from the portrait view of the film—from someone who had been in the crowd outside of The Glowing Monkey last night, showing the three kids brawling.

"The video being played was uploaded to the web minutes after the event."

Yeah, and once it's on the internet, it's there for good.

"Warning: this video may disturb some viewers. It shows the unsafe environment that our youth are being exposed to in the night."

Great. I get to watch my fucking mistakes mock me while I drink.

The video was shaky, and the yelling from the crowd drowned out all else as the three kids brawled. It was still clear enough to see the chain of events.

"Cops are here!" shouted one voice from the crowd.

The camera shifted over to two equally built police officers—Ace and myself—approaching the three.

I shook my head and turned back to my glass. The last thing I needed was to have my screw-ups rubbed in my face by the news report. I leaned back, surrendering to the rest of the whisky in the glass. I slammed it back down on the table.

Screams and gunfire began to erupt from the television. I didn't bother to look. It was too fresh in my own mind. I eyed the bartender, an older gentleman who had long white hair and a beard. He wore a plaid shirt with a blue denim vest.

"Another," I called out, waving my hand.

The bartender nodded, still watching the television. He was a master of his space and didn't need to look at where his hands were going. He reached for another glass and the bottle of J&B then began pouring my drink.

"Shortly after the video ended, the police opened fire on a civilian. Chief of Police Bob White had this to comment:"

Not exactly what I wanted the chief to know me for. I slouched on the counter, pressing my fingers into my forehead.

The television switched to a shot of a bald man with a moustache, the chief, at the scene of the crime. It was daylight in the video. "We are aware of the video recordings that took place and are looking carefully into the specifics of this case. Evidence suggests gang-related activity, but we're not ruling out other possibilities."

The reporter brought the mic back to himself, off camera. "What about your officers freely opening fire on a civilian? Was the gunman not already identified?"

"Yes, they had fired their weapons. As for the details, we are doing a full investigation. For the time being, the officer is suspended until we have a better understanding of the situation."

The bartender placed the new glass of whisky on my coaster and nodded at me.

"Thank you," I said, taking another sip.

"Utter chaos," came a voice from the opposite side of the bar. The man stroked his wrinkly neck and flared his nostrils, exposing the long hairs inside. He had been there since shortly after I got arrived. Another early drinker.

I straightened up from the high stool that I sat on and raised an eyebrow. "How so?"

"You got gangs running around shooting up the youth. The police have their hands tied. They do something and then get in shit for it. You'd think the city would want them to take action."

I nodded. "That, I agree on."

"There's nothing anyone can do but damage control on these criminals that keep popping up. It never used to be this bad."

"Nope." I relaxed my posture, resting against the bar again with both arms. "It all began when the Crystal Moths appeared."

"Yeah, well, they've been here for a while and no one took them seriously."

"What do you mean?"

"Think about it. There aren't enough cops on the force to deal with them. The mayor is pissing away our resources with grants and culture. The real crimes were being overlooked. It was incredibly easy for the Crystal Moths to swoop in and claim the streets."

I rubbed my chin and nodded. The old man had a point: the Crystal Moths did fill a niche that was completely overlooked by everyone. "To counter that, the mayor has been trying to raise money to pay for a lot of the advancements the city needs to grow."

"We can't even fill the damn potholes on the road! Fix the foundation we got first before expanding. Both in the literal sense and the metaphorical!" The man laughed—a raspy, crackly sound. "I've been in this city for thirty years and have seen it grow, yet this has been one of the most poorly planned developments I've ever seen." He took a sip from the brown bottle of beer beside him and cleared his throat. "All I am saying is that Mayor Chard is overlooking some serious issues. The whole city is. I bet the mayor thought you could make the drugs and gangs go away by closing down the other after-hours nightclubs. No, these people adapt. It makes you want to snap the necks of these fools."

I squinted. "How do you know so much about this?"

The man looked at me with his saggy eyes. "Because I used to be an officer myself. I was in the thick of it all." He leaned from his stool showing his leg. "It wasn't until I was shot in the thigh that I called it off. My wife was always worried sick about me, and I finally decided to retire. I'm a little bored, but I suppose that's retirement."

"Where was the shooting?"

"It's been a decade or so. I don't think about it much." He took another sip from his beer. "But it doesn't hurt my interest in the city. If anything, I want to stay on tabs with it all. I miss being involved. It's frustrating to see the good guys unable to do anything because of the fools in charge. You can't wipe your ass without the okay from the chief, the council, and the mayor."

"So you think the city's the way it is because of the mayor and its council?"

"I'm saying they don't help. Too many social sciences involved for anyone to do anything. Everyone is too damned sensitive. It's impossible to play by the rules and make any progress. You're better off taking things into your own hands."

I nodded and looked back at my whisky. The old man brought up points that I could not deny. There was no strong counter-argument to his statement, either. Or maybe there was, but I wasn't in the mood to debate. My misery was my fixation.

The city is a complex system with many moving parts. It has to keep the public in check and reassure them that everything is under control while dealing with all the grime in its gears. "Good chat." I raised my glass at the man.

"Likewise. The name's Donald. Donald Wickerman."

"Michael," I said before taking another sip.

It was refreshing to see I wasn't the only one who noticed the shithole that the city had become. He was right, too: the police have their hands tied. What can they do? I tried to push the limits within in the system and it brought me here.

I pray that this ends soon. I wondered what to do with myself. I guess the drinking could become a regular thing. It's not like I have any other interests in life.

I finished the whisky with a big gulp and decided that was it for now. I couldn't just hang out there all day. It wasn't healthy.

I need to try and get some real rest. Maybe the whisky will make it easier.

I cleared my tab with the bartender and put on my leather coat, reaching into my pocket to realize I didn't have any smokes with me. *Of course.* Smoking is something I do during breaks at work, and I rarely go out unless I'm in uniform. It felt odd to wear that coat. I didn't even think to put smokes in it.

I'll just hit up a corner store on my way home. I exited the bar—an old dive on the northern side of the city's core, quite close to a mall. I don't mind the area. It has cheap rent and a number of local restaurants nearby. Still, I rarely go out. I can't even recall entering that pub before.

It's only six blocks from me. This could become a regular thing while I'm suspended. I shook my head. *Fuck, I'm stupid.*

I began my hike home, hands in my pockets. The sun had already begun to set. I was probably at the bar for a good four hours or so. It's funny how time gets muddled when you're drinking—especially by yourself.

A shout came from an alleyway as I passed by during my drunk swagger home. The sound was followed by grunting, ruffling, and a clang of metal. Those weren't exactly normal street sounds. Naturally, my training kicked in and I looked over to the alleyway, putting my hand to my back and one foot forward—the old field position. Except I had no gun holster on my back.

Right. I'm a normal person, I thought.

Down the alley, about twenty paces, were two men roughing up an old man in tattered clothes. He had a rugged face covered in dirt, with blood oozing from his nose. The two men pushed him against the dumpster. He tried to fend them off, but he was too frail compared to his attackers. One was bulky, Caucasian. The other was Native and wore baggy clothes. He was abnormally thin—probably from too much crack.

The smart thing was to just walk away, considering my suspension. I could keep my head down, mind my own business, and wait to hear back from the sergeant. Just your everyday citizen, no different than the two men or the homeless guy in front of me. Why should I get involved? It wasn't my business.

No. I'm not just a civilian. I looked around to see that the streets were pretty empty. A few cars drove by, but they were moving too fast to see the brawl. *No one else is going to help him.*

I had to do something. I couldn't let another human being lay there defenseless against those two thugs. What kind of piece of shit did you have to be to gang up on some old homeless guy? What reason could they possibly have?

Their reason can't be better than my own to intervene. With that thought, it was decided. I rushed down the alleyway, taking my hands out of my pockets. I felt the blood pump through my veins and into my arms and legs. I was ready to rumble. Even though I didn't have a weapon and I was a bit boozed, I was still quite capable in hand-to-hand combat.

Bullies. Bunch of fucking bullies.

"Give it over, old man!" came the scrawny guy's snarly voice. He exposed his crooked teeth as he spoke, kicking the homeless man.

Only a couple metres away, I clenched my first and built up speed, charging straight for the thin guy. My fist slammed into his right cheek, throwing him off balance and knocking his head against the brick wall. His skull made a *thunk* as it rebounded off the brick. He collapsed against the dumpster and onto the pavement.

The large man glanced over at me with a confused glare. I rammed my boot into his kneecap, causing him to fall on one leg, yelping. I threw a fist into his face, followed by another. The two blows hit him straight in the nose, enough to crack the cartilage and leave him dazed.

I finished with a roundhouse kick right in the face. It sent him momentarily into the air before his head hit the concrete floor.

The homeless man watched in awe then eyed the two who lay beside him. His glazed eyes turned up to me while his head shook side to side. He slurred a *thank you* through his blood-filled mouth.

I extended my hand. "You might want to get out of here."

The man took my hand. It was rough, dry, and lacked any sort of grip. I used my strength to pull him back up to his feet. He wiped some blood from his nose and shook his head. "I found a wallet on the ground, and these bastards tried to take it away from me."

"Let's see it." I put my hands on my hips. I wasn't okay with beating up old homeless guys, but I also wasn't okay with taking random wallets that weren't yours. The most I could do was make right of this scenario.

The man's eyes widened. "I could really use the cash."

I shrugged. "Fine, but it's the other items in there that interest me. What are you going to do with them anyway?"

The old man swallowed some blood, his dangly neck moving the saliva-blood cocktail down his throat. "I don't know. It was the cash I wanted."

"Exactly. So hand it over."

The old man handed me the thin, grey leather wallet. I snagged it from his hand and flipped it open to find a twenty-dollar bill, a credit card bearing the name *Josh Ling*, and an ID card of this Josh character. Twenty-five, Asian, black hair, and brown eyes. The wallet also carried a debit card and a stamp card for a café.

I looked up at the homeless man. "Where did you find this?"

"Outside of that pizza place down the street. Tony's, I think."

I shook my head. "You did all of this for twenty dollars?" It amazed me the lengths people would go to for some petty cash. But then again, look who I was talking to. It wasn't like he had much else to go on.

The man looked to the ground. "I got nothing else but this jacket." He indicated his torn coat with feathers dangling from the liner.

I had to make sure the wallet made it to the pizzeria. This Josh guy would be looking for it. The homeless man couldn't have the twenty—it would be stealing. I also couldn't trust him to return the items, which meant I had to. I also couldn't steal a twenty from the wallet.

"You better use this wisely." I snarled, reaching into my own wallet and pulling out one of the twenties I had. "Here. Take it."

The man's eyes widened. "Are you sure?"

"Yeah. Now get out of here before these two get up."

"Thank you!" The man smiled, showing some of his teeth and the blood that sat between the cracks.

I pointed at him sternly. "This didn't happen. Any of this," I stated. I was suspended, wasn't on duty, and could get into some serious heat for kicking the shit out of some thugs.

The homeless man nodded. "Yeah, of course." He took a slight bow before leaving. "Bless you!" The man limped as he ran down to the opposite end of the alley, not looking back. He grasped the twenty with both hands.

He'd probably be wiser to hide that, I thought. It didn't matter, though. The deed was done. It had me wondering, was that the right thing to do?

It was. It was fully in my ability to break the fight up, and I knew it was my obligation to do so.

It's why I joined the force, I thought. *I can make a difference. Preferably, when I'm not suspended.*

I shook my head and put Josh's wallet into my pocket. As I left the alley, I scanned both sides of the street to see if anyone was looking. No, it was just as empty as it was before. A lucky break.

Time to get this back to its owner. Chances are this Josh fella would call the restaurant. It was the best place to bring it, and I didn't want to take it to the station. It'd just depress me.

It won't be that long. It's just a suspension, I thought.

It hasn't even been a day, and already I've decided to continue my duty. This might prove to be difficult.

Chapter 4
SIX MONTHS ON

It's November, exactly six months since the shooting. Not a day goes by without me replaying the scenario in my head. I can't stop analyzing every detail—from when Ace and I showed up to The Glowing Monkey, to the first gunfire, to me shooting the first man and then rushing into the alleyway.

If I hadn't misjudged and let my anger get the best of me, I thought—as I have several times a day.

The time off hasn't been like a vacation. No, the days are long, and I've had nothing else to think about. I've been rotting away in my own mind. Work was all I really had. When you have your passion taken away from you, you're left feeling hollow, constantly reliving what you did wrong to deserve it. The time off has been without pay too, so I've had to watch my cash.

Even though I'm still convinced that the gunman and the man I shot were working together, there just isn't any proof. None that I've heard of anyway. I've simply been waiting and hoping that the investigation would soon come to a close. I'm not sure how much longer I can spend doing nothing. Constantly thinking about it doesn't do me any favours either. I need to let it go.

Today was Sunday, the day I spend with my mom, Bonnie. I started the weekly visits the day that I moved back into town. At the time, I was still working security gigs and applying to join the force. When I got on, it took some creative shift-swapping and a lot of favours, but I managed to keep the day free. Now, it's been the only thing left of my old life. Suspension left me in anarchy. There's been no other structure to my days. Occasionally I've had Ace checking up on me—or internal affairs coming to review my statement. They've refused to share any information about the case because they didn't want it to tamper with my version of the story.

The routine with my mom has given me something to look forward to each week while I obsessively kept my phone by my side.

Mom and Ace are the only two I knew personally. People aren't for me. I've never shared a lot of common interests with them. Even with Ace, when he talks about simple things like that stupid automatic vacuum cleaner—during the night that I fucked up—I could hardly care less.

Despite not having much interest in anything lately, thanks to the depression, I've had good luck with the ladies. I always do when I put effort into it. It's pretty easy to swoop them off their feet when you start bragging about being a cop. It's always made me suspicious of those gals. If all it takes is a couple of crazy cop stories to have them drop their panties, how much character do they really have? That's probably why I've never had a lasting relationship. They date me simply for the thrill of having a cop for a boyfriend. They don't like me for who I am. They're just flings, so I don't get too attached to them.

Knowing me for who I am must be difficult for Ace and Mom. Poor Mom. If only she knew half of the things I've done. I didn't have the heart to tell her about the suspension or the criminals I've dealt with.

"How's work been?" Mom said, her voice shaky as she poured a cup of tea for me with her white and blue China tea set.

How long can I keep hiding the suspension from her? I thought. *Remember, it's temporary. Six months into temporary.*

"It's busy as always, thank you."

I just lied to her. It never came easy to steer her away from what was really going on, but I had to. It was for her own good. She can't handle more trauma after her latest trip to the hospital in the summer. All she needs to know is that I'm fine. She didn't need to know the frustration, the defeat, or the sorrow I've felt since May. That's something I've had to work through on my own.

"When will it ever slow down?" Mom asked, sitting down to face me at the table. She smiled, a wholesome one that filled her face. Despite the wrinkles and tired eyes, she was just as warm as I remembered her being when I was a kid.

I took a sip of the black tea and slowly put the small cup back on its coaster. "Well, I'm not sure. I really love my job, so I don't mind." *Temporary,* I thought.

"That is true, you were always a hard worker. It must come from your father's side."

Dad, I thought, recalling the swift hand he had whenever I disobeyed him or when he had too many drinks. Those are the most prominent memories I have of him. I wish I could say I had more. Truthfully, that's how we bonded. There was no playing catch or biking together.

"It must have," I said with a closed smile. "Are you keeping up with the news lately?" I've asked her the same question every week. I worried that she was keeping tabs on the incident that took place at The Glowing Monkey in the spring. It's unnerving that she might recognize me from the videos.

"I have indeed. Lots of gangs and reports about that serial killer. Did you know they still haven't caught him? It's been well over a year!"

"It's tragic, I know."

She shook her head. "The city is filled with so much violence. Let me tell you, it was never like this when I first moved to Edmonton four decades ago." She chuckled. "Doesn't that age me?"

"Ages you just fine." I took another sip of my tea.

Mom lives in a safe old folks' neighbourhood on the far northeast side of town. Not a lot of crime happens there, which makes me grateful. If she was ever in a constant state of danger, I'm not sure how I would handle it.

Probably not very rationally, like how I've handled my career.

Her place is a small, rented one-bedroom apartment. She moved out of my childhood house shortly after my father passed away. There was no use having such a large space to herself, and it gave her an opportunity to start fresh.

We didn't have much more to say after I asked her about the news. I stayed for the dinner that I cooked for her. She's getting old, and I don't like her having to work that much. It's the least I could do after she spent a good seventeen years raising me.

Why can't people be more like her? I thought, carefully pouring the water with one hand from the pasta pot and into the strainer, letting the noodles fall in and the water pour out the bottom.

Why is it so hard for others? My mom has never done anything worthy of being arrested. A flash of the man I shot outside The Glowing Monkey entered my mind—the smug face he had before I opened fire. *How could he not simply stop? Why did he reach into his blazer? I would have never have shot if he didn't.*

I shook my head and brought my focus back to the task at hand—making my mom a meal. It's never a big fancy dinner or anything, not like I'm a gourmet chef. It's just to be sure she gets some food and we get to spend some time together. I don't have any idea what she does all week, being retired. What do old folk do when they don't have work? Better yet, what do people do beyond work? It's a question I still haven't figured out with six months of free time.

Hopefully, I don't have to find out and this can all go back to normal with me working.

With my free hand, I moved the iron pan with the meat-based tomato sauce off the burner. Spaghetti and meatballs. Simple.

"Thank you, dear," Mom said.

"Of course, Mom." I prepared a plate for her and myself then placed them on the dinner table where Mom sat. It was a short wooden table with a white sheet, complete with bamboo mats and a glass of red wine for each of us.

The sad truth: Mom has no one else to take care of her. I'm her only son, her sister lives in Vancouver, and Dad's side of the family basically wrote us off when he passed. They did that because we were related to him, and he wasn't just abusive to me, but to my uncle, aunt, and their kids—who also don't live in Edmonton.

We ate in silence with the television turned to some drama show that I wasn't paying attention to. The tube was no more than white noise to me as I focused on eating, trying to keep my mind away from reliving that night.

"I quite enjoy his acting," Mom said, pointing at the TV with her fork.

I nodded, eyeing the man who had a fashionable haircut and chiselled jawline. Latino, based on the tone of his skin. It wasn't important, but it's tough to not profile everyone I see.

My phone vibrated in my pocket, startling me. The motion caused my knee to jerk. The buzzing noise vibrated from my pants against the wooden chair, catching Mom's attention.

"Sorry. Let me get this," I said, reaching into my pocket.

No one calls me, I thought. *The only two would be Mom or Ace—and Ace knows I'm with Mom tonight.* My heart skipped a beat when I pulled the phone from my pocket to see the caller ID saying it was the station.

This could be it.

I got up in a hurry, sliding the chair out of my way as I did and swiping the answer icon on the screen. "Hello?" I asked, stepping into the other room.

"Bradford," came the slightly distorted voice of a man from the phone's speaker. I didn't recognize the voice. It could be anyone.

"Yes?" I asked.

"The committee has reviewed your case. We want to discuss your current state with the force."

"Of course. When?"

"We were looking to wrap this up today. The board and the chief are here for a few more hours."

"Yes, of course I can. What time?"

"Sooner we can clear this up the better. I'm sure you'd agree."

"I do. I shouldn't be any more than an hour."

The phone hung up and I took a gulp. I kept staring at the phone as it switched over to the main screen full of various apps. This could be good news or bad—it was tough to get a reading on the man's tone or from the words he spoke. Most likely, he was a member of the committee. All I wanted was to clear this up and be back on the force.

Finally, I thought, feeling my heart race. *Six long months.*

"Everything okay, Michael?" Mom called out.

I stepped back into the kitchen and smiled. "Yeah, everything's fine. I just have to go back into the office. Let me clean up." I moved quickly, taking my plate and Mom's finished plate from the table. I rushed over to the kitchen to put them in the sink.

"Don't they know it's your day off?" Mom asked, getting up from her seat to watch me wash the dishes.

"They do." I plugged the drain and turned on the tap. "This is rather important, though." I took the soap bottle and squeezed some of the liquid into the sink.

Mom shook her head. "I know how important your career is to you, but you need to slow down. It's going to get the best of you."

If only you knew Mom. She would be worried sick if she knew how hotheaded I could get in the middle of action. It was better she never did. "I know, Mom, I will get a break. This won't take long."

"All right, don't you overdo it. Your body and mind need rest from your regular routines. Otherwise, it will burn out."

Thanks for the philosophical advice, I thought.

Without further words, I washed the plates, pots, and utensils and placed them on the drainer rack to dry. After a hug from Mom, I was out the door, feeling my palms sweat and my heart race as I hurried down the flight of stairs and out the front door to my vehicle. With a click of a button on the remote starter, the doors unlocked, and the engine roared to life. Next stop, the station.

God, I hope this is good news.

Not often did I go to the station on Sundays. It's always been my day off because of Mom. That didn't matter today—Mom would understand. I accelerated the car a little faster than normal, but I had to know what the committee's verdict was.

This is it. I squeezed the handle of the wheel a little tighter, feeling the sweat build up on my palms. Within about fifteen minutes, I made it to the station and parked my car along the side of the road next to several officer units and exited the vehicle.

The sun was already setting at six. I locked the car and marched up to the concrete building. My sweaty hands pulled on the steel handle, pulling the glass door outward and allowing me to enter.

The only officer on duty at the front was a blonde who nodded with a smile as I entered. I returned the gesture. Veronica was her name. We had become friendly enough, but now was not the time to exchange small talk. I had to meet the board and the chief and put this all behind me.

Shit. At that moment I remembered I didn't have my badge or key card with me and couldn't enter alone.

Sighing, I slowed my power-walk and approached the front desk, leaning myself against the counter beside the bullet-proof glass. "Evening, Veronica."

"Evening, Michael." She looked up at me with a smile. "Here to see the chief, I take it?"

"Yeah." It's no secret that I was suspended for the events that took place outside of The Glowing Monkey. I felt slightly embarrassed having to go to the front counter like some regular Joe. I'd spent years of my life on the force, and Veronica had only been with us for a couple years. Not to make it a seniority thing, but it was not how I wanted to be treated going back to the station.

"One moment." Veronica leaned over to the phone on her desk. She punched a couple of numbers on the dial pad and brought the handset to her face. "Hey, Robert. Michael is here. Okay, thanks." She hung up the phone. "Robert will come get you shortly."

"Thank you." I exhaled slowly, trying to remain calm. It's standard procedure for your sergeant to come get you if the committee wants to review your case. With any luck, they'd criticize my actions, like they've done before, and send me back on the street with a tight leash.

Let's get this over with.

The door leading to the back clicked open and a red-haired man in a white dress shirt and black pants marched into the main lobby. It was the sergeant. I hadn't seen him in six months.

"Bradford," Robert said with a nod. He waved for me to follow.

"Sergeant." I nodded back and walked up to him.

The two of us moved side by side and entered through the doorway.

Six damned months, I thought while wiping my face. The beads of sweat from my hand smeared across my skin. *I need this.*

"How are you?" Robert asked.

"Fine, sir. Fine. I was just having dinner with my mom."

"Excellent. Glad you could catch up on family time."

"Thanks."

Our steps were fast, echoing down the empty hall, and soon reached the bullpen. It wasn't quite as vacant as it was during the Saturday morning when Ace and I were filling out our reports. We passed a couple officers, both middle-aged men, who nodded and stepped aside for me and the sergeant to walk by. They recognized my face, as I did theirs, but our names were never exchanged. Funny how you can spend so much time in the same space as another person but know absolutely nothing about them. Honestly, I don't think I've ever spoken a word to the two besides *hello*.

We turned the corner at the end of the office where Ace's and my desks were. The desks were vacant, and the computers were powered down. To the left was the sergeant's office. We kept moving further into the station, heading for the back where the boardroom is.

Each step I took, I felt my heart beat. The sweat on my hands had intensified and could I swear I was getting stains on my pits.

Deep breaths, I thought. *Keep it together.*

"How's the time off been, Bradford?" the sergeant asked, looking over at me.

"Honestly, not very good," I said.

"Didn't get time to unwind?"

"Not quite. Truthfully, this moment has been in the back of my mind the whole time."

"I figured."

We came to a stop at the end of the hall where a wide door remained shut—the station's primary boardroom.

This is it, I thought.

Robert reached for the handle. "Let's cut the small talk, then, and get to it."

"Please."

Robert swung the door open, letting me enter the brightly-lit room first. On the far side of the large, oval boardroom table was the committee. The chief sat in the middle, directly across from me. All the chairs on my side were empty.

"Bradford," The chief said.

I took a bow. "Chief."

"Please, take a seat." He extended his hand toward the seat in front of me.

I glanced over to the sergeant who sat down a couple of seats away, arms folded. Sheepishly, I pulled out the chair and sat, adjusting it so I could sit straight. I eyed the committee members. Some stared right at me, and others were reviewing documents on the table—most likely related to my case.

The chief cupped his hands together. "Internal affairs reviewed the statements closely. You've had multiple strikes before."

"Yes, sir," I replied.

"We've let it slide in the past with expectation that you'd improve your aggressive behaviour"—he raised his hand—"but you haven't."

I swallowed heavily and looked over to the sergeant. He kept his head low. The sergeant is only quiet when the higher-ups are around—he knows it isn't his place to talk.

The chief leaned back in his chair. "Considering your lack of improvements and the evidence from the shooting in May, you haven't given us much of a choice. You're being terminated from the force."

My eyes widened. "Sorry?" I had heard him correctly the first time, but there was still a moment of disbelief.

"We're taking you off the force."

I felt the sides of my head begin to pulsate as my scalp tensed and my brows twitched. My breathing stopped for several moments as my lungs tightened. My hands clutched the armrests of my chair with so much force that my forearms were shaking.

"An officer will escort you to your desk so you can clear out the rest of your belongings," the chief said. "HR will deal with the termination forms. You're excused."

I took a deep breath and exhaled slowly as I stood from my chair.

This can't be happening. There wasn't much for me to say. Hell, what could I say? A part of me knew this was going to come if I didn't clean up my act—but when reality sinks in, it hits hard. It was unbearable to be near the chief, the sergeant, and the board after hearing the devastating news.

Six fucking months of waiting for this?

I was about to pull open the boardroom door when the sergeant perked up. "Bradford." The sergeant stood from his chair and walked over to me.

"I'm sorry it had to go down this way, Bradford," he whispered.

"Of course," I replied.

"It wasn't my call to cut you loose. Your heart was in the right place."

I wiped my palms on my pant legs and cleared my throat. "Thank you, Sergeant."

The sergeant extended his hand. "I'm just Robert now."

"Yes, of course."

Chapter 5

CHILDREN OF THE NIGHT

Crooked planks of wood made up the flooring where high-heeled shoes and steel-toed boots, covered in buckles, stomped rhythmically. Dozens of pairs littered the floor, stepping on the flooring with vigorous force in sync to the heavy bass kick blasting through the room.

Bookshelves lined the walls, accompanied by multi-coloured LED lights that were stapled to the running boards and ceiling. The room was crammed corner to corner with people of all ages dressed in black outfits. Some wore clothes made of PVC while others fashioned fishnets and chokers. Some danced alone, others in groups, and some talked in small clusters, trying to hear each other over the loud, distorted electronic music. The sound was being blasted through the studio monitors in the far corner where a bald DJ bobbed his head to the music while focusing intensely on his laptop screen.

A girl in knee-high buckled boots stood near the entrance of the room where a staircase led back up to the main floor. White cupboards could be seen on the main floor to the right of a screen door that led outside. This was not a normal club party. This club took place in an old bungalow.

A glorified house party, the girl thought.

This underground nightclub was tailored to the harsh electronic music scene known as industrial. The scene was small in the city, so when an event like this happened, word spread like wildfire. The events were popular because they were secluded from the main bar crowd, and the exclusivity was irresistible.

Not often did these events happen—maybe once every few months. They were risky. They were also highly illegal. They surpassed the sound barriers, booze was sold without a licence, and the maximum capacity for fire safety was breached. It functioned like a normal club, simply without any of the permits or regulations. Drugs were passed around like business cards. The underground house clubs were an infraction just waiting to get busted.

If only the bust would be like out of a Blade movie. Someone coming in here and arresting a bunch of vampire kids would be pretty bad ass, the girl thought, taking a sip of her rum and coke. She brought it in on her own booze by stuffing it in her purse. She wasn't going to pay for drinks. As far as she was concerned, she was just visiting a house.

Sometimes I wonder why I even come to these things. She knew the answer, though: she was drawn to the music, as was anyone in the scene. She also appreciated the fact that you could be accepted as an outcast among others. Everyone was dressed obscurely to the public eye. She didn't stand out like a sore thumb in her cat-print leggings and fishnet long-sleeve shirt.

"Lola Love!" erupted a high-pitched squeal.

The girl squinted to see a black-and-red-dreadlocked girl with pale white skin—unmistakably her friend. "Becky!" Lola said with a smile, extending her arms for a hug.

"Is that all I get?" Becky raised an eyebrow while stepping toe to toe with Lola. She grinned and leaned into her. With one hand, she pulled the back of Lola's head, causing their lips to press against one another's. The other hand slid along Lola's waist so their bodies were squeezed against one another.

Lola's eyes widened at first, but she relaxed and embraced her friend's spontaneous kiss—even if it did involve some tongue coiling. She could taste Becky's booze-infused saliva. They held one another for several seconds before stepping back. Lola caught sight of Becky's tight corset that pushed her breasts up.

"I like your outfit," she said.

Becky giggled and stroked Lola's long bangs from her face. "Loving your new cut."

"Thanks. I thought I'd try something new."

"It works. I didn't know you were coming! The announcement was pretty last-minute."

"Yeah, I know, but it's pretty easy to stay up to date on this scene," Lola replied.

"You here by yourself? Standing in the entrance all alone?" Becky tugged on Lola's black canvas skirt. "Come dance with me."

"I came with Brian."

Lola's words caught Becky off guard and she stopped her playful manners. She squinted. "Really? You still chasing that penis?"

Lola took a sip of her drink. "I'm not chasing him."

"Yeah, you are. How long have you two been fooling around?"

"We're dating—for a number of months."

"Right." She raised her fingers to mimic quotation marks. "Dating. I've never heard him use that word."

Lola felt her heart rate increase just from talking about it. The whole situation had her more stressed out than she wanted to be. "About four months, to be exact," she mumbled.

"Sorry? The music is loud."

Lola leaned into her friend's ear, noticing the studded piercings on her helix and the smell of sweat mixed with hairspray. "I said about four months."

Becky placed her arm over Lola's shoulder, keeping her close. "Yet he still keeps you two hush-hush?"

"He just hasn't opened up to someone this much before. He's got a lot of emotions."

"Bullshit. He's just using you. That's what boys do." Becky's attention was clearly lessening as she began to dance, swaying her hips side to side. Her arm slid away from Lola, moving up in the air. Her eyes closed as the beat to the music quickened and the bass thickened.

"We spent some time together earlier this week when he didn't have classes."

Becky opened her eyes and grabbed hold of Lola's hips in an attempt to get her to move with the rhythm. "It sounds like he's stringing you along."

Lola moved with her, starting to feel the rhythm of the music. "Look, I don't want to talk about it." She wasn't comfortable discussing her feelings for the boy. They were far stronger than what she was used to.

"It's just weird how he only spends time with you when it's convenient for him. Or, like, when other people are around I always see you by yourself. So where is blondie, anyways?"

Lola eyed the room. A large clump of people were by the bar on the other end of the room, getting drinks. Most of the crowd was still on the dance floor. The room was dark with a lot of black lights, which made it a challenge to see everyone's faces. But she knew Brian's tall, thin frame. She'd be able to spot him easily.

"He's around," Lola replied.

"I'm sure he is. Probably fingering some other chick." Becky frowned.

"No." Lola scratched her neck. *Drop it, Becky.* "There are actually a lot of people here I don't know. Isn't that weird?"

Becky nodded. "It's the newer EDM scene and the gangs. The lines between the scenes are blurring." She shrugged. "It makes coke easier to get."

Lola smiled. It was true, the increase of gangs on the street made finding any substance you wanted much easier. Of course, you had to be worried about them being laced. Some of the dealers were cheap and tried to increase their product's volume by cutting it with other substances. It's what made the drug scene so dangerous. It was a risk most people were either unaware of or willing to take to have a good time. Mostly Lola avoided drugs. She preferred liquor because she knew where it came from.

The two girls continued to dance. Lola wanted to try to get back into the party mood. It didn't help that their conversation brought up Brian.

He said he'd be right back, she thought, lifting her boots to the beat. She took a large drink of her highball. *Just have a good time.*

The DJ faded the track over to a new beat. It was minimal and clean, which lost the attention of some of the dancers in front of the DJ booth. It was a smart tactic to divide up the hit tracks and the less energetic ones to allow people to mingle, recover their energy, and buy drinks.

Well, this one's a dud. Lola leaned into her friend. "I'm going out for a smoke."

Becky nodded. "Catch up with you soon, love." She blew a kiss goodbye as she continued to dance. The girl was a warm-spirited person, despite being in a dark—often negative—scene. Occasionally it did attract the optimistic folk like her. It was why Lola appreciated Becky. She was not afraid to call bullshit when something was unfair.

Lola climbed the staircase to the main floor. *Brian.* It was difficult to remain hopeful while dating the boy. He was the one who asked *her* out, and he seemed excited at the time. But their "dates" were more often just hanging out at one another's places to hook up.

We clicked too well. Her memory returned to the first couple of months, which were quite exciting. It felt like they were both right for each other. Shortly after, he started distancing himself and coming up with reasons not to get together.

He seems to always have time to party, though. She had lost count of the times she'd either run into him at a club or see his photos online with friends and other girls she had never met before. The scene was small, so who were they?

Stop it, she thought, taking a deep breath.

The stairs from the basement led directly into the kitchen. To her left was the screen door leading outside. It was complete with wooden cabinets and an old, dirt-stained, white tile flooring. The main floor of the house was a little brighter, but it was just as full of people. Less of them were dancing— it had a casual lounge vibe to it. There was metal music coming from a DJ in the living room.

At the island of the kitchen was a second bartender serving drinks. He wore a spiked collar, skinny jeans, and an open black dress vest. At the moment, he was pouring a couple of shots for a man and a woman dressed in black PVC attire.

Lola pulled on the screen door to the side of the house. She stepped out into the dark where four other smokers stood—three of them having a deep, animated conversation. She couldn't make out their faces, but she didn't recognize their voices. One man was dressed in white cargos and a white tank top. The other two were in all black. The fourth smoker, away from the group, leaned against the house on the other side of the door, brushing his long, frizzy black hair aside.

Someone I recognize. Lola pulled out a smoke and lighter from her purse. She kept her self-rolled cigarettes—and joints—in a tin case. This time, it was just a cigarette. They were cleaner than the ones you could buy in a store.

"Hey, Donnie," Lola said as she lit her smoke.

The large man leaning against the house turned and waved at her. He adjusted his black denim jacket and exhaled his smoke. "Yo."

"I didn't think I'd see you here. Thought you were more into the metal crowd."

He shrugged. "Yeah, thought I'd give this a go. Change of scenery, y'know?"

She inhaled her smoke and eyed the night sky. Some of the stars were showing through—which was a surprise, considering they were in a central part of town where the lights and exhaust shrouded the cosmos.

Exhaling, she could taste the nicotine on her breath—a satisfying taste that helped keep her calm. "Yeah. I'm not really feeling it tonight. It isn't the same as it used to be." *It has nothing to do with Brian. It has nothing to do with Brian,* she thought, inhaling another puff of calm.

Donnie shifted closer to her and lowered his voice. "That's because the crowd is high out of their minds." He shifted his eyes toward the three smokers, specifically the one dressed in white.

Lola played with her black-and-blue-streaked hair that brushed against her shoulders, casually looking over to the group. The man in white reached into his pocket. With a closed fist, he pulled out his hand and slammed it into the other guy's hand for a firm handshake. It ended with a slide as they both closed their hands and put them in their own pockets—an obvious exchange of goods if anyone had any sense of observation.

Lola turned back. "So? That's been going on all night."

"Crystal Moths, Lola."

Her eyes widened and she took another puff of her smoke. "Is that one? How do you know?"

"The white clothes."

"That's their thing?"

"Yeah. Started showing up more in the metal scene, too. One ass-hat in white tried to recruit me."

Lola couldn't help but laugh. She knew Donnie for a while, and he was an exceptionally kind-hearted. Despite his threatening appearance, he was a giant teddy bear underneath it all. "They wanted you?"

"Well, I'm the front man for Blood Bathers. They know I'm well-connected. It would be an easy opening into a new stream of people for them."

"What'd you tell them?"

"To fuck off. Enough of that shit going around already. Anyone looking can find it themselves. I'm not going to be a pusher for that."

"Good for you," Lola said.

"There's something for your blog."

She swallowed heavily and took the last drag of her smoke, flicking the butt into the snow-dusted grass beside the house. "Yeah, I do need a new story. It's been hard to get any real info these days." Lola was passionate about reporting local, unfiltered news. She knew it was the people's right to be informed about what was going on in the city. The mainstream media always watered down the truth.

I didn't know they dressed in all white. Would be news to others, too. She eyed the Crystal Moth.

"I follow the blog pretty closely," Donnie said. "You post some real shit. I liked your last post about the Snapper."

"Thanks." Lola couldn't help but blush. "I really want to make it as a reporter." *And get out of that shitty café.*

"I think you got the chops. You take it seriously."

"I just gotta finish university." She looked to the ground. "What'd you like about the Snapper article?"

"News doesn't say much about the Snapper lately, which is weird. But I like how you archived all the reports on him."

"Hey, it's Edmonton's only active serial killer. Before the Crystal Moths really took off, it was the most interesting thing we had. The news jumps around fast on what's shiny and new that they leave important things behind."

"Yeah, place is going to the dumps. The Snapper, and now the Crystal Moths. Trust me, you'd like what I have to share."

"Could we grab a beer or something sometime?" Lola asked. "I'd like to talk about it."

"Sure. Pick a time. If I'm not working or playing a show, I'm good." Donnie said.

"Great. How about Tuesday?"

Donnie shook his head. "Band practice. Wednesday?"

"Sure, at the Black Dog?"

"Sounds awesome."

Lola tilted her head toward the door. "How about I get us a shot?"

"I'm down."

Donnie moved to the door and pulled it open, allowing Lola to step in first.

Lola reached into her studded black purse to pull out a twenty as she entered the kitchen, where the bartender cracked open a bottle of beer for a blonde girl who leaned against the counter, swaying slightly. Lola and Donnie lined up behind the drunk. The kitchen had about a dozen people in it, a little less crowded than the basement.

The music from the living room shifted to dancier metal—a remix of Hate Dept., from what Lola could recognize. She was pretty knowledgeable about alternative music as a whole. She owed that to her brother and dad who were also outsiders when it came to pop culture. She was born and raised as an outcast.

"How does Jäger sound?" Lola asked while she bobbed her head to the heavy guitar riffs.

Donnie put on a wicked grin. "Sounds excellent." He tapped his foot to the drum beat of the song.

The blonde took her bottle and exited to the living room, letting Donnie and Lola step forward.

The bartender's eyes widened as he acknowledged the two, emphasizing the eyeshadow he used.

Lola raised her two fingers. "Shots of Jäger!" She extended her hand with the bill.

The bartender took the cash and placed it in a steel tin then returned to her with the change. He then placed two shot glasses on the counter and poured the dark alcohol from a large bottle.

Lola took one with her index finger and thumb, showing her black-and-blue nail polish.

Donnie took the other with his thick, dirt-covered hand.

"Cheers to a new story!" Lola smirked as she clanged her glass against Donnie's. Donnie inclined his head silently.

The two tapped the shots on the table and lifted them up, pouring them down their throats in a single go. They simultaneously slammed them back down onto the counter.

The Jäger shot was the tipping point for her mind. The good news for her blog and another jolt of booze in her system made it a little easier to tolerate the party—even through her frustrations with Brian. It didn't matter now. She had some friends there and could have a good time.

I'll care when I'm sober, she thought. It was unfortunate, but it was probably the truth. That was the good thing about alcohol: it allowed you to endure situations just long enough to survive the evening without ripping someone's head off. The last thing she needed to do was cause a scene. Word spread quickly among the industrial kids and she'd be labelled as *bat-shit-crazy* or something.

Maybe I'm over analyzing this. Lola patted Donnie's arm. "I'm going to go dance to this!"

"Knock yourself out," Donnie called out as she ran toward the living room in excitement.

She stepped into the tile-floored living room. The walls were painted red with orange pumpkin lights mounted onto the ceiling and running between all four corners of the room. The windows had been blacked out with heavy curtains stapled to the wall, preventing any outsiders from looking in.

The DJ, a thin white guy who rocked thin black dreadlocks was set up at the opposite corner from her. He had his laptop out and headphones against his ear as he bobbed his head to the music.

Lola stepped side to side in rhythm with the heavy bass and guitar riffs of the song. The shot of Jäger began to kick in—her movements were slightly swayed with each step. She was finally having fun. For the remainder of the song, she lost herself to the beat, not keeping track of time or where anyone else was. She was just going with the music.

When the song came to an end, Lola continued moving with the new beat. It was a little faster and more aggressive. Finally, she felt like she was letting go of the tension from her school, her stagnating blog, and her boy troubles.

A night of fun, she thought.

The dance floor had cleared drastically for this song. Some people stayed and tried to start a mini mosh, but it didn't last long. There weren't enough like-minded people to get one going. Most of them eventually cut into conversations or left to grab a drink.

The clear space gave a better view of the whole room. Lola was able to see a red sofa to the left of the DJ booth where four people sat. The couch was only meant for three—a bald guy sat on an armrest chatting to another, larger bald guy. The drunk blonde girl from the bar sat on the couch. She had her arm over the shoulder of a blond, spiky-haired man, using her other hand to stroke the hairs on his chin. She was whispering in his ear while gently kissing it.

The hair, torn shirt, and PVC pants were unmistakably Brian's. He held the blonde's upper thigh as the bare leg wrapped around his.

Lola stopped dancing. She just swayed slightly as her jaw dropped. She felt her stomach twist, like the feeling you get at the sight of something too graphic. It fuelled a fire that channelled throughout her body and into her fingertips. It was a cocktail of pain, anger, and self-hate. How could she be so stupid to think that she and Brian were dating? Or why was she so willing just sit back and let this happen in front of her?

Am I that much of a pushover? she thought. Time seemed to be at a standstill. This situation had come up with Brian before, but she would just look the other way. Then again, he hadn't been this entangled with another girl. Just flirtatious behaviour and some questionable touching—something Lola wouldn't do with another man. This time, the new gal and Brian had crossed the line.

I can't take this anymore.

Lola stomped toward the couch, her boots creating vibrations around her. Her hands coiled into fists. She clenched her teeth, causing her jaw to tighten. Her fast, aggressive movements caught the attention of the two guys on the couch. The blonde and Brian were far too occupied with their intimacy to notice.

Only a foot away, Lola swung her leg, kicking Brian in the shin with enough force to get his attention. "What the fuck is this?" she asked.

Brian casually looked over at her. He kept a cool, relaxed posture. "Are you leaving?" he asked.

"Am I leaving?" She squinted and extended her hands. "Are you that thick-headed?"

The blonde looked over her shoulder at Lola, eyeing her from head to toe with a scowl on her face—clearly unimpressed with her arrival.

"We're chatting, here. I'll catch up with you in a few minutes." Brian turned to face the blonde again.

Lola felt her head throb on both sides from the rage that was coursing through her body. It took every ounce of her to resist pouncing onto the couch and tearing the blonde off of Brian. She wanted to slam her fists into that chick's face and choke the life force out of them both.

Then I'd be "the crazy bitch" among the scene. Her nostrils flared as she inhaled. Lola took a moment to think, especially since Brian was so well liked. He was able to put on a charm that was irresistible. They'd take his side. Lola and Brian weren't dating. Brian never agreed.

Lola shook her head. "Fuck you. I'm out." She gave one swift kick to Brian's foot and spun around, marching back to the side door exit.

"Hey!" Brian shouted. "Hold on! We're almost done talking here."

Lola ignored his call and rushed through the kitchen, slipping between people as quickly as she could. The alcohol caused her to misjudge her stride, and she bumped into a few people on her way out. Donnie wasn't by the bar anymore, but it didn't matter to her. Lola needed to get out.

She squeezed past the last group of people blocking the side door and swung it open, exiting into the night. She marched toward the back of the house and into the alleyway.

If Brian was following her, the darkness of the alley would be a better cover.

I'm done. I don't care if he tries to make up for his bullshit behaviour. She reached into her purse for her rolled-up hoodie. *I'm so stupid.*

Usually, there would be several inches of snow already, but it was an oddly warm November for Edmonton. Still, frost could be seen with each breath she exhaled. Her body shivered from the wind. Small snowflakes gradually fell onto her clothes.

She unwrapped her hoodie, which had a band logo screen-printed on it—her favourite band, Skinny Puppy. They were pretty iconic in the industrial scene. The hoodie brought her comfort, recalling when she saw them in Vancouver. It helped especially in times like this when she made a fool of herself with a boy. Somehow, it was a recurring event in her adulthood.

I guess that's my luck when dating within the scene. It's not like I'm perfect or anything, but I somehow find the best of the best.

Warmed by her hoodie, she pulled out a lighter and a cigarette, quickly lighting it and taking a puff. The smooth smoke ran into her lungs and brought a moment of clarity through her emotional, drunken rage.

I didn't say bye to Becky, she thought. "She'll forgive me," Lola muttered. She took another puff.

She power-walked for several blocks, inhaling her smoke and tensely hugging her own body to keep warm. The light hoodie wasn't enough to combat the winter wind, but it was what she had.

The alley gradually shifted from houses into commercial-style buildings and apartments. She was exiting the residential area just northwest of downtown and entering the heart of the city. By day it was filled with the working class, and by night it was littered with the city's finest underground community of gangs and prostitutes.

"I hate this part of town," Lola whispered. She grew up in Edmonton and saw the attitude of the city shift closer to that of a major metropolis with every decade. It was nowhere near the size of Toronto or Montreal, though—more like their little cousin.

A cry erupted from the alley up ahead just as she crossed the street.

Her eyes widened, and she stopped in her tracks. She opened her purse to pull out her switchblade. She never left the house without it, even concealing it into clubs. The cigarette was nothing but a butt now, so she dropped it to grab her knife. She pulled the cold, steel weapon out from the bottom of her purse, sliding it into the sleeve of her hoodie.

She took a few steps closer to the alley from the sidewalk, glancing down both sides of the road before entering—no other cars or people were nearby. The alley itself was poorly lit. The road dipped inward and was filled with potholes. There were several dumpsters, a couple of parked cars, and a cat running further into the alley. All typical stuff.

It's probably just some crackhead, Lola thought, looking down the sidewalk leading back to the main drag of downtown: Jasper Ave. It would probably be wise for her to just ignore the alleys from then onward until she made it back to the east side of downtown where she lived.

Another cry roared from the alley, then the heavy sounds of flesh being beaten. The ruffling of bottles and garbage followed until two men appeared from behind the second building in the alley. One of them had the other clamped by the neck and slammed their fist into the other's face. It was difficult to make out any details from the poor lighting behind them.

"Oh, fuck," Lola muttered. She stepped back and reached back into her purse. The first instinct was to call the cops.

The assaulter grabbed the other's face with both hands and, with a swift spin, snapped his neck. The alley was filled with the echoing noise of breaking bones.

Lola let out a scream as she jumped backward. *The Snapper*, she thought. The mysterious figure in front of her had to be the infamous serial killer. What else could it be? The brutish beatings followed by a signature neck snap was too iconic.

The sound of Lola's scream caught the attention of the man. He stood in a wide stance, staring at her as his victim collapsed to the floor.

"Oh God. Fuck—shit!" She dashed away from the alley toward Jasper Ave. Finally, Lola found her phone, pulled it out, and swiped the smartphone screen for emergency calls.

"Help!" Lola shouted as she brought the phone to her ear, hearing it ring a couple of times. *Come on!*

"Emergency. Are you in a safe location?" said a male operator's voice on the other end.

"No!" Lola glanced back to the alley. The man didn't follow. "I just witnessed a man being killed and the guy saw me. It was the Snapper, I swear! He was staring at me."

"What's the address, ma'am?"

"A couple blocks north of Jasper and 110th. Please help!" She began to cry, causing the mascara on her face to drizzle down her cold cheeks. "I don't want to die." Despite studying the Snapper for her blog, seeing the killer in person was beyond anything she could comprehend. He always seemed like an urban myth. No one had a description of him or even lived to see him.

"We have a unit on the way. Stay on the line with me. Is the man in pursuit?"

"I don't think so. He stopped. I really don't know." Lola glanced back again to double-check. Nothing.

The sound of police sirens filled the dead air. Red-and-blue flashing lights highlighted the road as Lola reached the corner of the block. She spotted the lights coming from a police car that roared through the next block's red-lit intersection.

"I think I see the car," Lola said. She panted several times and wiped the tears from her face. "Christ."

"What's your name, ma'am?" the operator replied.

"Lola. Yours?"

"James. Look, Lola, that unit is going to the scene of the crime. They see you, so stay where you are, okay? We have more units on the way."

"Okay." Lola looked around the intersection to see the traffic slow to a halt as the unit buzzed by her toward the alleyway.

The street was busy with traffic and pedestrians, despite the late hour. She was closer to Jasper Ave and 109th Street where a number of bars were located—and the night crowd that she would normally associate with. Now, she just wanted to go home.

This night has been too fucked up. She swallowed heavily. *At least this will be great for the blog. I should have taken a photo of the Snapper.* The thought amused her. Only moments before, she was crying for her life, but now her reporter intuition was kicking in.

She turned around to look at the police car. It came to a sudden stop at the alley a couple of blocks north. Two officers barged out of their vehicle, guns drawn. They held their weapons down as they approached the alley. One spoke into their walkie-talkie while they disappeared down the road.

"Those cops went into the alley," Lola said.

"Lola, are you watching the officers? Please don't interfere. They are trained professionals and will handle the situation. Are there other people around you?"

"Yeah, there's a lot of traffic by 109th. I'm a block from it."

"Okay, we have another unit coming to pick you up. Once they're sure you're okay, they'll get your statement."

"Yeah, of course." Her voice shook from the cold and shock.

Another set of red-and-blue lights came from the avenue she had walked from. The sirens weren't on, but the traffic moved out of the way, allowing the police vehicle to drive through and make a turn at the intersection where she stood.

The vehicle parked just at the corner and the engine stopped. The flashing lights remained on as the officer stepped out of the vehicle. He was well-built with black, slicked-back hair and a chiselled jawline.

"Lola, correct?" the officer said as he walked around his vehicle.

"Yeah," she replied.

"I'm Officer Ace."

"Hi."

"I'm here to take care of you. Are you hurt at all?" Ace asked.

"No, I'm fine."

"You're in good hands now," said the voice from her phone. "Just follow his instructions."

"Thanks, James." She hung up the phone and hugged it.

Ace extended his hand to his car. "Come on, let's get you out of here. This is now an active crime zone."

LOLA

YEGman

Chapter 6
REAL JUSTICE

Sunlight beamed through the tall glass windows and onto the large wooden floor of my open loft, complete with brick walls and an unfinished ceiling. The open space is divided by a leather couch and black countertop, creating two rooms. A spiral staircase leads into the bedroom overlooking the main floor. The sky outside was bright and cloudless—it had to be about midday. The brightness was enough to dry out the room, causing my eyelids to peel back against my dry eyeballs.

A pulsating headache rushed through my head as I rubbed my forehead, rolled onto my back, and stared at the ceiling.

What did I do last night? I thought, trying to recall the evening's events. *Oh yeah, I got fired.* I took a deep sigh. *Followed by excessive drinking and passing out.* The last time I drank that much was when Ace was shot a few years back. One of the few times I didn't fire but should have. Perhaps the guilt made me all the more likely to pull my gun.

At least when I drank then, I did it with Ace.

Monday morning, on a day where I normally would be getting ready to go to work. A day I would join my former partner in patrolling the streets and ensuring the safety of the people of Edmonton. Not today. Today, I started my new life as a civilian—like the rest of the people.

I stumbled out of bed, still in my jeans and white v-neck T-shirt. I held the railing carefully as I walked down the staircase, trying to ignore the skull-splitting headache.

Coffee was my only thought. I had kept to my shift schedule through the whole suspension—maybe half hoping that I'd be called back to work at any moment. The routine stuck, as did the urge to chug as much black liquid as I needed in the morning to stay awake. Especially now, I needed the extra push to start the day.

Old habits die hard, I thought, realizing that I didn't have much reason to be up.

In the kitchen, I leaned against the black tile countertop, sifting through the tray of coffee pods I had for the Keurig machine. Eventually, I found the strongest one I had. It was a red-labelled pod reading *Red Eye*. I hoped I could shrug off the grogginess with just one.

Placing the pod into the machine, I closed the plastic lid, set the machine to regular size, and pressed *brew*. With my other hand, I opened the cabinet above the counter and took out a mug, placing it underneath the Keurig's tap.

"Shit," I said, rubbing my face. *What am I going to do with myself?* Being out of a job is alien to me. I'd worked my entire life, and now I had nothing. It felt like something had been torn out of my very existence. Like I was a boat lost at sea. I had no purpose—no direction. There really wasn't much else now that I didn't have work.

The machine buzzed as it pumped the water into the pod and poured the delicious coffee into my red mug. Once the mug filled, I took the cup and wandered over to the open window to observe the northern downtown scenery. I've been paying off the condo unit for several years—since I got my first raise at work. Living just north of downtown has kept me close to the station and in the core of the city. The suburban lifestyle isn't for me. It's too quiet, and my skills were needed where there was noise.

Keeping the peace is all I'm good at, I thought, taking a sip of the coffee. The smell and taste tingled my senses and I embraced it with a large gulp.

God, I hate the taste. What is the city supposed to do now? Ace is the only effective cop left on the squad, but he plays by the rules. I need to get my mind off work. It's not work anymore. Maybe I need a hobby. It wasn't healthy to sulk around all day like I had done for the past six months. I had to keep my mind moving forward or I would be stuck thinking about the past.

Once I finished my coffee, I showered, brushed my teeth, and shaved my head, maintaining the bald image. Hair gets in the way, and this makes clean hygiene that much easier to maintain.

I found a clean pair of jeans, socks, a black button-up shirt, and my grey hoodie. Often, I use the hoodie for working out in, but comfort was my focus now that I was dealing with a hangover. After getting dressed, I exited the loft through the dark-green front door. It was time to find something new—starting with breakfast.

I've never been much for brooding. I hate it. I'd done it for half a year, and I couldn't keep doing it. Action is the only way to move forward, and I had to take it at some point. Today was as good as any other.

Waiting for the elevator in the white hall, I checked my phone in my leather jacket and noticed I didn't charge it last night. The battery was at about thirty percent. The time was a quarter to one, and I had one message and one missed call. Both were from Ace. At the moment, I didn't want to check it. As much as I like my former partner, chatting with him would just make me miss the force, and I had to clear my head of that life. I would only get pissed off at the whole situation.

Don't think about it. It'll only fuel this damned headache, I thought as the green elevator light lit up and a ring came from the speaker.

The stainless-steel doors opened, allowing me to step into the old, wood-panelled elevator shaft. An older lady was already in the elevator. She was about half my size, hunched and wearing a knitted black coat.

She looked up at me with her blue eyes, smiled, and said, "Good afternoon. Lovely day, is it not?"

I smiled at her. "Of course it is." I reached over to press the button for the ground floor, but it was already lit. I had seen the old lady before. She reminded me of my mom. Friendly, short, and always talkative with strangers.

My poor mom. What will she have to say about me getting fired? I thought. *I'll find out next week. I can't bear to tell her right now. I can barely handle the news myself.*

"I have plenty of shopping to do to get ready for the holidays," the old lady said.

"Starting early?" I said, cupping my hands in front of me. At her age, I would simply want to croak. Just doing errands and seeing decades of the world change around you would be enough to drive me mad. Not sure how Mom does it. The latest shift in technology has already been too much for me to be a part of.

"Yes, I want to beat the rush this year. You know what they say: early bird gets the worm! Besides, it gets a bit crazy once the snow starts coming in heavily."

"This whole city is rather hectic at the moment," I replied.

The old lady nodded. "That's right. Bunch of horseshit if you ask me."

I couldn't help but smirk. Hearing the old lady curse in her sweet voice was humorous on its own. "That, I agree with."

The elevator came to a stop, rang, and the doors slid open leading into the main hallway.

"Take care of yourself. The streets can be a bit dangerous lately," The old lady said as she pulled out a set of keys.

"You too," I replied, letting her exit first.

Leaving the building, I walked down the sidewalk leading from the residential area toward the downtown core. Walking the street out of uniform—especially knowing I wouldn't wear it again—made me feel like a lost dog. I always walked with a purpose, but this time I didn't have one. It made me question what exactly I was doing.

Food, I thought. That was the mission. But what after? Guess I had to figure it out one step at a time.

Walking down to the main drag, I saw a real change of scenery in the span of twenty minutes. From a neighbourhood residential area of apartments to glass towers, concrete buildings, and traffic crammed bumper to bumper. Clean-cut men and women in casual office wear or power suits. They chatted on their cellphones while walking to their next scheduled event. Still, in the corners and alleyways, I could spot the bums and drug addicts trying to take shelter by the dumpsters.

The higher-class citizens were not alarmed by the unwholesome sights. They simply went on with their day-to-day lives, ignoring the potential harm that was around every corner. Why should they be alarmed? Chances are nothing would happen. The scum saved that type of behaviour for after office hours when they could prey on some unlucky folk who happened to be alone.

I kept my hands in my pockets as I merged with the sea of people. The sounds of dozens of footsteps rushing through the street filled my ears. Car engines roared, horns honked, and tires screeched to beat the next red light. The white noise of the city's heart.

This is what I worked to defend, I thought, looking across the street to see that the opposite side of the sidewalk was equally busy. The lunch crowd was finishing their breaks and milling back to their workplaces. They had jobs to attend to.

Food. I thought again while passing a café. What I needed was something greasy to deal with my hangover. I decided heavy drinking really couldn't become a regular routine with the jobless lifestyle. I needed to keep my head clear and try to figure out the next stage of my life.

The lit sign of a sandwich joint caught my eye, and I decided it was as good a choice as any. A breakfast sandwich would have to suffice. I entered the restaurant and scanned the scenery—several people sitting and chowing down on their subs. One was a lone businessman staring out into the downtown view. Two casually dressed women sat together. Probably co-workers. Another guy sat by himself eating a sub by the window. He had to be no older than nineteen. He could have used a shave and a comb through his hair. What caught my eye was the white scrap of cloth that was tied to his left arm. It was wrapped tightly—his biceps strained against it as he leaned against the counter.

It isn't my problem, I thought, trying to convince myself that I should just ignore him and order my sub. Staring at the cloth brought me back to my last night on duty outside of The Glowing Monkey. The kid who was pegged in the head also had a white rag. Then there were the two men dressed in white.

The smug prick I shot, I remembered, realizing I never did get answers about that night. Who was that man? Who was he going to call on his phone? Who was the gunman? What was with the white rags?

No, I thought. *I'm not a cop anymore.*

"Hello, sir!" came a nasally voice from the short girl at the cash register.

I turned to look at her, realizing I had lost myself in thought for a good half a minute.

"Hi," I replied and approached the counter. "I'll just get a breakfast sub on white."

"Regular size?" the girl asked.

"Yeah."

"Would you like to make that a combo?"

"No, that's fine, thank you."

"Eleven twenty-five," she said.

I took my wallet from my back pocket and let my eyes slide over to the reflection on the glass separating the sandwich-building station from the customers. It was a clear mirrored view of the kid with the white rag was sitting by the window, peacefully eating his sandwich.

These white rags. I haven't seen anything like that since that night at The Glowing Monkey. Then again, I don't get out much. I took a twenty from my pocket and handed it to the cashier. *It has to be the Crystal Moths. Who else wears a white rag on their arm?*

"Thank you." She took the bill, popped open the register, and returned my change.

I took it without making eye contact, still staring at the reflection. The logical part of my brain once again told me that I needed to let this thing go. My gut told me I needed to do what was right for the city. It was eating away at my innards.

The force clearly didn't have the time investigate the white rags and their relation to the Crystal Moths. Whatever they were doing, they were going to keep doing it—expanding their progressively growing underground empire right under the noses of the police.

I can't let this go. I pressed my lips together as I stood at the end of the counter. This kid would know something about the death at The Glowing Monkey—or at least about the two men I shot. *I need to know.* My heart jumped, and I felt the blood rush through my previously sluggish body. It was the same rush I'd get at the start a shift.

Just to get closure, I thought.

"The hunt is on," I mumbled to myself, placing my hands into the pockets of my leather jacket.

It's not like the sergeant shared the results of the investigation with me. Ace most likely will if I ask, but I don't want to put him in a place that could jeopardize his job by telling me confidential information. I've probably put him in enough trouble already.

Once my sub was made and handed to me, I sat at a table for two that faced the glass reflection at the counter. That way, I could watch punk without giving myself away by staring directly at him.

I ate the sub quickly, seeing that he only had a fourth of his left—casually eating and tapping on his smartphone. What was he doing on there? Was he in contact with the Crystal Moths or just innocently messaging a friend? Unlikely. Everyone has something to hide.

The kid finished the last of his sub and crumpled up the wrapper, leaving his tray on the table as he got up to leave the restaurant. That was my cue. It was time to take action. It hadn't occurred to me that not being a cop gave me an advantage. I didn't have to wear my uniform and could blend in as a regular civilian.

Stuffing the last of my sub into my face, I chewed intently as I watched the kid walk out the door. He turned in the direction of the City Centre mall just a block down. The mall attracted all sorts of people from office workers to university students, drunks, and homeless. I had lost count of the number of times I'd been called there to pick up someone for some petty crime. There's always action there, and that punk was heading right for it.

Swallowing the remaining bit of food, I got up from the table, took my tray to the trash. and dumped the contents into the bin. I left the tray stacked with the others and hurried out the door.

"Thank you!" the cashier called out.

I smiled and nodded while exiting back onto the streets. My eyes followed the sidewalk the punk went down. He was about a dozen heads away in the sea of people. I could see through the crowd just enough to spot the white rag and his tattered hair.

I'm on to you, I thought, briskly yet casually moving in the kid's direction.

As I followed, the kid walked under the pedway that connected the east wing of the mall to the west. He stopped by the entrance, pulled out his phone and, began typing.

To avoid being noticed, I leaned against the side of the mall and looked in the opposite direction. *Just give him a few seconds.*

Moments later, I turned to see the kid stuff his phone into his pocket and continue past the mall.

Guess he's not a mall rat after all.

He continued to walk away from the mall—eastward toward Chinatown. I kept a good distance from him the whole time, so if the kid looked back, he'd be less likely to assume I was on his tail.

After we walked past the inner-city park known as Churchill Square, the punk continued east a couple blocks toward the rougher area with lower-income housing, pawn shops, and a burlesque bar—which is closed at that time of day. The further we went, the fewer people were around to give me camouflage.

The punk passed under the arch marking Chinatown—a red structure with rusty shingles and a lion sculpture on either side—then moved off the sidewalk and into a parking lot just behind the burlesque club.

What are you up to? Curiosity really got the best of me. I could have easily gone and looked at books or ski equipment—regular things that would be socially acceptable for a man of my age to do. Instead, I simply could not resist knowing what the white rags had to do with the Crystal Moths. I needed the peace of mind.

I was a good block and a half away from the kid now. He moved through the parking lot and disappeared behind the burlesque club. I picked up my speed to catch up with him. I couldn't let him get too far, or the pursuit would be a real waste of my time. Then again, I had nothing but time.

Passing the lion sculptures under the archway, I reached the dusty parking lot. It was at about a third of its capacity.

Come to think of it, this area is only about three blocks south of the station, I thought. But that really didn't matter. I had nothing to report to them anymore.

My eyes widened as I caught sight of the punk. He was headed toward an idling, white Mitsubishi Ralliart in one of the stalls. The windows were tinted, and the car had been modded based on the crisp sound of its engine, the white rims, and the size of the spoiler on the back.

The window rolled down as the kid approached. He reached into his pocket and pulled out a grey grocery bag from his cargo pants as he leaned against the window of the car—preventing me from seeing who was in the car.

Damn it, I thought, exhaling heavily through my nose. I hung back on the sidewalk beside some cars parked at the meters. If I got too close to the scene, they would probably back out of whatever they were doing. I kept my cool, grabbed a cigarette from my pocket, and lit it up. Just a bystander having a smoke in the street.

With my other hand, I fidgeted with my phone to make myself look more natural. I kept my stance toward one of the parked cars. It was pretty clean—clean enough to provide a clear reflection of the punk talking into the car.

The kid laughed and stood off to the side, nodding at the person inside.

A hand waved from the Mitsubishi showing the sleeve of a white blazer.

That's a clue, I thought.

The person the hand belonged to leaned up to the window, exposing his slicked-back hair and black goatee just under a smug smile.

No. My heart stopped momentarily. I leaned carefully to get a better look. It was the prick I shot outside The Glowing Monkey. How was that possible? Was there not enough evidence to book him?

That's more proof that I fucked up that night. The guy was clean—at least then. I couldn't let it go now. It was my one chance to see what kind of dirt this prick had.

The window of the car rolled up as the man leaned into his seat. The vehicle pulled into reverse, making a sharp spin before shifting into drive. It accelerated toward the exit. Toward me.

I inhaled my cigarette and brought my phone to my ear as if I were about to take a call. I rested my arm on the roof of the car, acting as if it were mine.

The Mitsubishi slowed as it reached the exit. It was impossible to see who was inside due to the heavy tint on the windows. The car roared as it took off onto the street away from the parking lot.

With my phone, I switched over to the camera and took a quick snap of the vehicle as it drove away before putting it into my pocket. Probably not a very good shot, but might come in handy if I could zoom in on a computer.

Time for this punk-ass kid to spill some answers. I took one last puff of my cigarette, then marched into the parking lot. The stupid kid hadn't even seen me. He was already on his way to the other end of the parking lot to who knows where.

I hastened my speed, surpassing his own while taking a quick glance around the area. The cars were empty and nobody else was around—just us.

I figured a sudden, intimidating appearance should be enough to get the kid to spill some info. Plus, not being in a uniform could again work to my advantage. One thing I learned from being on the force is that Crystal Moth members treated the police as a joke. They think they're better.

As I approached, I lifted my hood to help conceal my face. I counted each step I made in sync with my internal clock. *One, two, three,* I thought, only seconds away from the kid.

The kid must have heard my boots in the dirt because he turned around briefly, said, "Oh shit!" then attempted to pick up his speed.

"No you don't, you little punk!" I called out, close enough to grab on to his shoulder and spin him around.

The kid pulled a switchblade from his pocket and flicked it open. He backed up a couple steps and started circling. "Back off!" he snapped. His upper lip twitched just underneath his pencil moustache.

I raised my hands and shrugged at the kid. "Think you're a tough guy with that?"

The kid licked his lips and tightened his grip. "I'm not fucking around, man. Beat it."

"Who were you talking to?"

"None of your business, shithead," the kid taunted.

"What was in the bag?"

"You a cop or something?"

I smirked at him. I'll give them credit: scum like him can smell a cop a mile away. It had to be the way I stood, my mannerisms, or possibly my clean-shaven appearance—even with a hood up.

"Not exactly," I replied.

"You a snitch, then? Working for the cops?"

"Not at all. I got no affiliation with them. How about you just tell me what I want, and we can keep this civil?"

The kid glanced around and exhaled slowly. "How about you just fuck off?" His knife hand shook as sweat began to build up around his face.

His attitude was beginning to irritate me. That type of behaviour is no different from what I experienced in uniform. Although, unlike when I was on duty, I had no rules to follow. This was the street life.

"I wish you hadn't said that." I relaxed my stance and rubbed my chin. "You going to tell me what I want to know?"

The kid took a couple deep breaths and lowered his knife.

"There. Was that so hard?" I asked.

Without further interaction, the punk dashed from the parking lot, running as quickly as he could.

Little shit, I thought, sprinting after him.

His legs flailed wildly as he ran. He kept his arms low, still holding on to the knife. He did have the advantage of turning around and shanking me if I couldn't stop in time. I had to approach with caution. Luckily, he wasn't exactly a good runner. Catching up to him was a breeze.

I reached out for the arm with the knife, snagging on to his forearm and tugging on him tightly. The pull caused the kid to spin out of control. Still gripping tightly, I twisted his arm around. He yelped and dropped the knife, then slid face first into the dusty ground.

I firmly placed my knee on his back, holding the arm outward and stretching it until I could hear him grunt in pain.

"Stop!" he shouted.

I pressed harder with my knee. "Talk!" I shouted back, quickly glancing up to see if anyone was around. *This is crazy*, I thought. It was broad daylight and I was just a civilian assaulting a stranger.

Crystal Moths, I reminded myself.

"Okay! Don't break my arm!" the kid cried as he craned his neck to look back at me.

I let go of his arm and grabbed the collar of his jacket with both hands, yanking him to his feet. I swung him toward a nearby lamp pole, pressing his face into the metal by clamping my hand on to his scalp. My other hand snatched his arm, and I twisted, squeezing it vigorously.

"Who was the man in the car?" I demanded.

"Alex G." The kid breathed heavily and swallowed some saliva. "He recruits people for the Crystal Moths."

"They have an official recruiter now?" I asked, more so to myself. "That would explain the white rag."

"It's a sign of initiation into the Crystal Moths. Please, let go," he grunted.

"Come on, now you're making it sound like they're a cult."

"They're more than just the drugs. They're a way of life."

"Sure, kid. Every gang thinks they're a special little club. Let's get real. The bag you gave Alex. Drugs?"

"That was cash. I sold some drugs for him earlier. Just take what's left and leave me alone!"

"So, you're his pawn. Is that how you get into the Crystal Moths?"

"Look, man, I can't talk anymore! I don't want to get in shit for telling you all of this. They kill you if you squeak! They don't fuck around. Just take the cash and go."

I slammed his head into the metal pole and leaned in closer to his ear. "Speak! What is Alex having you do?" The sudden use of brute force was incredibly satisfying. Unlike being a cop, I had no procedures holding me back and could release that pent-up anger I had buried away. Now that I didn't have to follow the law to a T, I was making real progress. It was liberating. Punks just need a little shaking to make them talk.

"All right! Fuck! I don't know. I am just doing what he says so I can get in. None of the other recruiters have told me what they've done."

"What is he having you do next?"

"I don't know. They'll contact me."

"How?"

"However they want. Look, man, I don't know much else. I'm not a member yet. You don't want me."

A street urchin, I thought. He was being honest, though. It was clear from his wide eyes. The little prick had squealed everything he knew. There wasn't much use for him anymore.

"One last bit. Where does this Alex G. guy recruit people?"

"Anywhere, really. He gets references, or he finds people himself. Some of the other recruits said they were picked up around EDM clubs."

I nodded. "Good." I swung the kid from the pole and launched him away from me. "Beat it!"

The kid paced a bit and scanned the ground for his knife.

"Don't bother. Move your ass!" I shouted, shooing him with my hand.

The kid glanced over once more then scurried away.

I walked over to where he had dropped the knife and picked it up, closing the blade and placing it into my pocket. The kid shouldn't have a weapon. Who knows what the Crystal Moths would have him do.

I should have roughed him up a bit, I thought. The words didn't surprise me. I wanted to, but I suppose my training kept me restrained. Sort of.

I had to get out of there. The likelihood of the kid ratting me out to the cops was next to none. The chance of an eyewitness was much higher. I assaulted that kid in broad daylight, and my face was out in the open.

Alex G., I thought as I returned toward central downtown. Alex G. was the guy at The Glowing Monkey on the night I fired my gun. He was the man I shot—the one with the smug face.

If only the sergeant would have given me a detailed report of what happened that night. With the new information from the punk, I have some pieces to work with. Alex G. and the shooter were most likely watching their initiate perform whatever task they told him to do. Once the cops got involved, they decided he was too big of a risk and gunned him down before Ace and I could arrest him. Guess they didn't expect me to shoot so quickly. Not all cops are as ready to open fire. Not all cops are fired either.

I put my hands in my pockets and returned to the City Centre mall to figure out my next plan of action. Deep down, I know I shouldn't get involved. Backing away would be the rational thing to do. I can still hear the logical side of my brain screaming at me. But I can't do it.

I feel alive, I thought. Having a focus gives me purpose again. The conflict between my gut and mind fuels the fire. That little bit of information I have about Alex G. is far more than I ever got on the Crystal Moths while on the force.

Alex G.: the man who got away.

A part of me wonders if I should share this info with Ace so he can be aware of what the white rags symbolize. No. If I give him what I know, it'll just get lost with Major Crimes and nothing will come of it. Plus, I don't need him to know I've been out on the streets trying to do detective work. He'd lose his mind. And if I keep it up, he'd probably arrest me.

This has to be on the down low. If this is going to be my new pastime, I have to be smarter. Something about being a regular civilian is so unappealing. Once you have a taste of this freedom, it's hard to back away from.

The adrenaline—I've missed it.

Personal satisfaction aside, it's the right thing to do for the city. I'll stop this prick Alex G. from preying on the youth to join his gang. Perhaps it will be my final act to redeem myself for the violence I projected on the force. It can be the last bit of good I do before calling it quits for good.

ALEX G.

YEGman

CHAPTER 7

LAW-ABIDING CITIZEN

The steaming coffee was borderline scorching in the paper cup. The steam escaping the rim caused beads of water to bud. The small pale hands that held the cup shifted it from the back and forth frequently so that they did not get burned. It was the only thing that kept the girl awake at such an early hour. She was exhausted from a night of partying. The booze had long worn off, leaving her with a nasty headache to accompany her as the sun rose.

She sat at the downtown police station on a pleather green chair beside the desk of the officer that met her downtown. She was the key witness to the murder and needed to provide a full report. The office also had to profile her so no details were missed about the incident.

The Snapper. The girl shivered and closed her eyes. *Did they catch him?*

The vision of the silhouettes fighting, the large man snapping the neck of the other, the sound of cracking bones, and the collapse of the lifeless body were not things she would not forget any time soon. No, they would probably haunt her to the grave.

I have to be able to stomach this if I want to be a reporter.

She still had her phone, keeping it in the pocket of her hoodie. There was one text from her friend, Becky, but no one else. The boy, Brian—who she went to the club with—had never bothered to get in touch with her.

At the moment, it wasn't a major concern of hers—she had just watched a man die. The Snapper might be after her now. She was just grateful to be alive and that the cops didn't take anything from her purse, like her knife— or the rum, which she'd need later to wash the horrors she witnessed out of her mind.

"Okay," came the voice of Officer Ace as he typed at his computer. "I just finished typing in your statement, and the info is on record. Is that everything that you remember, Lola?"

Lola nodded. "Yeah. Can I go?" At this point, she just wanted to go home and get some rest. Lola had been answering the police's questions all night. Seeing the sun rise reminded her how much time had gone by since Officer Ace picked her up. She was about to fall asleep in her chair. No amount of coffee could help her now.

"Yeah. We'll call you back in if we have more questions, but for now, you're free to go." Officer Ace smiled at her.

He has a nice smile, she thought.

Ace had a wholesome expression, despite his tired gaze. Plus, he was fairly easy on the eyes. Lola didn't consider herself capable of finding a cop attractive. Her type was always the weird, thin alternative guys. Perhaps it had to do with the fact he rescued her.

I'm so tired, I'm not making sense. "Thanks," she said, getting up." *I'm getting the hots for cops now.*

"I'll walk you to the door," Officer Ace said as he stood.

He led Lola out of the office and down the hall to the front entrance. Lola's phone began to buzz in her hoodie pocket.

"Try to get some rest. You saw a lot tonight. Us keeping you probably didn't do you any good either." Officer Ace said, swiping his key card to unlock the door to the lobby.

"Yeah. Okay." Lola smiled and checked her phone. The display read *Becky Bubs*. Her smile faded. *Why is she calling at seven in the morning?*

"You need a ride back home? It's the least we can do," Officer Ace asked.

"I'm good, thanks!" Lola called out while swiping her phone to answer and rushing out of the station. She didn't look back at the man and covered one ear with her hand, rushing out of earshot. Becky liked to hang with questionable people at times, and she didn't want the officer to overhear. Plus, this early in the morning, she was probably still partying and doing lines. Two things that a cop would want to know about.

"Hello?" she said, pushing the second set of doors open with her shoulder.

"Lola! My love!" Becky shouted from the phone.

"What's the deal?" Lola replied, squinting as she adjusted to the orange-hued daylight. *My makeup is probably a mess from crying*, she thought. She hadn't thought to fix it at the station.

"Where did you go? I went looking for you everywhere," Becky said. Her voice was slurred.

"I really don't want to talk about it." She bit her lip and eyed the street.

"Did it have to do with Brian?"

"Yeah. Well, no. It's a long story."

"I'll have another bump," Lola said. Her voice was quieter—likely directed at someone else.

"Are you doing blow?" Lola asked.

"Maaaybeee," Becky replied before bursting into laughter.

"Where are you?" *Sometimes she can be such a pain in the ass.* Lola had to mother Becky when she got a little out of hand with partying. Becky returned the favour when Lola cried her heart out over idiotic boy problems.

"At Alex's place."

"Who the fuck is Alex?"

"He showed up at the club. I don't know where he is right now, but he wanted to keep the fun going and invited some of us over." The sound of a quick sniff came over the speaker, then more sniffling. "Oh my God, you wouldn't believe who showed up here!"

"Honestly, I don't care. Where is this Alex's place?"

"Amanda was here, that bitch!" Becky began to snicker and muttered something Lola couldn't pick up. "Thank you, dear."

A man's muffled voice came from the phone's speaker in response.

"Okay, Becky, I'm coming to get you, but I need you to tell me where you are." Lola didn't like the idea of Becky partying with a bunch of random people so early in the morning. The excessive drug use and the shady people brought out the protective instinct in Lola. She had to get her friend back to safety.

"You want to party too?" Becky asked.

Lola let out a sigh. Trying to reason with a coked-out drunk was not easy. Especially when you were hungover and up all night having to recount the details a murder. "Yeah, I do!" she replied, trying to fake excitement.

"Really? Okay, good, because pretty much all the cool people here have left." Becky lowered her voice. "These guys look like they're in the Backstreet Boys. Dorky white suits. Did you see them at the party?"

Crystal Moths, Lola thought, recalling what Donnie had told her at the club. Becky mustn't know about the gang dressing in white. Lola hadn't. "Okay, I could really use some fun. Where you at, sweetie?" Lola acted.

"It's not far from the other place. A couple blocks over. Hold on." She moved the phone from her face, but Lola could still hear. "What's the address here? Yeah. Okay." The phone made a shuffling noise. "Hey, Lola Love, it's just by that shitty donair place. Like, a block up from there—the three-storey green apartment called Hillside Manor."

"Okay, I'm coming to you. What's the suite number?"

"Two-oh-eight. Just ring the buzzer and one of the boys will let you in."

"Okay, great. I'll be there shortly."

"Don't keep me waiting." Becky giggled.

Lola hung up and sighed. "Shit." Now she had to get her friend out of trouble. *This night never ends.*

The donair shop was too far to walk, so Lola kept her phone out to call a cab.

She knew the number by heart. Calling a cab was a common occurrence when living by night, and there was always one nearby in the downtown area.

Sure enough, a yellow cab pulled up in minutes. She climbed into the back seat and directed the driver to the donair shop.

"It's by 122nd Street and Jasper. You can't miss it." Lola figured it would be better for her to walk to the apartment from there. If Becky was partying with Crystal Moths, no one needed to know where Lola was going—even the cab driver.

The ride took about fifteen minutes—Monday morning traffic hadn't begun yet, and it was a holiday.

Remembrance Day. Of course, Lola thought. That's why there was an underground club event on a Sunday evening.

The cab driver was not one for conversing with passengers. He just spoke into a Bluetooth earpiece in a language Lola didn't understand. She eyed the high-rise apartment condos just north of the river valley. It was the tail end of downtown before you got to the river that split the city in half. The other side was home to Whyte Ave—another place where the night brought a drunken infestation of hooligans and violence.

Lola shuffled over and looked in the rear-view mirror to see her mess of a face. Her eyes widened at the sight of her tattered hair, smudged makeup, and tear trails made of mascara.

Oh God, she thought, reaching for her purse. She snapped it open and stumbled around through the items, looking for her makeup and a tissue.

I already made Officer Ace deal with my ugly-ass face. I can't go into some sketchy apartment looking like a mess, she thought, fixing her eyeshadow.

"Dis good?" The cab driver pointed to the large green-and-blue sign of the donair shop. The lights around the sign were off, chairs hung up on the tables.

"Yeah," Lola said and reached into her purse. She found herself spacing out at the scenery and hadn't noticed they had arrived. Lola enjoyed car rides because they allowed her to let her mind wander. Unfortunately, now was not the time to daydream. She was beyond tired, and she had to focus on finding Becky before she did anything stupid.

Lola eyed the meter on the cab's dashboard then sifted around for cash, pulling out a ten-dollar bill and some change. The cab shifted into park right in front of the shop, not bothering to take a parking stall. He was obviously ready to leave and find his next job.

"Here," she said, dropping the amount into the driver's hand.

"Thank you," he said in monotone, taking the cash. Before Lola could leave, he continued his conversation on his Bluetooth.

Not very friendly with his clientele, she thought.

Once the door closed, the cab shifted into reverse and swung right back onto the road from the parking lot. It didn't even stop at the sidewalk to watch for traffic.

Cab drivers. Lola shook her head and started north toward the Hillside Manor apartment complex. She had a general idea where it was. Most of the apartments in this area were brown, red, or limestone-coloured, so a forest green was easy to spot among the others. After a couple of minutes, she spotted the three-storey apartment made with green stucco and dark-grey steel bindings on the corners. Each unit had its own concrete balcony with chipped black railings. Lola marched up the stairwell, walking underneath the curved awning with *Hillside Manor* in a golden script. Behind the text was an illustration of hills with a sun beaming over the valley.

It's odd how all these shitty apartments have such lovely names, Lola thought while opening the lobby door. The grey, red-speckled carpet was stained with dust and brown dirt—probably from years of boots trampling over it and poor maintenance. The cream walls were cracked and chipping in numerous areas. The glass doors dividing the lobby from the hall were smeared with greasy fingerprints.

The resident legend and metal intercom were off to the right. The laminated paper was so old that it was tinted yellow. Names were written on it with a black sharpie behind the glass.

Lola moved to the intercom and punched the metal buttons for two, zero, eight, then the pound sign. The chunky button clicks reminded her of the old telephone booths that used to line the sidewalks.

Whatever happened to those? They had a charm to them.

The intercom rang a couple of times and then the door buzzed without a word from the speaker. Lola pulled the door and entered the hallway. It smelled smoky, and the heat was cranked up way too high. She took a right into the stairwell, passing the brown-painted door frame. The staircase was made with the same grey carpet and the trim was brown plastic.

God, this place is a wreck, she thought, moving up the staircase.

On the second level, she wandered down the hall and scanned the black metal numbers screwed into the brown doors. *Two zero one, two zero two,* she counted. In the stuffy hallway, the smell of smoke intensified her headache and grogginess, but she pushed on. Becky needed her.

Two zero seven, two zero eight. Lola stopped at the door and knocked lightly a couple of times. It echoed down the hall. She glanced both ways down the corridor to see that it was empty. The lifelessness put her on edge. Then again, it was still early on a holiday morning.

A shout came from inside the unit, muffled by the closed door. Several seconds later, the knob twisted, and a bald man wearing a white tank top and blue jeans opened the door. He had a long, black goatee, a bald head, and thick eyebrows above his oval eyes.

"Lola Love!" came a voice from inside.

"Hi," Lola said to the man. He returned nothing but a stare. "I'm here with Becky." Lola stepped forward, expecting the man to move. He remained still and continued to glare at her. He was about a head taller than her, which made her uncomfortable. The man could easily overpower her.

I really should have tucked my knife into my sleeve. Her fatigued state made her slow, and she was not planning her steps ahead. Rescuing Becky was an impulse.

Too late now. Let's just keep it cool. Lola stepped closer. She was only an inch away from the man, who kept his gaze on her. "Excuse me," she said, frowning.

"Lola!" Becky called out again.

"Coming!" Lola squeezed past the man, forcing herself to brush up against him. She kept her forearms close to her chest, avoiding as much contact with the man as possible. *Creep.*

Once inside, Lola noticed the blinds were all closed, limiting the amount of light in the room. The right doorway led into the kitchen and a hall to the bedroom. The left hall led directly into the living room. The shaggy carpet was a light grey. The walls were white, cracked, and chipped.

She noticed there were no shoes in the entranceway, so she left hers on. Besides, she'd need them on if she and Becky had to make a quick escape.

Lola marched through the entryway, glancing down the empty hallway to the right as she passed. There were three closed doors. Entering the living room, she scanned the area to see two leather chairs, a couch against the wall dividing the kitchen and living room, and a black coffee table. A couple of girls cuddled with each other in one chair. One man sat on the ground by the coffee table, his back against the couch. He held a credit card that he used to push together lines of white powder. Both of his arms were covered in tattoos from his fingers to his upper arms, vanishing under his white T-shirt and reappearing on his neck.

Another man sat on the couch, leaning on the armrest nearest to Lola. His spiky hair was the first thing that caught Lola's attention. On the far end of the couch was a dreadlocked girl who rested her head on the other armrest.

Bubs!

Becky raised her head, eyes popping open. A dopey grin spread across her face. "Hey, love! I'm so glad you made it!" She extended her arms and waved for Lola to come to her. "Join me."

Lola stepped into the room, catching the attention of the other two girls on the chair. Their sensual movements with one another were sloppy. One lay on top of the other as they pressed their heads into one another, breathing heavily. Sweat ran through their dirty hair and down their necks.

That can't be coke, Lola thought. She was just thankful that Becky had a better head on her shoulders than those girls—most of the time.

The two men eyed Lola before turning their gazes back to the flat-screen television that was mounted on the opposite corner beside the chair with the girls. The men were intensely watching some old western movie that she didn't recognize.

She stepped around the coffee table and walked toward Becky. Lola smiled at the girl and kneeled down to her level. "Hey, Bubs."

Becky rubbed her legs together and giggled. "My Lola Love." She placed her warm, clammy hand on Lola's cheek. Lola was disgusted to see how high her friend was. The remnants of booze and cigarettes could be smelled on her breath. At least she was able to come to her friend's aid.

"How are you doing, lady?" Lola asked, placing her hand on the moist bandanna that wrapped around her friend's forehead.

"I'm good!" Becky pointed to the man sitting on the ground. "John's just getting us another line. Want to join?"

Lola bit her lip and thought for a moment. *We need to leave. She's had enough fun.* "I'm really tired, to be honest."

"This'll wake you up."

"No, like a lot happened last night and I want to share it with you."

Becky sat herself up and brushed her hair from her face, blinking twice. "What do you mean? What happened? I lost you at the club."

Footsteps came from the hall, and the bald man from the entrance casually walked over to the empty spot on the couch. He stepped over the man on the floor without care and planted himself down, staring at Lola.

This is creeping the hell out of me. Total rape vibe, Lola thought, quickly glancing at the man and then back at her friend. "Want to go for a quick walk and come back? You might need some fresh air."

Becky squinted and shrugged. "Maybe. I'm digging this couch though." She pointed at the bald man. "This is Mika. Beside him is Chuck, and that's John on the ground." She gestured to the two girls on the couch. "They were here already—Jessica and Ashley." Becky giggled. "They're having a good time over there."

The man named John chuckled, it was a raspy smoker's laugh. "They're stealing all the fun for themselves, eh?"

"I know! Where's the love for us?" Becky snickered and started playing with Lola's hair with her index finger.

John raised an eyebrow. "How about I give you some?"

Becky ran her tongue around her upper teeth while staring at Lola. "I'm good. I got my love."

Lola forced a smile. "I'm happy to see you too."

The doorknob at the front of the apartment twisted open, catching the attention of everyone in the room. The clicking of dress shoes echoed in the entrance. The three men straightened their postures. Their faces tensed.

Lola eyed the hallway, holding on to her friend.

The footsteps grew louder as a new man in a white suit entered the room, stopping at the entryway. The light shined on his gelled, slicked-back hair. He stroked his goatee with one hand as his other fiddled with a set of keys. His narrow eyes scanned the living room, eyeing each individual: first the girls on the chair, then the three men, then Becky and Lola.

He grinned, exposing his bright white teeth. "Who's the new girl?" he asked in a natural Maritime accent.

John, who had finished lining up four separate lines of coke, looked up at the new man. "One of Becky's girls. She's here to hang."

The bald man identified as Mika looked up at the newcomer. "Alex, we about to do lines. You in?"

Alex shook his head. "No can do. We gotta meet the recruit in a bit here, for the pickup."

Mika wiped his face. "Right, let's hope he didn't fuck up like the last time."

Alex chuckled, "Yeah, that was a shame."

John perked up. "Speaking of, any news on Joe's release?"

"Nah," Mika replied. "The cops caught the dumb shit red-handed, remember? He's not getting out."

"Shit," John said.

Alex pointed to himself. "Yeah, and I got shot! Bullshit." He gestured to Mika. "So, you're driving?"

Mika nodded. "Yeah, that's cool."

"Good. After that, we gotta get more ice to cut down on the power. Those freezers aren't cheap."

Fucking gang operations, Lola thought. She looked over to Becky and leaned into her ear while stroking her hand. "Let's get some fresh air."

Becky nodded with a sigh. "Okay." She got up from the couch with a slight wobble. Lola helped her get up safely.

John widened his eyes at the girls. "Yo, you sticking around for another line?"

Becky grinned. "Yeah, I'll be right back, stud. We're just going to step outside for a second."

"Girl gossip." Lola smiled politely at John, gently pushing Becky's back to direct her forward.

John rubbed his chin. "All right."

Becky moved first, arms swaying lightly as Lola guided her toward the hallway, passing Alex.

The man nodded at the two as they walked by. He winked at Lola as she passed.

Creep.

Lola smiled back, still guiding her friend to the door. When they reached the entrance, Lola quickly opened the knob, pushed Becky out into the hallway, then closed the door.

"All right." Becky swatted Lola's hand out of the way. "You don't have to move me around like I'm some old lady or something." She brushed her dreadlocks out of her face as the two walked side by side.

Lola brought them to the staircase, taking each step carefully. Becky still had poor balance and couldn't move fast. Lola was just glad that her friend was out of that party.

"So what's the deal?" Becky asked once they had reached the ground level.

"Let's just get some fresh air okay?"

"All right, but what's with all the 'not wanting to talk about it'?"

Lola sighed and rubbed her forehead. "I left the party at around one or something and was just going to walk home."

"What made you leave?"

"Brian. But that's not a priority right now."

Becky groaned. "Go on."

"I was on my way back, and I heard a fight in the alley between these two guys. It was really dark, and I couldn't make out who they were. One of the guys got the upper hand and . . ." Lola stopped for a second, feeling her throat close up. Saying it out loud again was difficult. "He snapped the other guy's neck."

Becky's eyes widened, and she lowered her voice. "Oh my God, like he killed him?" She glanced around, stopping at the front lobby door.

"Yeah, dead. I think it was the Snapper."

"Oh God."

"I called the cops, but they didn't find the guy. I had to write up a police report at the station."

"Sweetie." Becky pulled Lola in for a side hug as they stepped into the daylight, shielding their eyes.

"Let's get you to bed. You had a rough night."

Lola swallowed and wiped a tear from her face. "Don't you want to go back?"

"I do, but you're way more important to me. I'll stay with you. Besides, I can come back to party with those guys later. They got my number."

"What the hell were you doing in there?"

"What do you mean?" Becky smiled. "We were doing some coke. They were the only ones who wanted to keep the party going after the club."

"You do realize who they were, right?" Lola added.

Becky squinted and shook her head.

"Dressed in all white?" Lola said.

"What's the big deal about that?"

"All four of them? Doesn't it seem a little weird that they're offering a bunch drugs? Talking about a pickup? Donnie told me last night that all-white meant Crystal Moths."

Becky shrugged. "Crystal Moths or not, who cares? People have coke all the time. They just wanted to party. Plus, that John guy was kind of cute. He was so trying to get into my pants. That's why they were giving me all the free blow."

Lola looked back at the apartment. "What about the other girls? Shit, we shouldn't have left them."

"They're fine. Alex is a good guy. He takes care of people. Just wants everyone to have a good time."

"How did you meet him again?"

"I've met him a couple of times at some clubs. He was at the opening of The Glowing Monkey in May."

"When the shootings took place?"

"Yeah, that was pretty intense." Becky rubbed Lola's shoulders. "Come on, let's just get you home."

"I'm just glad you're safe." Lola smacked her friend's shoulder. "You had me worried sick."

"I'm fine! Try not to worry so much. You're the one who saw a guy die."

"It's hard not to. The whole night was fucked, and these streets are littered with trouble. We've really got no one to help us out. Cops didn't do shit about the murder I saw, and you spend a whole evening hopping from one illegal party to the next. Now you're hanging out with the city's worst gang. No one is doing anything about the mess we have."

"You blog about it." Becky smirked.

"Yeah, that's all I can do."

BECKY

YEGman

Chapter 8
A HERO IS BORN

Justice. It's more than just a word. It is meant to bring right. It is meant to render judgment upon those who have done wrong. It is meant to keep order and reduce the number of creeps out on the streets. It is meant to allow good civilians to carry on with their lives. It *was* meant to.

The one thing I have learned about justice is that it's entirely subjective. It's not about what's right or wrong. The unfortunate thing with justice is that it's defined by those who created it. It's bound by those constraints. It isn't governed by a sense of morale. Unfortunately, justice can also be wrong. It can be slow. It can be evil.

Because of all the laws, there are loopholes to be found by sleazy lawyers looking to make a profit. Crooked cops and crummy politicians. The damn leeches don't have any sense of what's right and wrong. That's why justice fails.

The series of circumstances over the past six months brought me to a unique situation. Here I was, removed from the justice system and left with a burning desire to lift this city out of the shithole that it found itself in. I needed to be able to do what justice coudln't. I want to provide the city with something that I couldn't while I was constrained by the system. Chasing that punk, I had no laws binding me. It was freedom. I had the ability to provide real justice.

I shouldn't, I thought as I sat in a bar in the core of downtown. An old Irish pub—small, with dim lighting. I sipped on my bottle of beer, holding on to the glass neck with my index and middle fingers. I stared blankly at the people through the window who stood outside for a smoke.

It was a quiet evening. Considering it's a Wednesday, that was no real surprise. *Happy Hump Day.* I took another sip of my drink. At the far-right corner, at the front of the bar, there was a small stage where a man sat on a stool. He wore a red plaid shirt, fashioned a long beard, and had his hair tied up into a bun. A guitar rested on his lap. The man had his eyes closed, tapping his foot to a tempo while strumming the guitar and singing into the mic by the stool. It was some folk song that he wrote. Open mic night.

Not many of the patrons seemed interested in his music. They were either there with friends or sitting and watching the game that was on TV. But he continued to play. I appreciated his lack of care for those around them. It was clear in the confidence expressed through his voice and the fluent strumming of his guitar. He was playing the music for himself. He was free. The type of freedom that I had never known before. Not until this week.

Chasing that Crystal Moth punk was exhilarating, I thought, remembering how I got the info I needed with ease. *That was freedom. I operated under my own laws.*

Before that moment, my job was to follow orders. Although I never followed them very well, it was how I functioned. I grew used to the restrictions set on me by my superiors. And the justice system that watched my every move like Big Brother or something. Not anymore. Now I could think on my own and freely make my next move.

I should really drop the Crystal Moths thing, I thought, trying to convince myself. I took another big drink of my beer.

The idea of going after them was very attractive. I felt—still feel—a burning desire to figure out what they're up to. *I could become a private investigator.* There isn't anything wrong with that. However, I would need to be hired for the occasion. Plus, doing freelance investigation on my own might earn the disrespect of my old co-workers. PIs are a nuisance for them, always sticking their noses where they shouldn't.

Like how I did on Monday. No, I'm not going to, I thought again, tapping my hands on the table. Being fired is my opportunity to grow and expand. There's more to life than the law—good and evil—right and wrong.

I can get into camping. I couldn't help but laugh to myself at the thought. *Christ.* It's something so peaceful that I couldn't visualize myself doing it.

My phone buzzed in my pocket, and I took it out to look at the notification. The pop-up display showed it was a text message from Ace, reading: *Hey Michael, just checking in again. You alive?*

He just doesn't give up on me. I sighed. I've been avoiding him all week. He's tried to contact me every day since Sunday. I've also been staying clear of my mom. Then again, I've been keeping contact with her to a minimum for the past six months—except for Sunday. She just assumes I'm busy.

I exhaled heavily and took another gulp of my beer. The thought of Sunday struck a chord. I lost my life that day. *Will I ever find something new? Rebuild what I had?* They were tough questions that weren't going to be answered in one night of drinking alone.

Swallowing the last of my beer, I got up from the table. *I should get home,* I thought. *But for what?* Really, I had no obligations. I could keep drinking until I vomited or got kicked out. But that would be a slippery slope into alcoholism. I still have enough discipline from my years on the force to not completely fall off the deep end.

Looking into the Crystal Moths would be exactly that, I thought, walking out into the brisk air. *I'm fixated on it. Fixated on that night. Alex G.* I zipped my jacket up and exhaled, seeing my breath in the air. Winter was soon. The group of smokers near the entrance were all staring toward the street, wide-eyed.

"Bruce just got knocked down," one man with glasses said. He was one of the bartenders from inside. He had a smoke in one hand and was on the phone with the other.

I followed the group's gazes to the middle of the road where six people were brawling—five men and one woman. The girl, wearing a black wool coat, was screaming. She was struggling to get a man in a leather coat off of her. Three other men, wearing rugged clothing, were beating on one man who wore a blazer and jeans. He tried to defend himself, but the blows were coming in too strong for him to hold them back, and he collapsed. Another man was on the ground a couple feet away. He was out cold. It was the bartender from the front of the bar. He had checked my ID earlier. He must have tried to break up the fight.

I squinted and looked at the smokers. There was one girl and another man by the bartender. The girl stared in awe while the other guy looked at his phone. He held the girl with his free hand.

"Are you all just going to stand there?" I shook my head at them and rushed toward the fight. *People are too afraid of getting dirt on their hands. I prefer the dirt.*

My eyes were on the three men beating on the lone man who was on his knees, still trying to fend off their blows. I glanced over to the girl who struggled with the one man in a leather coat. He pulled out a knife. This was about to get serious. I couldn't have anyone get harmed. I had to stop them.

The man had his back turned to me as the girl fell to the ground, crying. She cringed as tears poured from her eyes.

"No, please don't!" she cried.

My footsteps grew louder as I charged, catching the attention of the man with the knife. He spun around—his long black ponytail flung back as he swung the knife at me. He missed as I came to a halt, barely dodging the attack. He roared and slashed a couple more times—both misses. On his downswing, I snagged his arm and slammed it into my knee, forcing him to drop the knife.

With one tug, I pulled him into me, ramming his face into my forehead. The sound of crushing cartilage erupted and I threw an uppercut into his jawline. It pushed the man back. He stumbled, trying not to fall on his ass.

I stepped forward and gave a swift kick to the back of his knee. He tripped, hitting the back of his skull on the pavement.

One down.

I rushed over to the group of three who were kicking the downed man. One of them was scrawny and missing a tooth. He had noticed my attack on their buddy and he turned to face me.

"Hey!" He came running with his hands clenched into fists. The man swung at me, sloppy and with a lack of coordination. The blow was easy to avoid by stepping to the side. He exhaled heavily, exposing a distinct stench of liquor. I snagged his open arm and twisted it, causing it to snap. He curled inward and cried in pain. I finished the attack with an elbow to his nose. Blood poured down his face as I rushed past him to the last two men.

The sound of the man's cry caught the others' attention, and they switched their focus to me. One was a larger and had several acne scars on his face, while his partner was tall, broad shouldered, and stood with confidence.

The acne-faced man rushed at me first and attempted to trample me with his weight. I intercepted his charge with a swift boot to his shins. The blow stunned the man, throwing him head first. It gave me enough time to recover my stance and coil my fist. I launched it into his face as he fell toward me. The blow knocked him back upright. I could feel the pressure in my wrist from the intense impact—that's going to hurt tomorrow.

I followed my attack with a right hook to the side of his skull, causing him to stumble backward to the ground.

The last opponent stopped in his tracks several feet away. He reached into his long jacket and pulled out a metre-long metal chain. He swung it a couple times, holding it with both hands. The man spat on the ground then started circling me.

This is where I can't fuck up, I thought, eyeing the man. That chain would be a critical blow.

He stepped between me and the front of the bar where the smokers stood. The bartender, who had finished his call—with who I assumed was the cops—now had his phone pointed toward the fight. The girl and the man also did the same.

Are they recording me? I thought. That wasn't good. I didn't need evidence of me beating the shit out of people, even if it was to protect a couple on a date.

The large man bellowed and rushed toward me. He swung the chain, extending his reach with the heavy metal. If I hadn't moved, it would have collided with my face and knocked a couple teeth out. I leaped to the side, rolling on the ground as the chain rushed past me, slamming into the ground with a loud *clack*.

The man swung again in a fluent motion, following my movement with each strike he made. I dodged the second attack with a leap, but the third was too quick and it scuffed my ankle.

I grunted. *Just the system warning the brain*, I reminded myself. Pain is inevitable in life, and I learned to build up an endurance. It only exists in the mind—although that didn't change the fact that it was going to bruise.

I can't keep dodging this guy. His reach was too great, and the only way I could get an advantage in the situation would be to rush him head-on. On my good foot, I leaped forward as he readied another attack.

The man lifted his arm up and swung down toward me. I accelerated before he could lash the chain, tackling the man. The two of us went flying and landed heavily on the pavement with me on top. The blow was enough to knock the weapon from his hand. It skidded away.

It was a standard tactic that I learned in training, and it finished with grabbing the seized suspect by the arms with cuffs. Unfortunately, I didn't have cuffs. I did have fists, though, and that guy had pissed me off.

Getting upright, I sat on the man's chest. I clenched my hand and brought it down to his face before he had a chance to lift his arms in defense. My other hand mirrored the first, colliding with the man's nose.

He winced from the pain and tried to cover his face, but he was too slow to stop the third punch. This one was dead centre and caused his head to rebound off the road, knocking him out cold.

"Piece of shit," I mumbled between breaths.

I rose from my opponent and surveyed the other three men on the ground. The pain I had unleashed on them was too much for them to handle, and they had clearly given up. I was the victor. A little battered, but I won.

The victims, I remembered, noticing the girl had moved. She knelt beside the man in the blazer who sat on the road, rubbing his head.

"Are you hurt?" I asked, rushing over to them.

The man shook his head and lifted his hand to see there was blood on his skull from where the men were kicking.

"God, thank you!" the girl in the red dress exclaimed.

"Keep your hand on there to stop the bleeding. You should get checked for concussion." I turned around to see that the three smokers were now accompanied by several other people who were previously inside the bar. Most of them had their phones out. They cheered and shouted with excitement.

Shit, I thought. This was not the type of publicity that I needed.

"That was astonishing," the girl beside me said.

I looked over at her as she brushed her brunette hair from her face, looking up at me.

"You saved our lives."

I can't stick around here, I thought. The pub is also in Ace's patrol. He could easily be the first to respond. Even if it wasn't Ace, I didn't want any cops finding me. Being recently fired, brawling with people on the streets wasn't the brightest move. My past wasn't going to work in my favour.

"You're welcome. Take some self-defense classes." I started off, looking for the least busy street to turn down.

"Wait!" came a man's voice from the crowd.

"Come back!" a girl called out.

That's the last thing that I would want to do, I thought as I jogged into an alleyway. *What the hell was I thinking?* But I wasn't thinking. That was the same type of bullshit that got me fired. At least they can't kick me off the force this time. They could throw me in jail for using excessive force, though.

My heart raced as I ran through the alley, checking over my shoulder a few times to see if anyone was following me. Thankfully, no cops had shown up yet. There wasn't anyone from the bar trying to catch up with me either. I rushed through the side streets for about another block.

It seemed quiet, so I decided to return to the main streets, pulling up the hood of my grey hoodie. I could use the pedestrians as camouflage on the walk back home. As I stepped onto the sidewalk, a police car buzzed by the main drag, sirens roaring. Traffic steered off to the side, providing room for the unit to zoom through.

I got out at the right time, I thought.

My senses felt heightened, picking up on all the sounds around me. I noticed every detail on the sidewalk. It was a typical adrenaline high I got from fighting. The same rush that I got when I was on the force. The same thrill as when I was confronting that Crystal Moths punk. The gratifying feeling of freedom.

There's more to it than the high, I thought. Those two needed my help, and the other people outside weren't doing anything. What would have happened if I hadn't intervened? The witnesses were the typical cowardly generation of anxiety-filled, cellphone-abusing pansies who can't actually stand up to anyone, let alone throw a punch. They'd rather stay off to the side with their dicks in their hands.

That's not me. I took action. It felt satisfying to be able to bring some real justice. The good justice that protects people. That young couple was safe because of me. The shits that attacked them would probably think twice before causing trouble in the future, too.

I reached into my pocket and pulled out a cigarette, leaning it into the flame of the lighter I ignited. *Perhaps it isn't such a bad idea to keep looking into the Crystal Moths*, I thought. Maybe I was on to something with this newfound freedom—or maybe I was still on a high from the fight, feeling like I could conquer the world.

The rest of the walk home had me nervous. I worried that a cop car was going to pull up at any moment. I kept my stride calm and stayed near public areas so I could blend in with the downtown night. After an hour of walking, I made it back to my condo complex and into my suite. I kicked my shoes off and wandered over to my fridge. A fight like that required a drink to celebrate.

I'm not going to drink that often, I reassured myself. The victory was just too good not to celebrate, even if it was by myself. I pulled out a bottle from my fridge and cracked it open, tipping it into my mouth to let the cool bitter ale run own my throat. Satisfying.

Ace would have enjoyed the brawl. I deeply wanted to call him up and tell him about what happened, but I knew he would not be impressed. I couldn't let him know how I took the law into my own hands.

This will have to be a secret victory, I thought, walking over to my couch to turn on the TV—something I was trying to use more often. Especially after tonight, why not unwind?

I grunted as I sat down. My ankle and wrist were warm—the subtle swelling before the pain. *I'll sleep it off.*

Turning on the TV brought up the news, which was the last channel I had watched. Two newscasters sat at their long marble table. At the bottom left were the words:

MAN   MURDERED   EARLY   MONDAY   MORNING
Another Snapper victim?

I shook my head and sighed. *I was hoping that sick fuck would have vanished by now.*

The blonde anchorwoman looked straight into the camera just as the text at the bottom of the screen faded. "We will now be joining Tom for a live report of an indecent that people are already talking about online. Tom, over to you."

The screen switched to a news reporter who stood in front of an ambulance and a police car. Off to the right was a small Irish pub—the one I had just come out of.

That didn't take long. I turned up the volume to hear the reporter.

The curly-haired reporter held his mic close. "The couple was leaving a bar in downtown Edmonton and were confronted by a group of men. The group immediately attacked the two, and one of the bar's staff members attempted to intervene before a mysterious man joined to help. The scene of the crime has been sealed off momentarily so the police can interview the witnesses and victims."

The feed switched over to a video of the four men, the girl, her date, and a bald man in a hoodie: me. It was taken by one of the cowards standing by the bar entrance having their smoke.

"Shit." I took another drink.

Just below the video was a caption from a social media post. It had the typical profile photo, a post date of today, and a video description that read *Edmonton's Mysterious Hero.*

The reporter continued to speak as the video played. "As shown in the video, we can clearly see that a man came to the rescue, defending the young couple. The bartender suffered a concussion, but is recovering quickly."

Watching the thugs get their asses handed to them on video made me chuckle. At the same time, it had me concerned. I looked different with a bald head, but the police might still be able to identify me.

The camera switched to the man and woman who were smoking with the bartender. They smiled as the mic pointed toward them. The man held up his phone. "As soon as that guy ran into the fight, I started filming it. Whoever he was, the city needs to see what happened. It's blowing up online!"

The girl stood straight. "We uploaded it right away, saying our city has its own hero running around the streets of Edmonton. The conversation exploded, and people are sharing the video under hashtag YEGman."

Hashtag YEGman? I thought. I had heard the term hashtag before. It was used to categorize online posts to easily find similar content. I've never been very involved with social media, but I could piece together the clever title that the people chose. *YEG* was the airport code for the city, and *man* was playing off superhero comic books.

The reporter brought the mic back to himself. "The video of the mysterious vigilante performing this incredible feat of bravery is blowing the city away and taking the internet by storm. We'll have more details once the police make a public statement. For now, the internet is praising the heroic actions of hashtag YEGman."

MICHAEL

YEGman

Chapter 9

FLY INTO THE LIGHT

Crumpled black clothes littered the laminated flooring of a bedroom where a steel frame contained a mattress covered in bunched black-and-navy sheets. A flashing smartphone on a round, circular nightstand played loud, bass-pounding music with distorted snares.

A groan came from the human shape underneath the bed sheets. A small, pale hand poked out and reached around for the smartphone.

Shut up, Lola thought as she struggled to find her phone. When her hand found it, she slid it over to her face. She swiped the screen, turning off the loud music. She had set her phone's alarm to play one of her favourite bands: Combichrist.

Her alarm only went off when it was late afternoon. She was more of a night owl and preferred to sleep in. Most of her classes were after lunch or in the evening, so there was no reason to be one of those morning people. Her shifts at the café were in the evening too. Besides, days like yesterday were long with classes and work. She needed the extra hours to sleep.

"Shit," Lola mumbled while looking at her phone's notifications—twenty-one, to be exact. Social media was difficult to deal with when she was so busy juggling her regular life. *How do people have time to manage all of this?* It was a challenge to also find the time to maintain a blog. Her site was the best way for her to get the news to people. It also served as a living portfolio, showing she had experience in reporting. That would be a big help in getting an internship.

Then there was her social life. She swiped her phone's unlock code and found a majority of the notifications were for social media—as she expected. One of them was a text—from Donnie. *Hey Lola, we still meeting up today?* the text read. It was about a half hour old.

Donnie, she thought, sitting upright. *He had some dirt on the Crystal Moths.*

She quickly punched in a reply, her fingers rapidly pressing the screen from muscle memory. It was easy for her to communicate through typing at any time of the day. If she had to talk to someone without a coffee, though, she would struggle to translate her thoughts into words. Life was intolerable without morning caffeine. *Yeah, Black Dog at 8?* she typed before hitting send.

Lola browsed the rest of her notifications to see if anything was of interest. Nothing. Mostly reminders about events or comments on her posts and selfies. Nothing from Becky for the past couple of days, and still nothing from Brian.

She sighed and looked up the ceiling. It was difficult not to think about the boy. After her dramatic exit at the party, he had made no effort to contact her. What was she doing wrong? She knew that Becky was not a fan of him, and he didn't treat Lola well. The times that she could spend with him alone, though, were like magic.

Fuck feelings, she thought. It was normal for her to be grumpy when she hadn't had her morning coffee yet. It was true, though: if she and Brian didn't like the same fashion, the same music, and have the same sense of humour, she wouldn't bother. It also didn't help that he was such good eye candy—and was good in bed.

That curled stubble on his chin, she thought, feeling her heart rate increase. *No, not now.* She got herself up from bed and glanced around to see where her clothes were.

Clothes, coffee, then get ready to see Donnie—for the blog. Blog. She had to keep herself occupied so her mind wouldn't wander to thoughts of Brian. It was easy to be distracted by thoughts of him when she was alone—when she wanted the comfort of his arms or to taste his lips.

Stop! "Christ." She picked up her crumpled, black skinny jeans from the pile on the ground. "Coffee," she reminded herself as she sifted through the pile of clothes to find a top to wear. A band shirt was the first to grab her attention due to the white-and-red pop-art-styled illustration of a girl slapping a man. KMFDM—another industrial band she was fond of.

Throwing the shirt on, Lola brushed her hair aside. After sliding into her jeans, she tucked her phone into her back pocket and left her room. She squinted from the dramatic change in light. The west-facing living room windows that led to the balcony had no curtains.

Lola plodded to the kitchen, avoiding the light as best as she could until she was around the corner. She went to the Keurig brewing machine by the sink. She was thankful that her roommate owned one. The pods for the brewing machine were far more cost-effective than going to a café.

Jenna always has her shit together, Lola thought. They were both going to university and worked jobs to pay the bills. However, Jenna was more organized and more focused than Lola. Lola had a hard time following rules and naturally gravitated toward the underground night scene. Jenna was more of a daytime person, which also made their roommate arrangement work well—they rarely saw each other.

Lola turned the machine on and opened one of the white drawers to pick out a coffee pod from the drawer. At this point, she didn't care what flavour it was. She just needed coffee. She grabbed her favourite a mug from the cupboard—a matte-black mug in the shape of a skull. It was one that Brian gave her on their second date.

It's like he lost interest and doesn't want to talk anymore. Am I boring?

The machine made bubbling noises and the *ready* light flashed. She placed her pod into the machine, closed the lid, and pressed start.

As the machine began to pour, her phone buzzed.

Brian? was her first thought. Lola grabbed her phone from her pants pocket only to see it was Donnie texting back. Her heart sunk slightly. It shouldn't have, but any time the phone buzzed, she hoped that it would be

Brian apologizing or checking to see how she was doing. No luck. The boy was selfish.

Why do I do this to myself? She swiped the phone to read Donnie's text, which read, *That's awesome. See you there.*

Come on, just forget that idiot, Lola thought, putting her phone back into her pocket. She had a lot going on in her life and didn't need to cloud it with a stupid boy. She was about to get some information on the Crystal Moths—finally some new, juicy content for her blog. She hadn't been posting as much as she normally would. She wasn't putting in as much effort into searching for new content—which was directly related to her preoccupation with Brian.

He's just a distraction, she thought.

When the machine stopped pouring, she grabbed her cup and took a sip of the dark liquid. The bitter smell jump-started her brain, and the taste was all so soothing.

Coffee, done. Now to put my face on, she thought, wandering over to the bathroom. Lola couldn't stand being in public without having any form of eyeshadow or eyeliner applied. It was equally as important to put on foundation and lipstick.

Stepping into the backroom, she saw a reflection of her bare face: pasty skin, half-shaved blonde brows, washed-out lips, and dark bags under her eyes.

Ew. That is not me, she thought, placing her coffee on the counter. Lola never did identify with how she naturally appeared. Perhaps she'd been insecure since high school, or maybe she looked too much like her mother back east. Who knew. She didn't spend much time thinking about it. She simply knew how to fix it. Lola felt truly like herself with her gothic attire. Applying makeup and being able to change her appearance as she saw fit gave her a level of control and confidence that was unmatched.

Lola began applying her everyday makeup. She didn't use heavy eyeshadows or primers like she would when going out for a night on the town. Wednesday was her day off from school and work, and there weren't any parties or bands playing. It was supposed to be the day she would focus on her craft.

No boy to distract me either, she thought while applying the final touches to her face. Lola leaned back slightly to analyze her eyes in detail. She examined the arches of her pencilled-in brows, the darkness and length of the eyeshadow, and the blending of her foundation.

Could be better, she thought. She barely put effort into her outfit and hadn't even touched her hair. Truthfully, she could spend all day working on her appearance—but if she did, she would be there for hours and poor Donnie would be waiting at the Black Dog.

Good as it'll get. Lola took a brush and cleaned up her hair, then gathered the rest of her items for the trip out: her notebook, her phone, her laptop, and her purse—which had an assortment of daily necessities of its own.

Once she was finished, it was a little after seven, which gave her enough time to get over to the Black Dog. It was always a favourite of hers. One of the few good places you could drink alone without looking like a complete loser.

Lola slipped into her black Doc Marten boots and tied the laces. She then threw on her leather jacket, purse, and laptop bag. She was ready to head out.

She felt her phone vibrate in her pocket again and pulled it out. Zero notifications.

Phantom buzz, she thought. Simply her mind playing tricks on her. The phantom buzz happened a lot. She had a knee-jerk reaction when it came to checking her phone. She also spent a lot of time on it.

Lola unlocked the pastel-blue front door of the apartment and stepped out into the white, narrow, wood-floored hallway. She locked the door and began to hike down to the lobby of her apartment complex—only four levels high, it had no elevator.

She reached the main floor after three flights of stairs and twisted the steel handle to open the door. Stepping outside, she could feel a slight brisk breeze pick up even with the sunny sky. That was a winter chill—the type of cold that came when summer was long over and the seven months of frozen hell had begun.

Lola started walking toward the Black Dog. She lived a good half an hour away from the bar, which was located on Whyte Ave. The avenue was the city's arts district, complete with a farmer's market, boutique shops, cafés, and bars. It was close to the university too, making it popular for the young crowd—especially during the night.

She made it out of her quiet neighbourhood and began walking west to Whyte Ave. She found it easier to put her silly thoughts of Brian aside now that she was out of the house. Her senses were stimulated by the cars buzzing, people walking, and the nearby construction of new buildings.

It's a good day, she thought. *I'm finally going to get some good information on these Crystal Moths. Get the blog some real hits. Maybe get the attention of a news channel.* She felt like the day had a purpose. It was a nice change from the numbing feeling she'd had over the past few months of chasing Brian.

By the time Lola made it to the Black Dog, she had worked up a bit of a sweat even through the cool wind. On a Wednesday, the bar was fairly quiet and casual. During weekends, they'd have a couple of bouncers out front to check IDs and to steer the crowd. Today, there was no bouncer and no lines.

Lola walked up to the burgundy and forest-green building, directly under the chain-hung sign with a black dog on it. She pulled open the wide, chipped door and stepped into the dimly-lit bar. She had been there dozens of times and walked in with comfort, ignoring the framed paintings and metal signs on the aged wooden walls. To her right was a set of stairs leading up to the second level.

The main floor had about a half a dozen people besides the waitress and bartender behind the bar near the stairway. At a table in the far-left corner, Lola spotted a larger man with long black hair who was watching the TV mounted just above him. It was Donnie.

She smiled with excitement and approached him with a friendly wave. "Hey," she said.

Donnie looked over and raised his drink. "Hey."

Lola opened her arms for a hug. Most guys, she wouldn't be so willing to hug. But she considered Donnie to be a friend and knew he wasn't a perv who would abuse the situation for a boob press. Plus, his size and warmth made her comfortable.

She gave him a squeeze while leaning against his large shoulder as he lightly patted her back. Lola sat herself beside Donnie, carefully hanging her purse and laptop bag on the chair and looking up at the TV. It was playing the news channel—which wasn't common for a bar to do in the evening, but the Black Dog staff liked to mix it up depending on the time and day.

Donnie shifted in his seat, aligning himself to face Lola. "How goes?"

Before Lola could answer, the waitress showed up. Her curly black hair bounced as she came to a halt. "Hey! What can I get for you?"

"A Keith's works," she said.

"Pint?"

"Yeah, thanks," Lola said. She recognized the waitress. They didn't know each other personally, but they had seen each other just enough times that she wouldn't need her ID checked.

Lola shrugged. "I'm doing all right." *You know, as all right as a person can be after seeing someone get their neck snapped. Not to mention the other drama I have going on.* She knew full well that she wasn't going to give Donnie that level of detail. "How about you?"

Donnie shrugged and took a sip of his beer. "Not bad. Left the club a bit after you on Sunday. Band practice on Tuesday. Getting ready for the show coming up. You stormed out pretty fast that night. What was up?"

Lola sighed. "Boy troubles."

"Brian?"

"Yeah, he pissed me off. I saw him with another girl."

Donnie shrugged. "Yeah. Sounds like a douche, from what you've said."

The waitress arrived and placed a pint filled with golden ale beside Lola.

"There you go!" she said, moving on to the next table.

Lola took a large gulp of her beer. She knew Donnie was being truthful, but it still aggravated her. She felt a need to defend Brian—probably because he was a reflection of herself and her interests.

She shrugged. "Yeah, well, we'll see what I'll do about that. I'm trying to focus more on my studies and the blog for now."

"And like I said, your blog is good. It's to the point and you cut out all the bullshit. Plus no click-bait blog titles. "

Lola blushed, as she did the last time Donnie complimented her on her blog. Any time someone complimented her on her craft, she felt a surge of warmth throughout her body. "Thanks. That's encouraging. I really can't neglect it anymore like I have been. Shouldn't be getting distracted with boys."

Donnie chuckled and took a sip of his beer. "I could use a distraction myself."

"Not with your show coming up, trust me. This stuff sucks. I hate having feelings. Sometimes I wish I was a robot and didn't have to deal with emotions."

"Way to fill the industrial-goth stereotype."

She smirked. "Yeah, well, it makes sense. Sometimes I wish I could just push it all out. Be free from all of those emotions."

Donnie raised an eyebrow. "Wanna know a solution to that?"

"What?"

"Meth."

Lola and Donnie laughed.

She brushed her hair aside, exposing her neck. "Well, if you know where to get some."

"Isn't that why we're here?" Donnie jokingly replied.

"Indeed. Let me just get my recording app and notebook." Lola dug through her bag for a moment before pulling out her black leather-bound notebook with an embossed skull on the front. She flipped it open to a blank page. After, she found a pen in her bag and placed it by her phone on the table. Finally, she opened the recording app on her phone.

Donnie took a sip of his beer and cleared his throat. "Ready?"

Lola crossed her legs toward Donnie and pressed the record button. "So, you said a Crystal Moth tried to recruit you?"

"Yeah, at a show I was playing at. Right after we finished opening for Soul Guzzlers. These two guys showed up: one named Mika, the other named Alex G."

Alex G.? Lola thought, remembering the man named Alex who she met when rescuing Becky from the apartment.

Donnie continued: "They caught my attention because they were in all white at a metal show. Normally it's a sea of black, y'know? And word had already gotten out that dressing in all white meant Crystal Moth."

"Yeah, something I know now. What'd these two look like?"

"One had slicked-back hair. Tall. Thin. The other was a little shorter. Asian and bald. They didn't belong there."

"Wait, was the bald guy buff? About this high?"

"Yeah. You know him?"

Lola took a sip from her beer. "I ran into him at an after-party. I was getting my friend, and he was there. The other guy too—Alex G."

"Shit, you were at a Crystal Moth after-party?"

"Yeah, it was sketchy as fuck."

"No doubt."

"Anyways, go on," Lola said.

"These guys approach me—compliment our show. Normal stuff after a gig. Mika says they're new in town and not familiar with the metal scene. We chat about it, and I ask where they're from. Out east, they said."

"Alex G. had that easterner accent, hey?"

"Yeah, he sounds retarded. Eventually, they asked if I wanted any coke. I told them no, I don't do that shit. They seemed okay with it. Alex G. stepped closer as Soul Guzzlers played. He said that he saw I had quite the influence on the scene."

"Weird," Lola said, jotting down notes.

"Yeah. I thanked him. He went on to say he was looking for more people to join their organization. I cut him off and said I knew about the Crystal Moths and didn't want anything to do with them. Said that they weren't going to infect the metal scene with their shitty drugs."

Lola nodded. "Rock on, man. How'd they take that?"

"They laughed. I thought for sure they were going to get pissed off and start a fight. Nah, they agreed with me. Mika spoke up and said that they weren't interested in selling drugs."

"Really?" Lola shook her head. "They fooled the rest of the city."

"That's what got my attention. You don't get approached by the Crystal Moths every day. I asked what they wanted from me."

"Alex G. said the Crystal Moths were much more than drug distributors. They simply used it as a goods exchange—like currency. As if any other gang hasn't tried to use that cop-out before. What's interesting is what he said after that. He said he'd be straight with me: there are a lot of lowlifes in the city. Underground music scenes are attractive to them, much like the drugs. They're attracted to them like a moth to a light."

"Symbolic."

Donnie smirked. "He said they were looking to make them useful to civilization again. They were the light and could help those people contribute to the higher classes of society. They would become heroes and wouldn't have to waste away."

"What does that mean?"

Donnie shrugged. "Not sure. Probably to deliver their drugs? I asked if it was some sort of new-age cult. Alex G. said they weren't into religious propaganda. They were in the business of people."

"Of people? Like human trafficking?" *Alex G. was talking about something when I rescued Becky.* She could barely remember. She was far too traumatized that morning to recall all the details.

"I asked that too. He said they weren't involved in the sex industry."

"What, then?"

"I asked him what he wanted because I was getting tired of their vagueness and was exhausted from the show. Alex G. said he couldn't elaborate in a public place. He needed to know if I was interested."

Lola couldn't help but snort. "Yeah, so he can stab you when no one else is around."

"I'm serious. That's what he said." Donnie took a sip from his beer.

"Sounds like a crack-monkey to me." Lola took a drink as well. "Got anything else?"

"Yeah. He said he liked my straightforward nature and said if I wanted to know more, I should join him after the show. They were going to have a get-together with their new recruits."

"Did you go?"

"I said thanks, but no thanks and went to leave. Alex G. put his hand on my shoulder and handed me a card. He said I could be a part of something bigger than the metal music." Donnie reached into his pocket and pulled out a white business card with black text. He handed it to Lola.

She flipped it over to find a moth-silhouette illustration on the front with a triangle surrounding it. On the back side, it had the number *999-1111.* Lola looked up at Donnie and shook her head. "No Area code?"

"Weird, eh?"

"What is it, then?" Lola asked.

"I'm guessing a phone number. Interesting choice, though."

"Why?"

"1111 is often associated with uniformity. From what I read online, it represents going through a cycle. Manifesting into form."

"What?"

"Some shit I read on the internet. I dunno."

"Did you call this number?"

119

"Fuck no." Donnie took another drink. "It's too weird—I don't wanna get involved. I keep my life simple. But like I said, I knew you'd want to know about this."

"Yeah. Can I keep the card?"

"Go wild. Just be careful."

"I'll be fine, honestly. I've been through enough shit that a creepy cult-gang isn't going to scare me away."

Donnie raised his eyebrow. "Just lookin' out for you."

"Thanks, Donnie." Lola went to touch his arm just as her phone buzzed. *Brian?* she thought. *Fuck, I gotta stop doing that.* Lola paused the recording and swiped down to see a notification with a picture of Becky. It read, *Becky has tagged you in a video.*

"One sec—just going to see what this is." Lola unlocked her phone and tapped the notification. The post was for a video on a social networking site. Becky was known to send her random things.

The video was originally from someone she had never met before. Perhaps Becky knew them. Regardless, it was a live streaming video with over two hundred viewers. Lola swiped down to the comments section. New comments were pouring in: *Good job! YEG's Hero! #YEGman!!* Lola swiped back up to the video. It was of a bald man fighting a group of thugs. A man was on the ground beside a young couple who were in awe. There were several other cellphones held out, recording the scene of the bald guy dodging a chain weapon held by another man.

"Holy shit, Donnie, check this out." She turned her phone over to Donnie.

Donnie squinted at the video. He laughed. "Hashtag YEGman? What is this?"

"Looks like some guy is rescuing these people. That's downtown, isn't it?"

"Yeah. Why's everyone else just standing there?"

"Scared? Who knows. People suck," Lola said.

"Not this guy. Look at him!"

Lola looked down at the screen to see the bald man defeat the last thug and check on the wounded people. The crowd cheered loudly. The man glanced back before running away while the crowd called out to him.

Lola fiddled with her hair. "Looks like Edmonton is finally getting some real justice."

Donnie smirked. "If only he could kick those Crystal Moths out of the city."

"Yeah, right?" Lola placed her phone back on the table and downed the rest of her beer. "Hashtag YEGman. That's catchy."

"Yeah." Donnie finished his beer and slammed it down. "Want another?"

"Let's," she said with a smile. Lola's phone buzzed, and she instinctively looked down at the lock screen. It was a text message from Brian.

Fuck. She felt her heart skip a beat. She unlocked her phone and read the message: *Hey, sorry I'm a shithead. Can we get together today?*

"You okay?" Donnie asked.

Lola put her hand on her chest. "Yeah, I'll stick around for one more beer."

DONNIE

BLOOD
BATHERS

YEGman

Chapter 10
YOUNG AGAIN

Reports of a vigilante are a red-hot news topic. The talk of the town. It's in every newspaper, on every local channel, and dominates the internet. The video of me beating the living shit out of the four thugs is everything the media loves. It's filled with action and a sense of real justice. For too long have the people of Edmonton needed to see someone helping the city. Now they have that hero: the mysterious man in the video that demonstrated that the city isn't going to stand for the thugs and lowlifes anymore.

From what the news has shown, the internet hosts a swarm of videos, posts, and fan drawings categorized with the tag #YEGman. The articles in the newspaper speak about me like I'm a saviour—far more than what I actually am.

I do want to do good for this city, I thought, putting down the paper. I had to wonder: was the choice I made to help the folk or did I simply have some anger to let out?

The answer's still unclear. Perhaps I latched on to the hero persona because of the glorification from the papers. It feels good to give real results and be appreciated for it. Then again, the appreciation could end at any moment. I've seen it in the news before. The media likes to spin events with catchy headlines to engage viewers and then hop onto the next thing. It's a cheap tactic, and it distorts fact from fiction. They'll do anything they can to find or fabricate the next story. People are gullible for a feel-good story, and my act of kindness happened to be the most positive thing in months—if not years. Especially thanks to all the buzz from the Snapper and the Crystal Moths.

As long as the cops don't find out that it was me. That was the primary concern. Thankfully, it was dark and there weren't too many witnesses. The bartender probably got the best description of me. I've watched every recording I could find. Luckily, the poor lighting and video quality made it impossible to make out my face. Being a bald white guy makes it easy for me to blend in. Still, the paranoid side of me can't help but wonder if it's only a matter of time before someone recognizes me.

I stood from my couch and walked over to the window, looking at the downtown scenery. My wrist and ankle were still a little sore from the brawl. Only minor bruising. It didn't affect my walk anymore like it had earlier this week.

It's Friday night, and at the time, the sun was beginning to set. As with every Friday, it reminded me of the shooting outside of The Glowing Monkey.

Six months since I've been on patrol, I thought as I finished my cup of coffee. With all the YEGman stuff floating around, there hasn't been a lot of time to think about the Crystal Moths. For the past couple of days, I've kept my visits outside to a minimum. I didn't need any more trouble. I stayed at home, watched the news, and read some novels to keep my mind off of the recent events. But how long could I really keep myself entertained? I never enjoyed those activities before, and my mind always wandered to the city's crime.

The Crystal Moths aren't slowing down, I thought. It was disturbing to think that they had an entire sector dedicated to recruiting the youth. The thought crossed my mind that the prick, Alex G., would be farming The Glowing Monkey for more thugs.

I could intervene, I thought. It was worth a try. As it was, I didn't have much else to go on. The only working piece I had was knowing he liked to prey on young and gullible druggies. It sickens me to think that someone's so willing to feed off those who are easily manipulated into that dark world.

I should read a book. Again, the rational side of me tried to bring in reason. *I shouldn't take this any further than I have.* The brawl I had with the four thugs was a clear sign that I got away lucky.

It just felt so right, I thought, recalling the rush from giving lowlifes what they deserved. The satisfaction of saving that couple on a date. The freedom of real justice.

The city needs it. It's so obvious from the reaction to the hashtagYEGman video.

I knew the Crystal Moths investigation would need to be on my own time. I'm not hurting for cash—sure, the six months of unemployment burned a chunk of that, but I've been smart with how I've handled my money. Realistically, I could follow their activities in the evenings and juggle a part-time gig during the day. That would still let me take Sundays off for Mom.

I took the last sip of my coffee and watched the sun disappear below the horizon. It left the sky dark with only the skyscrapers and street lights bringing life to the night. *Looks like I'm going clubbing*, I thought.

My phone suddenly started vibrating in my pocket. The sudden motion caused me to jerk, and I reached for the smartphone. Pulling it out, I saw that the caller display read *Ace Borne*.

Ace, I thought. *I've been ignoring him.* I have a hard time expressing my emotions to a person if it doesn't involve beating the shit out of them, but truthfully, I've missed him. I knew he'd been swamped with work and his personal life, adapting to living with his girlfriend since the spring. I didn't want to be just another situation for him to worry about.

I shouldn't keep ignoring him, though. It's been all week. I swiped the answer slider on the phone's touch screen and brought it to my ear. "Hello?"

"Hey, Michael!" came Ace's cheery voice.

"Ace!" I couldn't help but smile. "How've you been?"

"Busy, to tell the truth. I've been pretty buried since—well, you know."

"Yeah, no doubt. I can't say I'm surprised." I chuckled. "It's been the complete opposite here."

"For sure. Thought I'd give you a buzz. Glad I could finally catch you. What have you been up to?"

"Outside of the excessive drinking? Not much."

"I get it. Hey, listen. I got some time tomorrow. Want to catch up?"

"Yeah, I'd like that. Wait, don't you work tomorrow?" I asked.

"Yeah, Delta Four though."

"You're right there."

"Great. I got to start a shift right away, but I wanted to call you before I got sucked into work."

"Of course. Want to meet at the usual spot?"

"Yeah, let's aim for around eight."

"All right, Ace. See you then. Hey, rough up some street urchins for me."

Ace let out a hearty laugh. "Yeah, we'll see about that. All right, good finally to hear from you, Michael."

"Likewise. Ciao." I hung up the phone and sighed. "I miss having a partner," I muttered to myself. "Time to get focused."

If I were to hunt down the Crystal Moths, I would need to be more careful—especially since I knew Ace was about to start his patrol. The Glowing Monkey is right in his area. I couldn't let him see my face there or anywhere nearby.

The YEGman video was a lucky break. Now, I can't take any major risks. My outfit is pretty clean: a T-shirt and jeans. No uniform. What I needed was something to cover my face. Thankfully, here in Edmonton, winter is the longest season. Toques and ski masks are a common thing to own.

I sifted through my box of winter clothing and found a couple scarves, leather gloves, and the full-face ski mask I use when I shovel Mom's walkway.

That will work for now, I thought, pulling out the deep-blue mask with an Oilers crest on it—the city's hockey team.

I looked through the rest of my clothes to find something that would help blend me into the night scene. Preferably something besides a plain T-shirt. Unfortunately, that's all I could find.

I might have to go shopping for a new wardrobe at some point. I changed from my jeans into a pair of dark-grey cargo pants to go with my white T-shirt. These clothes had a little more flex space than what I'd worn in the last brawl.

Now I was ready to hit up The Glowing Monkey and hunt for some Crystal Moth scum. I didn't have a real plan yet. The first thing would be to try to find that recruiter, Alex G., and extract some information from him. It would be impossible to get him arrested just for recruiting people into the gang, so I'd need to go deeper.

It pisses me off, I thought as I jammed my wallet into my pocket. *He got away after I shot him and continues his operation untouched.* I eyed the clock by my bedside to see that it was a quarter to ten. The nightlife often begins around then. It was time to head on out into the streets.

I left my apartment, holding the ski mask in my leather jacket pocket. I marched down toward the sidewalk, heading for the main drag. By the time I got to The Glowing Monkey, it would be closer to 11 PM, which is when the real chaos started. One thing I learned from the night shift is that the kids start to come out once their drugs kick in. That means that the street urchins won't be far behind.

Cars buzzed up and down the street at high speeds as I walked south. Some were fast sports cars and others were shitty beaters—then there was the odd cop car. Everyone was getting ready for the night's excitement. Most were probably out looking for a good time. Others were only out to prey on the weak.

That's where I come in. It was more motivation to voluntarily do this work. *If I can discourage the city's scum from continuing their shit, I've done my duty.* Going out on a stealth mission made me feel like I had a real purpose again. I had to do it.

About forty minutes later, I arrived near The Glowing Monkey. I wanted to get a sense of the surrounding area for tonight's agenda. If I had to chase anyone down, it would be beneficial to know how active the area was with pedestrians, cars, and police.

The night was loud. The roads were filled with vehicles crawling down the jammed roads. Swarms of people crossed the streets, huddling close together to stay warm as an icy wind blew between the downtown towers. Some flakes of snow began to fall, melting as they landed on the ground.

Thankfully, I would be in a stuffy, crowded club soon, and the cold wouldn't be an issue. I put my ski mask on, rolling it up to fit over my forehead. Wearing it as a hat while I walked in was less suspicious than having a full ski mask tucked into my pocket. Before I left home, I made sure I had nothing unusual in my pockets. Only a phone, wallet, smokes, a lighter, and keys. This would make me as least suspicious as possible.

Satisfied with my preparations, I approached The Glowing Monkey. It's the most brightly-lit venue on the block—much like how it was in May. The bass-pounding music could be heard, muffled, through the concrete walls. I eyed the familiar neon lights mounted onto the building.

Just as I remember it, I thought, pulling a cigarette from my pocket and lighting it up. Casually, I strolled up to a large pack of other smokers who stood on the sidewalk. There was a lineup outside of the entrance where they had two large bouncers in bright green shirts. One was checking IDs, and the other took pictures of each person that came in.

Damn, I thought. I should have seen it coming. Most clubs at this level have some sort of ID system, photographing each person that enters. The plan was getting risky. I'd just have to keep cool inside the club. Any sort of action would have to be outside, away from the club.

The crowd outside was mostly young, wearing bright clothes, beads along their arms, glow sticks, and furry hats. The girls laughed with each other and the guys bobbed their heads to the bass. They were all probably high out of their minds. Rave kids on drugs are a lot like moths: attracted to bright neon lights. Put those on the streets, and they'll start fluttering in by the dozens.

I strolled up to the crowd, casually slipping into the mass of smokers. I scanned each person that I passed, looking for white clothes or white rags.

So far, so good. Most of the people were eighteen to their early twenties. Some of their eyes flickered, some were glazed over, and others were wide as their owners talked rapidly to their friends. A mash-up of people on a variety of supplements.

Blending in has always been difficult for me. I've been told I'm too stiff and don't look natural. I guess if I was an animal, I'd be a bull rather than a chameleon. With that in mind, I just tried to relax.

Finishing my cigarette, I threw it to the ground and slipped through the rest of the crowd until I found the end of the lineup. I took my place in the back.

Shortly after, a few other people lined up behind me: a guy and two gals who were fairly young. One girl wore a masquerade mask, and the other two had animal masks on—complete with makeup to finish where the masks didn't cover.

"Have you been here before?" asked the blonde girl wearing a lion mask, with cat whiskers painted on her nose.

I glanced back to see that she was staring right at me with bright-blue, dilated eyes. "No, this is my first time," I replied.

The girl in the masquerade mask brushed her black hair from her face and smiled at me. "Oh my God, you're going to love it." She said in her naturally squeaky voice.

The guy with a mouse mask had his hands in his pockets and some glow sticks attached to his tank top. He smiled. "It's a ton of fun."

The blonde tilted her head, looking around me. "You here by yourself?"

I shook my head. "Not quite. I got some friends inside," I lied.

"They went in without you? That's not much fun," she replied.

I shrugged. "I don't mind. I'll get to see them soon."

"Well, hang with us for now while we wait." The blonde put on a warm smile and stepped to my side. The other two moved closer, initiating me as part of their group. It couldn't hurt to have them as camouflage. That way, I didn't look like some weird older guy going into the club by himself. I don't exactly fit the electronic-dance-music-kid stereotype. Same problem I always have when I try to act casual: I can't.

Blend in, I thought. Just then, an idea hit me. I asked the group, "Hey, you have any more glow sticks?"

"Sure!" the black-haired gal said excitedly while reaching into her bra. "Want a bump too?" she whispered.

I shook my head, knowing she was referring to coke. "Not yet. Too close to security."

"They're generally cool," the blonde said. "But better safe than sorry, hey?"

The black-haired girl pulled out two sticks from her bra and snapped them so they lit up. One was blue, and the other was green. "I'm Vicky, by the way," she said with a toothy smile.

I took hold of the sticks and shook her hand, smiling back. "Mike." I snapped the sticks around my wrist to form bracelets.

As badly as I wanted to use an alias, I couldn't. My ID was going to be up on the screen once I passed it to the bouncers. I didn't want to jeopardize the alliance I had just made with the three kids.

The girl named Vicky slid her hand away from mine in a sensual manner, running her fingers against my palm. "Pleasure to meet you."

"Jeff," the guy said, extending his hand.

I shook his weak and sweaty hand—the drugs he took were surely oozing out of his skin.

"Amy." The blonde waved.

"Your guys' first time here?" I asked, shifting closer to the group.

The line moved forward and the four of us walked as a single unit.

Vicky shrugged. "I haven't been here since May."

Jeff's eyes widened. "Were you here for the shooting?"

"Yeah. It got really weird when these two guys started beefing it out. Normally fights are no big deal, but this time it was a little over-the-top, y'know?"

Amy nodded. "Yeah. Sounds like it was really fucked up."

Vicky nodded and looked toward the entrance of the club. "It happens. Whenever you just want to have a good time, something always goes down."

The group was quiet through the rest of the lineup. Their eyes stared in random directions while they bobbed their heads to the music and swayed their bodies. Whatever they were on was peaking.

Substances are something I never got into. I do enjoy drinking now, but the abuse of drugs is beyond my understanding. It seems like a real waste of time, spending hours a night on making a fool of yourself. You act out of character, potentially get into trouble, and then deal with the recovery over the next day or two. If you ask me, people who do that simply aren't willing to face life head-on.

Cowards, I thought as I pulled out my ID, now next in line for the bouncer.

I watched as the girl in front of me handed her ID to the first bouncer then stood in front of the camera.

Follow her lead, I thought. She took her ID back and walked into the club.

"ID," came the deep voice of a large, bald guard with a ginger beard—eyes stern and brows flat as he stared at me.

I handed him the card. He checked it and nodded at me. "In front of the camera."

I took my ID back and put it in my pocket then stood in front of the small, round camera.

The bouncer behind the camera had shaggy hair and operated the computer with a few presses of the touch screen. He nodded at me after a couple seconds. "You're good to go."

I nodded back, climbed the single step, then walked through the wide-open door. The music became crisper as I entered toward a booth that a skinny girl dressed in a skimpy, low-cut top stood behind. She smiled at me while I approached and flicked her straight brunette hair out of her face.

"Hey! It's twenty-five tonight."

That's a little steep, I thought—although I suppose they need to make money somehow. They probably don't make a lot off the drinks, considering most of their club goers are into drugs.

I pulled the cash from my wallet and handed it to the girl.

Vicky came up from behind me and leaned on the counter. "How much is it?"

"Twenty-five," I replied.

She widened her eyes. "Wow, it's gone up."

I got my change back from the booth girl and she put a stamp on my wrist—a monkey eating a banana. I smiled at the girl then turned to Vicky to see that the other two were now beside us.

"All right, see you guys inside," I said, turning to step deeper into the club.

Time to dance.

Chapter 11

DANCE, MONKEY, DANCE

After getting patted down by a second set of bouncers, I stepped further into the narrow hallway inside The Glowing Monkey. I put my toque into my pocket and walked into a large open room finished with violet walls, black flooring, and a green ceiling. On the far-right side of the room was a stainless-steel, die-cut sign of the monkey logo. Green lights were mounted behind, emphasizing the shape in negative space.

In the centre of the large room was a split island bar. To the left side was a row of tables and couches. The bar had shelves lined up with a wide range of bottles in the middle of it. A couple bartenders tended to pouring drinks. Behind the island contained the dance floor and, further back, a raised stage. The dance crowd poured past the bar and near the entrance. A man with a backward cap and white hoodie stood on the stage, bobbing his head while adjusting dials—the DJ.

White top, potentially a Crystal Moth. What else do we have? I thought.

Off to the left of the entrance was a staircase leading to the second floor. The main floor was packed with people talking along the corners or leaning against tall tables. Others were sitting on the lounge-style leather couches, flirting and laughing just behind the row of tables. My eyes continued to examine the outfits of the crowd. The black lights made it easier to spot bright colours. So far, I'd noticed some white on people's outfits, but no full white or rags on arms. Everyone seemed energetic and smiley. Not the cool, cold attitude that the Crystal Moth members displayed.

A cheer came from behind me as Vicky came bouncing to my side with her arms in the air. "I love this DJ!" she shouted.

I smiled at her and bobbed my head to the music, moving my torso along. *Blend in. Blend in*, I thought. *This is not me.* Throwing a fist felt far more real than this.

Jeff and Amy rushed past us, arms rhythmically moving to the gritty bass line. Vicky smiled at me and took both of my hands, guiding me into the crowd with her friends.

Damn it, I thought. I wanted to scope out The Glowing Monkey, not go dancing. I supposed it was a plus to blend in with those kids. At the same time, I didn't want a girl probably under half my age dancing with me. For all I knew, she wasn't even eighteen.

Just blend in. God, I hate going undercover.

Vicky guided me past the bar and deep into the swarm of dancers. My eyes moved quickly back and forth, watching the people that we passed. I wanted to get a better look at each of them so I could put them in my memory bank. They were all kids. Some had their eyes closed, dancing on their own. Others bounced together. They all shared the common stench of sweat. An aura of heat radiated from their bodies.

Vicky brought my arms closer to my chest and moved her body only millimetres away from mine while she began to bounce to the beat. Her legs and hips brushed against my leg as she moved to the music. She patted her hands on my chest to the kick of the track.

Move with her, I thought, extending my stance and shifting my feet to the bass line. I probably danced like an old man. Still, I had to keep rhythm with her or I would seem out of place. I guess I could have walked away saying I was gay, but that would probably wreck the cover I had established. I didn't want to draw unnecessary attention.

I placed my hands on her hips to move with her body. Vicky flung her sweaty hair back, whipping it past my face. I caught a whiff of her naturally soft aroma. It had been months since I last picked up on a scent like that, or was that close to a girl.

No. My rational thoughts came into play, destroying the moment of ignorant bliss. *She's half your age.* I was undercover and had to keep my mind on finding Alex G. That was the goal.

I'll take in whatever I can from here and scope out the rest of the venue later, I thought, exchanging a smile with Vicky who now rested her forearms on my shoulders, biting her lip.

I kept my eyes partially closed, acting as if I was "getting lost" in the music as best as I could. Vicky closed her eyes completely and bounced her head side to side, hair flying with her. She bought into my act. It also helped that she was high out of her mind.

My gaze moved over the sea of heads that bounced with the beat. The DJ at the top of the pedestal swung his fist in tempo as he held one side of his headset against his ear. The crowd was at his fingertips. It amazed me how easily people were willing to give themselves up to a single person. Especially one who was just looking at a laptop screen.

Off in the far end of the venue, away from the DJ, I eyed the black leather couches that faced the crowd. They were filled with people. It was difficult to make out how many there were through the dancers and tall tables in front. That area would be worth examining. There was also the upstairs that I hadn't seen yet.

The DJ shifted to a slower, melodic track—a cooldown period, allowing the crowd to ease up and catch their breath.

"You're a fun dance buddy!" Vicky said, patting my chest.

"Listen, I'm going to try and find my friends. I'll be right back!" I squeezed her hips. "Not done here." I winked at her.

"Okay!" Vicky leaned up and pecked me on the cheek before stepping back. She raised her arms in the air, moving with the synth-driven melody. She waved at me while stepping back into the crowd.

I waved back then squeezed through the people, using my hand to guide several out of the way who were too blitzed to have any spatial awareness. Eventually, I reached the outskirts of the dance floor where I had more space to move around. Groups of people at the edges of the venue shouted to each other over the music—mostly guys wearing tight-fitting designer shirts that complemented their muscular figures. They watched the girls on the dance floor with lustful eyes.

The night scene never changes, I thought as I moved deeper into the club.

At the back of the venue were a number of raver kids with glow sticks, bouncing along to the beat on their seats. Some leaned against the wall and stared at the ceiling, waving their hands around. Most of the women wore skimpy dresses, and some men wore clean blazers. It all looked normal—at least for The Glowing Monkey.

Wait, I thought, noticing three men sitting in the lounge area. They wore white dress shirts. One had a white blazer. Each of them had a girl in a white dress at his side.

Bingo. I slowed my pace and watched as the three men stared at the dance crowd. The girls were calm, looking out into space, their eyes flickering. Probably accompanying the men for free party supplies. Groupies are common within the gang life. Just another reason I despise them and the underground drug industry. They affect so many lives around them. It's not just about the business as most of them claim.

This is why I'm here, I reassured myself.

I walked over to the opposite side of the lounge area, away from the presumed Crystal Moth members. Being closer to them, I could see that one of the men was bald, Asian, and had a thin, black goatee. In the middle was a Caucasian man with black, slicked-back hair, a goatee, and a smug grin on his face – that was Alex G. The girls with those two were both brunette and in their early twenties. The last man on the far end had spiky hair with frosted tips. The girl with him was blonde and near the same age as the others.

I spotted a nearby empty seat beside two guys on a couch near the washrooms. One was a thin, dangly kid with shaggy hair, stubble on his chin, and an abnormally large Adam's apple. The other had a short, spiky mohawk. That spot would provide a good view of what the three Crystal Moths were up to. They were clearly watching the crowd, but what for? Were they looking for potential recruits? Or were they watching an initiate perform a task? It was hard to say, but I needed to find out.

I can't just go in there and ask them. I need to send in a scout. I nodded to the two guys as I sat beside them. They glanced over at me, blank stares on their young faces. They held their drinks with both hands—a sign of nervousness.

These guys might work, I thought. It was either sit around and wait for the Crystal Moths to make a move, or make the first move myself. I'm not one for waiting around.

"You guys new here?" I asked.

They nodded. The kid with shaggy hair smiled. "Yeah. This place is awesome!" He shifted his feet, which made me notice his black PVC pants and biker boots.

I smiled back. "Welcome! I've been in the scene for years, and this is the best place we've had in a long time."

The two kids exchanged glances. "Awesome."

"What are your names?"

"Brian," the guy with messy hair said.

"Mike," I replied.

The guy with the mohawk leaned closer. "I'm Robby." He wiped one nostril. "You know where we can get some blow?"

I glanced over to see that the three Crystal Moths were still watching the dancers.

"Yeah, as a matter of fact, I do." *These two kids are exactly what I need.* A part of me considered the immorality of what I was about to do. Then again, I had no rules to follow but my own. I had the upper hand on the Crystal Moths. I needed to take advantage of it.

These kids are going to get coke one way or another. I convinced myself. *At this point, I might as well use them—see how the Crystal Moths handle an exchange.*

I cupped my hands together and pointed my pinky finger to the three Crystal Moths. "See the men dressed in white? They can help you out."

The two kids nodded.

"You didn't hear that from me, all right? We keep the operation on the down low."

"Okay," Brian said.

Robby got up and patted his friend on the shoulder. "Let's get this party going."

Brian got up, and the two of them left on their mission, leaving me on my own. I kept an eye on them. They weaved through the lounges to get to the other side—to Alex G.

The scene is set, I thought as I leaned back on the couch, placing my arms on the backrest. I had never witnessed first-hand how the Crystal Moths interacted with their customers. Normally, these things are done quickly in passing—either on the spot or in a hidden area like a washroom or in the thick of a crowd. I was about to learn how my target operated.

The two kids approached the three men with Robby taking the lead. He nodded and leaned closer to the spiky-haired Crystal Moth. Their lips began to move. The blonde girl watched, playing with her hair.

Alex G.'s gaze latched on to the newcomers. He fiddled with his goatee while watching the two discuss business.

If only I could hear what they're saying.

The spiky-haired Crystal Moth got up from his seat and adjusted his blazer. He started walking without acknowledging the other two Crystal Moths or the kids. The blonde shifted over, giving room for Brian and Robby to sit. The blonde placed her hand on Brian's knee, and they began to chat.

Interesting turn. I eyed the Crystal Moth who had left the others. He strode in my direction.

I looked toward a couple of girls sitting across from me, playfully grabbing each other's legs and whispering to each other. When in doubt, make yourself appear like a horny dog and you'll be left alone.

The Crystal Moth walked past me toward the men's room, and I turned over to examine my target again.

Brian gently squeezed the blonde's shoulder while she flirtatiously played with the stubble on his face. The two laughed. Robby and Alex G. were chatting, Alex's face was stern, and he didn't make eye contact with the kid. His eyes were fixated on the dance crowd. His lips moved after Robby spoke. The two chatted for several minutes and then the two kids got up. Alex G. and the other Crystal Moth stayed. The blonde waved at Brian.

At the same time, the third Crystal Moth came from the washroom, passed me, and returned to his seat. He nodded to the kids as he did. The two kids walked away, making a beeline for the entrance of the club.

Where are they going? I thought. From what I saw, Alex G. didn't move at all. Perhaps they had another member who was going to give them the drugs.

Hold on. The bald Crystal Moth pulled out his cellphone from his blazer's inner pocket and began to type something. Once he finished, he put it back into his pocket, nodding at Alex G.

That's not what I expected. I got up from the lounge. I had figured they'd do a quick exchange in the club. It was time to follow those kids. Alex G. wasn't going anywhere for the time being.

I squeezed through the group of people at the front of the lounge area and away from the dance floor. I spotted Jeff, Amy, and Vicky dancing together, but they were too distracted by the music to notice me passing.

The two kids, Robby and Brian, were easily spotted leaving The Glowing Monkey. Robby's mohawk stood out like a sore thumb. As they stepped outside, they paused at the entrance where they were met by a girl with straight black hair with blue streaks and bangs. She wore a black corset under her leather jacket, fishnet stockings, and a black leather miniskirt. She folded her arms, gazing coldly at the two boys—mostly keeping her eyes on Brian. The three of them chatted for a moment then Robby pointed down the street with his thumb. The girl rolled her eyes before following them.

I followed them casually, stepping out into the crisp night air. The three kids had crossed the street already. They moved around the corner of the block, disappearing down the avenue. I hurried up the street, staying on my side of the road to watch where they were going. They crossed onto the next block and walked down the first alley. They had to be meeting a Crystal Moth dealer.

I marched across the street toward the alley, picking up speed to catch up with the kids. I couldn't miss anything that was about to happen.

I slowed my pace as I neared the alley. I reached into my pocket for the ski mask and put it over my head. If anything were to go down, I couldn't have my face exposed.

Strolling up to the alley, I peeked around the corner to see the three kids. They walked further down the pothole-covered road. Brian and Robby were on each side of the girl. Their voices echoed, but they were too far away to pick up what they were discussing. The only clear thing was the girl's louder and more aggressive tone.

She's pissed off.

The alley had a crossroad in the middle, splitting the four buildings. The three kids moved past the intersection just as two men appeared from the sides. They were fit, had short haircuts, and wore white rags around their arms.

Alex G. is getting the recruits to do the deals. It was a smart idea. It kept the real Crystal Moths away from any potential threat. Plus, recruits are disposable, as I saw back in May.

I saw their movements clearly as they talked. The man off to the right reached into his pockets and pulled out a small bag with a white substance inside—the cocaine. He also casually kept his one hand cupped inside his coat, most likely concealing a weapon.

The group talked quietly with one another for several seconds, followed by a long pause.

What are they waiting for? I thought, eyeing the recruits. One still held the small bag, gripping it tightly.

Robby folded his arms and looked around nervously.

"Look who wandered away from the fun," boomed one man. It projected from the far end of the alley.

They're trapped. It was time to move. I crept into the alley and kept myself pressed against the brick wall. Hurrying to the nearest dumpster, I crouched beside it and peeked over. Several metres from the kids and recruits were two of the three Crystal Moths from inside the club: the bald guy and Alex G.

The three kids exchanged glances as the two Crystal Moths approached, their footsteps echoing.

Alex G. let out a chuckle and brought his hands together.

"We got the cash," Robby said, glancing between both pairs of men.

Alex G. shrugged. "Oh, I know you're good for it. What concerns me more so is how upfront you were about asking. Who do you think you are?"

"Brian," the girl whined. "This is why I hate these rave clubs."

"Not now, Lola," Brian said, brushing his hair from his face.

"Guys, I really don't like this," the girl identified as Lola complained, glancing nervously at the recruits as they stepped closer.

Alex G. pointed at the girl and licked his lips. "Weren't you at the apartment the other night?"

Lola looked over at him and folded her arms. "Yeah, so?"

Brian grabbed her arm. "What were you doing with him?"

"That's none of your concern, pussy." The bald man snarled and cracked his knuckles.

"Watch who you're talking to." Brian turned to face him.

Lola gently touched his arm. "Brian."

He shrugged her off. "Not now."

Alex G. stroked his goatee. "Now, you see, I don't know who you kids are, but I don't like you openly asking about my operations. We run a very tight ship."

Robby shrugged. "Everyone knows if you dress in white, you're a Crystal Moth. I don't get the problem."

The bald man shook his head and chuckled.

Alex G. shrugged. "Yes, we do dress in white. Something you missed, though: you never, ever, approach us."

The recruit on the right flipped open the knife that was previously cupped in his hand. It caught the attention of all three kids.

Alex G. grinned. "We approach you. That's how it works. We choose who gets the goods. We're not a vending machine."

Damn it, I thought. This was probably why I never saw the Crystal Moths do an exchange in person—they did the targeting and set up the time and place. *I'll have to break this up before it ends badly.* It was a dangerous situation, and I couldn't have any of the kids hurt. There were four Crystal Moths, and chances were these kids couldn't throw a decent punch.

"All right, we're sorry. It won't happen again," Robby said, raising his hands in the air. "It was a mistake."

"Damn right it was!" Alex G. shouted. "We have rules for a reason. You don't approach us. We're not your on-demand service, you self-entitled fuck. We have a reputation to maintain."

"Yeah, of course." Robby nodded.

"You knew about our dress code. How the fuck were you so stupid you didn't know how to interact with us?"

"I don't know! We thought one of your guys told us to talk to you!" Robby exclaimed.

Brian shook his head. "We'll walk away and never do this again."

"No, you won't ever do this again. One of ours didn't approach you, and we'll make an example of you for it." Alex G. stopped about a metre from the kids.

"Example made!" Brian argued.

Alex G. smirked. "You see, if we request that no one approaches us, and someone does approach us, our word is no good. No one is going to respect it unless we give them a reason to."

Brian lifted his arms in the air. "Okay, we won't get anything. That's cool—we'll go." He turned around and started to walk toward the recruits, who had boxed them in.

"Brian, no!" Lola pulled his arm, trying to get him to stay still.

"Your lady is smart," Alex G. said. "You're just pissing me off now." He snapped his fingers, and the three others rushed toward the kids.

Lola screamed as the men closed in.

Here we go. I burst from the dumpster as the two groups began to brawl. A loud cry echoed through the alley—one of the kids got stabbed.

I spotted the recruit with the knife pull his weapon out of Brian's gut. Lola tried to grab hold of the man's arm to stop him from attacking, but she was too weak to stop him. The other two thugs easily overpowered Robby and began pounding their fists into him. He collapsed to the road.

Alex G. snagged Lola by the hair, dragging her back. He wrapped his other arm around her chest. "We never got a chance to properly introduce ourselves!"

All four of the Crystal Moths were engaged with their targets and hadn't noticed me approaching. I ended my charge by slamming my foot into the kneecap of the recruit who stabbed Brian. The sound of snapping bone filled the air, and the man yelped in pain. He gripped the broken bone that strained against his pant leg.

I grabbed hold of the man's skull as he leaned down. With a forceful twist, I snapped his neck, causing him to fall to the ground.

The noise caught the attention of the other three and they turned to face me. The second recruit rushed at me. A glimmer of light reflected off his fists—he wielded brass knuckles.

Oh shit.

He swung at me and I dodged to the right, avoiding his attack. I grabbed him by the collar before he could recover and head-butted his face. He stumbled back as I let him go.

The bald man rushed into the action as I threw a swift boot into the recruit's chest, throwing him into the oncoming Crystal Moth. The bald man used his forearm to hit the man approaching him, smacking him in the face and knocking him clear from his path. The man's nostrils flared as he rushed toward me, his face painted with a nasty scowl.

He swung first, and I had no time to deflect it. The blow hit me dead in the face and threw me back. He hit me again—this time in the chest, knocking the wind out of me. The man went for a third swing, but this time I raised my forearm and deflected the blow downward. I threw in a left hook, hitting his face. The blow didn't disorient him, and he swung at me again. I threw a lower kick at his leg, causing his body to jerk and misdirecting his punch.

"Bitch!" shouted Alex. G.

I glanced up to see the girl gnawing on his hand, causing blood to spew down his wrist and onto his white blazer. Alex G. used his other hand to punch her ribs several times. The blows forced her to let go, and she wobbled to the ground.

"Help!" Robby cried from the ground. "We're being attacked. Please, a block north of The Glowing Monkey—in the alley." Blood poured down the boy's face as he clutched his stomach with one hand, holding on to his phone with the other.

"Mika!" Alex. G. shouted.

The bald man identified as Mika had his fists ready for the next round. He took a step back and exchanged glances with me, eyebrows twitching. He clearly wasn't over our fight. Mika quickly backed off, keeping his eyes on me as he regrouped with Alex G.

"Shit." Alex G. said, pulling a phone from his pocket. "Let's go!"

Mika pointed at the recruit with the brass knuckles—still on the ground. "We can't let him squeal."

"I don't got a fucking gun on me!" Alex G. argued as he ran. Mika said nothing more and the two rushed down the alley, leaving me alone with the three kids, the knocked-out recruit, and the dead one.

A part of me wanted to run after Alex G. and peg him down now that the police were on their way. I would have the opportunity to stop the prick in his tracks and prove that when I shot at him months ago, it was for a good cause.

No, I can't. It was too risky. Mika was a challenge. And besides, Alex G. mentioned he'd seen the girl before. I could avoid risking a dangerous brawl with the Crystal Moths and being caught by the police. The girl had something I could work with. I had to let them get away.

"The cops are on their way, you fucks!" shouted Robby.

"Not now, Robby!" Lola said. "Oh my God, Brian. Brian. Brian," she repeated, crawling over to him. She took the boy in her arms. He clutched the wound in his stomach.

"Let me see it," I said, glancing around to see if the police were nearby. So far, there were none. The sirens subtly roared nearby. Time was limited.

"Is he going to be okay? Brian." Lola began to cry.

I examined where Lola and Brian pressed on the wound to see blood seeping through their fingertips just under his ribs. The boy grimaced and kept his eyes closed. He was in deep pain, but he would live. "Yeah, he'll be fine," I said, standing up. "Don't take your hand off the wound until the paramedics get here. I can't stay here, but we need to talk."

"About what? Who are you?" She looked up at me. Her makeup had smeared, making her look like a sad clown.

It was risky to give the girl more information. However, I didn't have any leads on the Crystal Moths. She was my in. With the cops on their way, I didn't want to be hanging out there with a ski mask over my face. I certainly couldn't take it off and reveal my identity to the kids or the police.

I've got to take a risk. The only way I could meet up with the girl again without giving any personal information was to find a common meeting place. "You want answers?"

"Yeah." Lola sniffled. "Why did you help us?"

"Meet me tomorrow. Beaver Hills House Park. Midnight." I stared at her for a second, and our eyes locked. I wanted to be sure she was serious.

The sirens gradually became louder. They were near.

She nodded quickly, not blinking. "Yeah, all right."

I turned and ran down the alley, returning to the main street. About a block away, I flicked off my ski mask, adjusting my movement to a casual stroll. Running at this point would make me look suspicious. Quickly, I unsnapped the glow sticks on my wrists and stuffed them into my pocket—another easy identifier.

The sirens began to subdue the further I walked. I didn't spot any red-and-blue lights—I was clear.

I twitched my nose, feeling that my right nostril and cheek were swollen where Mika had hit me. That was all right, though. I finally had a lead. It's a shame that the kids took a beating for it. Maybe it'll teach them not to go looking for coke. I should feel ashamed for using them as bait, but it was necessary to allow me to gather more information.

They had to learn that life's a bitch at some point.

CHAPTER 12

TOUGHEN UP

L ola sat on a pleather chair, knees shaking, and fiddled with her sticky hands that were covered in blood from Brian's wound. Two officers sat across from her at the steel table. Shortly after Robby called the cops, the first response team arrived followed by a swarm of police units.

The cops joined Brian and Robby in separate ambulances. Robby was beaten pretty badly and needed medical attention. Lola had known Robby for a number of years—before Brian. The two of them had been good friends since high school. Actually, it was Robby who introduced her to Brian years later.

Brian was clearly in serious condition and was loaded into the first ambulance.

Lola, the only one not hurt, was taken in for questioning by the police. Oddly enough, she got Officer Ace again. This time, he had his partner with him. Their ride to the station was silent—besides Lola's sobbing in the back seat.

Officer Ace and his partner brought Lola into the station, then Ace interviewed and profiled her. It was like out of some crime TV show: the cuffs, photos, the lights, and the dried blood sampling.

They can't find out what the three of us were trying to do, she thought. Lola could only pray that Brian and Robby were smart enough not to tell the cops that they were buying coke. With any luck, the one Crystal Moth that was left behind would keep his mouth shut too. There was no guarantee their stories would align, though.

We're so fucked. Lola shuddered and swallowed heavily. The officers hadn't even let her wash off the blood yet. They had taken some samples of the semi-dried liquid for forensic testing, and they told her she could wash off once they were finished. It wasn't soon enough. Having Brian's blood all over her made her nauseous.

"Can I please just wash this off?" she asked, looking over at Officer Ace.

His eyes were slanted inward and lips pressed tightly. He was clearly getting frustrated with the situation. "When we're done," he said.

Lola sighed. She wanted to get the blood off and call Becky for some moral support. She didn't like being interviewed by the cops while trying to emotionally recover.

Becky is always there for me, she thought. It's not like she could call her parents. They weren't exactly a fan of her friends, and they didn't even live in the city. Besides, they didn't like her approach to her reporting career or how she chose to spend her free time. *They'd tell me to focus more on school and quit the nightlife. Not the kind of support I need right now.*

"Okay, start from the beginning," Ace said with his pencil in hand, pressed firmly on the notepad.

Becky would know what to tell them. Lola wiped her face with her forearm, smudging her makeup. She looked over at Ace. *I probably look like a crack-whore right now.* "Okay, you want to know what happened?"

Ace nodded. "Yeah, you're the only witness we have to work with right now. One man is dead, three severely injured, and three got away?"

I'll tell him the truth, Lola thought. *Minus the drugs and the point where that mystery man asked to meet with me.* She didn't want the cops to ask her a ton of questions. The masked hero was strange enough, and he wanted to talk to her.

Meet me tomorrow. Beaver Hills House Park. Midnight. The voice of the man echoed in Lola's mind. What did he want to know, and why did he save them from the Crystal Moths?

It happened so fast. I don't even know how he did it. Despite the chaos, her desire for good blog content made the meeting very attractive. She could deal with that later. For now, she had to cooperate with the cops.

Just keep my statement simple. I didn't do anything wrong. We were ambushed. "Yeah, that's right."

Ace shook his head. "Okay, go on."

"Brian, Robby, and I were just out at The Glowing Monkey. It was just a night of fun and we wanted to get some fresh air."

"Okay, back up. I need you to explain everything in as much detail as you can."

"All right." Lola told the story to the officer in vivid detail, describing how they entered the club and how she went for a smoke outside.

"Brian and Robby stepped out after a few minutes. They wanted to go for a walk. The club gets pretty warm," Lola lied.

She kept the part where the two guys in the alley and the Crystal Moths cornered them.

"They taunted us, and that's when they tried to rob us," Lola said. She was careful not to give Alex G.'s name or the bit about knowing where he lived. She feared that if she did, the cops would bust it. That was too big of a risk for Becky, considering she partied with them.

Almost the full truth. Just leave out enough details to protect my friends, she thought, continuing the story. "Then, out of nowhere, a man in a ski mask came up and beat the shit out the man who stabbed Brian. I heard bones crack—I think he snapped him like a twig. I don't know, it was all so fast. One of them had me by my hair and I was struggling with him. Maybe I'm getting mixed up with last week."

Ace raised his eyebrow.

Lola went to brush her hair aside but stopped when her red-stained hands caught her eye. *This is disgusting,* she thought. "This masked man took on the other two with no problem, and I bit the hand of the creep who had me. The man with the ski mask was struggling with the bald, brawny Crystal Moth, and I guess Robby took his chance to call 911. He yelled loud enough that it caught everyone's attention. After that, they all fled the scene."

"Even the man with the ski mask?"

Lola nodded. "Yeah, it was the weirdest thing."

"That is all that happened?"

"That's all."

Ace sighed and dropped his pencil.

She cupped her hands together and looked to the ground. "Is there anything else you need? I really just want to call my friend and get to the hospital."

He wiped his face and exhaled. "You're our prime witness for a couple of cases now. We'll be in touch for sure." Ace got up and looked down at Lola. "We'll get that blood off of you and I can drive you to the hospital."

Lola let out a deep breath of relief. The last thing she wanted to do was talk more about the event. She needed some comfort, and Becky was always affectionate with her no matter how serious the situation was.

Officer Ace escorted Lola to where she could wash off Brian's blood. *I don't get why no one helped me get this off.* She was still in shock and couldn't comprehend police procedure.

After she washed off the blood, Officer Ace led her out of the station to where his unit was parked. Lola sat in the back seat. She stared out into the dark downtown scenery while he drove her to the hospital. Lola wanted to call Becky right away but didn't want Officer Ace snooping in on her conversation. It seemed like a bad idea to tell Becky the full story of what happened with a cop in the front seat.

The drive to the hospital was silent. Ace and Lola did not exchange a single word. It took about twenty minutes for them to get to the hospital. Ace parked the vehicle right out front of the emergency entrance.

"Thanks," Lola said as she pulled on the unit's door handle.

Ace nodded. "Get some rest. We'll be in contact."

Lola got out of the vehicle and closed the door, allowing Ace to drive off. She glanced over to the hospital entrance and marched through the automatic sliding doors, passing a security guard in front of a row of monitors. Behind a glass barrier, the front reception desk faced the automatic doors. The sound of beeping came from an unknown origin, and footsteps came from every adjacent hall.

Lola rushed over to the receptionist—an older woman in burgundy scrubs. The lady didn't make eye contact and continued to sift through some papers.

"Hey, I'm here to see my friends," Lola said.

"Names?" she asked in a raspy voice.

"Brian Moor and Robby Harris."

The nurse rolled her chair over to her computer. She made a couple of clicks with the mouse, her eyes squinting to read the screen. "They're not available to be seen right now."

"Sorry?" Lola asked.

"They're in surgery. Unless you're family or their emergency contact, you can't see them."

"Have their families been notified?"

"I can't share any more information with you. You can wait in the seating area until they arrive."

Lola exhaled heavily. "For how long?"

"Hard to tell. We're very busy right now. You're welcome to wait."

Shit. What do I do now?

Becky, she thought. She sifted through her purse, sniffling, and pulled out her smartphone. She located *Becky Bubs* in her contacts and pressed the phone icon next to the name.

The ringer went a couple of times before the girl picked up on the other end. "Hey, Lola Love," she said flirtatiously.

"Becky, I need you," Lola said hastily as she walked over to the waiting area.

"Yeah? What's going on, doll? I'm just at the Empress right now. You caught me outside having a smoke."

"Brian got stabbed." Lola swallowed heavily.

"Oh my God. Where are you?"

"I am at the hospital downtown. Robby got the shit kicked out of him too. They're both in the ER."

"I'm on my way now. What the fuck happened? Are you okay? I'm getting a cab."

"I'm fine, yeah. I'm fine. It's a long, fucked-up story. I was at the station giving my statement to them—like last week. Seems to be a recurring thing, hey?" Lola couldn't help but laugh. She wasn't sure if she found it funny or if she was laughing due to her nerves. She still felt sick to her stomach from the shock. "I didn't know what happened. it all went by so fast. Please just come here."

"Fuck. I'm on my way. Downtown, right?"

"Yeah, and I have no idea what to do. I can't see them—I'm not family."

"Shit. Okay, I'm on my way. The Empress—it's like thirty minutes away."

"Please hurry."

"Okay, Lola Love, I'll be there soon."

"Love you, Bubs," Lola said before hanging up the phone. She closed her eyes and slowly exhaled.

God, I hope they don't find out I was lying, she thought.

Lola waited in the lobby by herself, fiddling with her hands. She tried to get into Brian's or Robby's room again when the front-desk clerk changed. They shooed her away too. It was difficult for her to just sit there and wait while Brian and Robby were in agony. She had no updates on how they were doing and no info on who or where their families were.

Hurry up, Becky.

About half an hour later, the sounds of jingling and boot stomping came from the direction of the automatic doors. The familiar dreadlocked girl came rushing in with her star-print leggings and leather coat, which caused the jingling. She marched straight toward the visitor chairs.

"Lola!" she exclaimed, extending her arms for a hug.

Lola got up from her seat and collapsed into her friend's arms, sobbing. They were tears she had been holding back, but seeing a friendly face lowered her guard.

"Everything went by so fast."

Becky hushed her and gently stroked her hair. "It's okay. I'm here. Let's clean you up a bit."

The two went into the women's washroom, which was meant for one. Lola was thankful her friend rushed to her aid. Despite Becky smelling like booze, it was comforting.

Becky helped clean the makeup off Lola's face so she wouldn't look like a dying raccoon. When Lola was out clubbing, she preferred to wear heavy eyeshadow and eyeliner with lipstick to match. Now, she was far beyond the mood to make herself look pretty and just wanted it gone. Once the makeup was washed off, it was difficult to identify with the girl in the mirror.

That isn't me, she thought, analyzing her pasty skin and pink lips. Becky continued to wipe the last bit of smeared eyeliner from her face. The face in the mirror was simply a girl, not the spooky, edgy badass she normally presented herself as.

"There's my beautiful girl," Becky said, leaning in and kissing her on the cheek.

Lola smiled—it was hard not to when Becky was around. Somehow, she was always perky, even in the darkest situations.

The two exited the washroom and sat back down in the waiting room. Becky took off her coat, exposing her tattooed shoulders.

"Is anyone coming for Brian and Robby?" Becky asked.

"I would assume so. They wouldn't let me in to see how they were doing. There's no reason for me to be here."

"Have you met their parents?"

Lola shrugged. "No. Brian has always kept things super secretive with me. I have no idea what they look like."

Becky sighed. "Okay, you need to back up. What the fuck happened? Last time we chatted was at that apartment party."

Lola's eyes widened. *Alex G.* Her memory flashed to seeing the man's smug grin at his apartment. "Okay, Becky. You need to listen. Stay clear from Alex G.," she whispered.

Becky squinted. "Why?"

Lola swallowed heavily. "He's the one responsible for what happened this evening."

Becky's eyes widened, and she shook her head. "How? I know him—he's good stuff."

"Okay, so I invited you to come out tonight, right?"

"Yeah, but I already had plans."

"That's fine. So I got together with Robby and Brian instead. Brian and I chatted this week about what happened between us and we wanted to put it in the past."

"Did he invite you out?"

"No, Robby did. But that's not the point." Lola said.

"Anyways."

Lola brushed her hair from her face. "So the three of us went to check out The Glowing Monkey. I was out for a smoke when Robby and Brian came out and said they were going to get some blow."

Becky squinted. "Okay, stuff started to go south from there?"

"Yeah. We met these two men in the alley, both a little rough looking. They had white rags tied around their arms. I think it has something to do with the Crystal Moths. They weren't much for talking. Then Alex G. and that bald guy—Mika?—showed up."

Becky's jaw dropped. "No."

"I'm not shitting you. He recognized me too and I was so scared, Becky." Lola started crying again and fell into her friend's lap.

Becky stroked her head.

"I didn't tell the cops his name in fear of your life. There's no way I would put you in danger. I am so worried right now. Alex G. doesn't fuck around. Please don't go back there."

Becky nodded. "Okay, I won't, now that I know how much of a freak he is."

"Thank you." She paused. "Something else weird happened."

"Oh?"

"A masked man came and saved us. Just as the Crystal Moths began to attack us. He came out of nowhere. He fought them, and I think he snapped the neck of one of the men. He took them down easily." Lola shook her head. "It's like he's brawled before. He was so quick. And after Robby called the cops, he told me to meet him tomorrow night at the park on Jasper Ave."

"What?" Becky asked.

"He said we needed to talk."

"Okay, yeah, that is the fucked-up part. Did you tell the cops that?"

"No, I kept my story vague. We were out to get coke—I couldn't tell them what we were doing. Besides, this is some real dirt I can use on the blog."

"Your blog? Lola, don't be crazy. Didn't you see some guy snap someone's neck last week?"

"Yeah," Lola confirmed.

"And now you saw this masked man snap a neck this week?"

"So?" Lola asked.

Becky shook her head. "Who have you been blogging about for the past few months?"

Lola's eyes widened. "No."

"Yeah. The Snapper. Lola, if he wants to meet you, he's probably going to try to kill you."

Lola stared into space. Was he the Snapper? She had been in shock from Brian's stabbing, so it hadn't really occurred to her. But she would be dead already, wouldn't she?

"He can't be the Snapper," Lola said. "From what I've researched, the Snapper kills all of his victims. He doesn't leave witnesses. If he was the same guy from last week, he could have killed me tonight—or at least the rest of the guys he fought. He wants to meet me. We're missing something."

"He probably got freaked out when the cops arrived."

"No, it doesn't make sense. Why would he have fought off the Crystal Moths? He took on all four of them at once. The Snapper has always attacked his victims one at a time. Rubbies, at that. Who rescues people like he did? No one."

Becky scratched her head. "Unless you're in a viral video."

"You mean that YEGman video?" Lola got up from her seat and glanced around to see if anyone was listening. No one was. There were only a handful of other people in the room: a couple in a deep conversation, one girl asleep, and another guy on his phone.

She sat back down. "I did see that video you tagged me in. The video was pretty shitty quality."

Becky nodded. "But he took on those guys with very little effort too. Did you see it?"

"Oh yeah, I watched it a couple of times."

"Lola Love." She put on a wicked grin. "Do you think?"

Lola shrugged. "I don't know."

"Well if you don't think he's the Snapper, then I think the city's superhero wants to meet you."

"Yeah, but why?"

Becky giggled. "You got a secret admirer. Are you going to do it?"

Lola scratched her neck. "I don't know, should I? What if he isn't YEGman and tries to do something to me?"

Becky nodded. "Yeah, that was my first concern. What if I joined you?"

"Do you think he would be willing to meet me if I brought you?"

"Doubt it. I wouldn't be beside you. Let's say I was across the street or something. Pretending to wait for the bus. That way, I could watch the park from afar and call for help if anything starts to go down." She patted the purse she kept to her side. "Plus, I got some bear mace with me at all times. I can give you that."

Lola fiddled with her fingers. "It's not a bad idea. I got my knife."

A drunken grin went across Becky's face. "So, what do you say? Want to meet the city's vigilante? Maybe it will be like those comic superhero books where you fuck him."

"Stop it. This is serious"

Becky began to make mocking moaning sounds. "Oh YEGman, thank you for saving me!"

"You're fucking stupid sometimes." Lola shook her head. The humour was incredibly disturbing considering Brian got stabbed and Robby was beaten. It was even too dark for Lola to enjoy.

"If you don't, maybe I will." Becky played with her hair. "Maybe he can save me from this dry spell I've been having."

Lola sighed. "Okay, fine, let's meet him and find out what he wants. I do need it for my blog. I've already lied to the police. I might as well see this through." *Maybe it will help support the info Donnie gave me.*

Becky clapped her hands. "Hashtag YEGman, we're coming!" She giggled. "Catch what I said there?"

Lola sighed. *"Yeah. Very funny."*

BRIAN

#YEGman

Chapter 13
RECAP

Sunlight barely beamed through the tall windows of the room. A thick layer of fog covered most of the downtown scene outside. Only the immediate couple of blocks could be seen from the high-rise. The sun appeared as a small glowing ball in the grey-and-white sky. Even inside my warm condo, staring outside, I could feel the cold touch of winter was here.

No need to get ready for work, I thought, buckling up my jeans. Today, in the late morning, I would have normally been getting my uniform ready and mentally preparing for my shift. Six months' time was not enough to break a routine I've had for years. Especially since I was going to meet Ace as I used to do every Saturday.

I got to get with the now, I thought while stepping away from the window. For a weekend, it was going to be a full one. I suppose that wasn't unusual when I was on the force.

First, I meet Ace this afternoon. It'll be good to catch up with him. I missed chatting with my partner. He's the only person I've been able to relate to. Well, half the time. It is probably because we worked together—had common goals. Regardless, hearing how he, the sergeant, and the other guys and gals from the station were doing would be refreshing.

Second, I meet that goth girl. My investigation into the Crystal Moths isn't over. That girl from last night knows Alex G., but how? I need answers from her, and I can only hope she'll show up tonight. If she doesn't, maybe it'll be a sign to drop all this nonsense.

A part of me kept thinking back to the last couple of encounters I had on the streets. Specifically, the Crystal Moth punks and that young couple outside the bar. Both scenarios would have played out differently if I was still an officer. Being a regular civilian provided camouflage so I could get the jump on them. I was getting results that the people were praising through that YEGman hashtag. I was giving people hope.

Or am I chasing a high? I thought as I left my condo. I locked the door and walked to the elevator. *Am I simply holding on to my old habits of being a cop?* I pushed the button directing the machine to bring me down. It's difficult to know the answers to these questions. And honestly, for how lost I've been feeling, it didn't make sense to question what I was doing. Being impulsive and cracking down on the gang is liberating. Who knows, maybe I really will become a private investigator. I'm good at this.

Then there's tomorrow when I'll meet Mom. I couldn't help but smirk just as the elevator rang and the chrome doors split open. I'll have to explain the black eye to her. *My poor mom.* She still has no idea that I was fired and even less of a clue about what I've been doing with my spare time. She'd freak out if she knew half the things that went on while I was on the force, let alone this.

I sighed as I stepped through the doors, thinking about how today was going to be extremely long. A lot of it depends on the results of meeting the goth girl. If she shows up and cooperates, more than likely I'll try to find out where Alex G. lives tonight. The Crystal Moths seem most active in the evening, so it's the opportune time to strike.

The elevator rang again, and the light flashed on the *M* as the door opened. I stepped outside and marched out of the entryway and into the streets, tucking my hands into my jacket. Normally, I would have driven my vehicle like I did for work. Lately, I haven't been feeling the need to drive. What's the point? It wasn't like I had anywhere pressing to be. I was just going for a drink with a friend. Like a normal chum.

I took a deep breath, feeling the cool air enter my lungs. As I exhaled, the trail of my breath shot into the air. As I walked, I kept my head down low, looking at each crack in the sidewalk, marching to Ace's and my favourite place: Pub 1905. We used to meet up there after a shift or when we were off duty. It's right downtown, which made it convenient for us to go there. Plus, it was owned by a former cop, so we were welcomed.

That girl better show up tonight, I thought. It was difficult to think of anything else besides meeting that kid. Last night was far more than I bargained for, not to mention ethically questionable. I encouraged two kids to buy coke. I used them as bait to lure out the Crystal Moths. They got severely injured and then I murdered a man.

A Crystal Moth. He was a piece of shit, I reassured myself. If I hadn't intervened the way I did, that kid could have died. It was the right thing to do. Taking someone's life is something you hear a lot of controversial opinions on. Some say it changes you for good and others say each one makes it worse. Personally, it's never had much of an impact. If the cause is just, then I see no reason to feel anything.

Besides, it's not like it was my first kill. There were a few times on duty where I had to kill in self defense. Still, what I did on duty doesn't matter anymore. Now I'm just some self-righteous civilian who figures he can change the city on his own. It's true though: I'm making real progress, unlike Major Crimes. Where the hell are they on busting the Crystal Moths? Nowhere, that's where. That's where I come in.

I don't need to justify it—just act. But today, it's been tough not to, considering all I've had to do besides the meetings is think. It's not like I have a lot of people to talk to. I'm a loner. It makes brewing crazy ideas way too easy.

I hiked down south to Jasper Ave, walking hastily to build up some blood flow in my system to battle to subtle chill in the air. Being bald didn't help the issue either. It was nice to get out on the town—appreciate it as a civilian as best as I could.

Of course, passing by side streets and alleyways, you could spot some of the rubbies. They were minding their own business. Nothing to be alarmed about. Downtown is often dead during the day on weekends, when working class folks go home to their suburban lifestyles. The clubbers don't show up until later. That leaves the core of the city to rot in limbo.

After a long stroll, I looked up to see the familiar forest-green-and-burgundy building with gold lettering. Pub 1905. The good old watering hole.

I pulled open the door and stepped in, moving across the green carpet through the well-lit bar. There were a few grizzled old men scattered around the seating area. Otherwise, it was just the two waitresses, the bartender, and me. Ace hadn't arrived yet.

The decor of the pub is nothing special, but it's quiet and there's plenty of seating. One of the charms of the place is the motorcycle model directly above the bar. I sat myself at one of the booths against the wall. Placing myself on the pleather bench, the waitress—a tall, slim girl in a black tank top and short skirt—came from the bar.

Her long, thin black hair bounced as she approached. "Hey. What can I get for ya?" she said, resting her tattooed arm on the bench across from me.

"I'll grab a house lager," I told her.

She tapped the bench and nodded. "Coming right up." She marched back to the bar.

I looked around the pub again, double-checking that I'd spotted all the customers. Yes, only the old men. Two of them were together, and the other two sat alone—drinking while watching the news on the TV mounted behind the bar. The screen showed a bald man with a moustache, wearing a white dress shirt adorned with patches and pins. He was talking into a mic.

Bob, the chief, I realized. There were several other mics from reporters trying to get good spots. On the left of the screen was the title of the report: *Vigilante: Hero or Criminal?*

The tacky 80s pop music in the bar was too loud for me to hear what the TV was saying, but the subtitles in black boxes and white text were visible from where I sat. Squinting to read, I focused in on the text as the chief spoke.

"By no means is anyone to take the law into their own hands. We are well aware of the popularity this man has received through the viral videos. He did save the couple in danger, but he did it in an unethical and violent manner. This is precisely why vigilante behaviour is highly illegal. As I said, no one is to take the law into their own hands—not this YEGman or anyone else. The law is to be handled by the police and by the city."

The waitress returned to my table with my drink and placed it on a coaster she brought. "There you go!"

"Thanks," I said as the girl walked away.

The mic returned to the reporter as the subtitles continued. "What are the police doing regarding the case of YEGman?"

The mic tilted back to the chief as he took a deep breath before speaking. "Well, as I said, we highly discourage all vigilante behaviour. We are currently investigating the situation and gathering witness statements. We are aware it is a popular belief among civilians that the deed was heroic. The public needs to know it was also criminal. The combat tactics shown in the videos are evidence of formal training, which classifies it as the use of a deadly weapon."

Bull shit, I thought.

The sound of the front door to the pub caught my attention. I turned back, spotting a man with emerald eyes and slicked-back hair—my former partner.

"Ace!" I called out, raising my glass.

"Michael!" Ace smiled at me and opened his arms. He wasn't in uniform yet. Rarely have I seen him in common clothing like jeans and a shirt.

I extended my hand to shake his, but he continued to move toward me. "Come here, you!" He gave me a tight hug while standing, which made it an odd squeeze, but I let him embrace me. I've never done well with physical contact that expresses likability. Most people enjoy it, so I've had to conform. Truthfully, unless it's violence or getting off, physical contact seems rather pointless to me.

Ace let me go and pointed to his face. "What's with the eye? Get roughed up?"

"Drinking a little too much lately, remember?" I smirked.

Ace shook his head and slid over to the bench facing me. "Bullhead. How are you? It's been weeks since I've seen you."

"I know, I know. I've been ignoring your calls." I admitted, taking a drink.

The waitress appeared from nowhere and smiled at Ace. "Hey, what will you have?"

"Just a cola," Ace replied.

"Coming up," the waitress said, stepping away.

Ace glanced at the TV, shaking his head before leaning in on the table. "See that bullshit about an Edmonton superhero?"

"Yeah, people are desperate to believe anything."

"It doesn't help that all of those superhero movies are on the big screen. It just makes people's imaginations go wild."

"Yep, and viral videos just add fuel to fire. That's the last sort of distraction we need." I cleared my throat. "I mean, you need."

Ace shook his head. "I know what you meant. On that note, how are you?"

The waitress returned with Ace's soda before I could speak. She placed it on a coaster, saying nothing, and hurried off as one of the older gents waved for her.

I sighed. "Well, it's been weird, that's for sure."

"Guess it forces you to relax a little bit, hey?"

"I suppose."

"That's never been your strength." He raised his glass to me.

I raised mine to his, and the two glasses clanged. We both took a sip of our drinks before I cleared my throat. "Other than that, everything is pretty normal. Still spending time with my mother every week. Honestly, it's no different than how the past six months have been. Only thing now is I know for sure I'm not coming back."

"Yeah, that's true. How is your mom?"

"She's fine. I haven't told her anything yet."

"Still? Come on, Michael."

"I haven't been able to work up to it just yet. I'll get to it. I will admit, I'm bored as fuck some days. This just leaves me thinking a lot."

"Yeah, about what?"

"That last night on duty. Thinking what I could have done different."

"Stop it. You did everything you could. It was a mistake."

"I messed up big time, and it got me the boot. What were the results of the investigation anyway? The gunman was a Crystal Moth, wasn't he?" I knew the answer, but I had to hear it from my former partner. I wanted to know if the force was doing their job.

Ace shook his head. "I really shouldn't be talking about this stuff. You know that."

"Come on."

Ace sighed. "All right, fine. Just because you're still my partner in my books."

I smiled at him and nodded.

"Like you said, it was pretty obvious that they were all Crystal Moths from the white clothing. The gunman was taken into custody. Open and shut case."

"What about the other guy?"

"The one you shot? Well, his name was Alexander Gabehart. Some Newfie. Other than that, we had nothing to go on. He was straightforward with us when we interviewed him. He said he wasn't going to press charges, and that was it."

"That seems rather odd, doesn't it?"

"Yeah, most people would jump on an opportunity like that in a heartbeat. Get some support from the press and cash in a ton of money. That right there was a clear sign that this Alexander character's fishy. He doesn't want attention." Ace shrugged. "I left it with the sergeant and Glenn Hayes. Not my business anymore."

"Right, Glenn has bugged me a bit over the summer." I shook my head, thinking about the name. Glenn Hayes, the detective in Major Crimes. Ace and I met him numerous times when we stumbled upon a big scene.

"That's odd. Isn't that an internal affairs job?"

"Yeah, they bugged me too. The whole thing is still bullshit if you ask me."

"I know, you getting fired pisses me off too. It's just not the same without you."

"Yeah? I don't doubt it. Who are you supposed to rant about your girlfriend to when you should be working?" I laughed.

Ace rubbed his neck and laughed nervously. "Yeah, right? No one. It sucks."

"How's the rest of the station? I miss them."

"Pretty much the same. The sergeant is stressed out. I was solo for a bit until Stacey got promoted."

"Nice. Glad to hear."

"Are you?" Ace smirked and took a sip of his drink.

"Well, no. But you know what I'm saying. I'm glad you can keep at doing what you're doing."

"Where does that leave you now?"

I shrugged. "I don't know. Maybe become a private investigator. Who knows. Right now, I'm just letting the whole thing sink in—and drinking a lot."

"Of that, I have no doubt. You don't often ignore my calls."

"Yeah, well, I needed time to process all of this. Work is all I've really known. It's all I wanted to do."

"Maybe it's a good thing. Maybe you can actually find something healthier. As a friend, let me tell you that the way you went about it was self-destructive. You need more in your life than just work."

"I know."

"Speaking of, go out on some dates. When was the last time you got laid?"

"It's been too long—trust me."

"Well, there you go. There's something for you to chase." Ace chuckled.

I couldn't help but smile too. Whenever I'm around Ace, my mood lightens. He has a way of shrugging off the shitty things in life and enjoying the good. A lot of the time I think he's being a fool, but whenever I'm in my darkest place, his good-spirited ways are rejuvenating.

"How do you do it, Ace?" I asked.

"Sorry?"

"How do you keep it yourself together?"

"Well, I have sex for one. You should try it," he said.

We both laughed and took a sip of our drinks.

"Really, though. How?" I asked.

"Well, besides that, hobbies help keep your mind off work. Exercise, as you know. I suppose finding a greater purpose outside of work so you don't snap."

I nodded. "Yeah, that makes sense."

Ace glanced around the bar and then looked up at the TV as it showed a reporter in an alleyway in daylight. At the end of the road, a monkey sign could be seen—neon lights off.

"Oh, look." Ace said, pointing to the TV. "I was just there last night. Man, that was a long shift."

"Yeah?" I took a gulp of my drink. *I was there too.*

"It was obscure. Some kids got into a mess with the Crystal Moths."

"That sounds pretty normal."

"The weird part was that someone intervened and saved the kids."

"Really?" I leaned onto the table. *Shit, are they on my trail?* I thought. I was quite careful not to get injured too badly and leave a trail of blood or any torn clothes, but maybe I was sloppy.

"Yeah, the one girl I interviewed seemed to be hiding something. The kids were rescued, her two friends were badly injured, and one of the Crystal Moths had their neck snapped. She claims this person just ran away without saying anything."

"Wow." I pretended to act surprised. It was relieving to hear that the girl didn't tell Ace about her encounter with me in detail. It's a good sign. Maybe she will show up tonight.

"I know, as if we don't have enough neck-snapping from the Snapper." Ace said.

"You thinking it's him?" I asked.

Ace shook his head. "I doubt it. He only targets the rubbies."

"Or maybe he's changing targets," I said, swallowing heavily. It made me nervous to talk to my former partner about the scene. Especially lying to him. We were both there, and I was responsible for the death. That's the kind of trouble I don't need.

"No, I highly doubt it. Snapping a neck doesn't automatically make the murder related to the Snapper. It's off my plate anyway. I got the girl's statement and Glenn took over."

"It seems odd, don't you think? How many neck-snapping-related murders do we get? Not a lot," I said. I wanted to steer Ace away from thinking of anything else other than the Snapper. It wasn't like I meant to snap the recruit's neck, but it was instinctual to neutralize the target. If I could use it to my advantage though, I would. Anything to reduce the chances of the cops discovering that I was there.

"No, it doesn't make sense. Trust me." Ace took the last drink from his soda. "I had a report of a Snapper case last week. That one was more his style."

Guess the Snapper is still at large. I lifted my glass, tipping it upside down so the last of the ale could go down my throat before slamming the glass down. "Maybe you're right." Initially, I convinced myself to look into the Crystal Moths as one last good deed for the city, but should I stop after that?

The city doesn't stop hurting after the Crystal Moths go down. What about the Snapper? I thought.

"It's been great, Michael, but I gotta head out. I got a few more things to do before I start work." He reached into his pocket and brought his wallet out on the table.

I reached for my wallet just as Ace shook his head. "Don't worry. I got this," he said.

"Really? You sure?" I asked.

"Yeah. You grab the next one." Ace smiled. "Gives you a reason not to vanish for weeks."

"Thanks, Ace," I said, looking down at the table. I felt humbled to have a friend like him. Ace always has my back.

Ace flipped open his wallet and pulled out his debit card causing a couple of other cards to slide out. One was a gym membership, and the other was a business card for a Dr. Lang. I recognized the dark-blue card and bold text from Robert's office back in May. I was fixated on it when the sergeant had that unforgettable bitch-fest.

"You seeing the same doctor as the sergeant?" I asked, pointing at the card.

Ace looked down to his wallet and tucked the cards back into the slip. "Yeah, changing it up from the previous one. He wasn't very good." Ace looked back to the bar and waved at the waitress.

"That makes sense," I said.

The waitress came by with a debit machine and let Ace pay up. Once he was done with the machine, the two of us left the pub, exiting through the front and stepping out into the cool air. It had warmed up slightly from when I had first walked down to the bar, being just past midday.

We stopped in the middle of the sidewalk as Ace pointed out west.

"I parked over there. Gotta head back to the house to grab my stuff," he said.

"No worries. I'm heading back home."

"You walked?" Ace squinted in confusion.

"Yeah, thought I could use the walk." I raised my arms in the air. "It's not like I'm pressed for time or anything."

Ace shrugged. "Well, for now. You'll get up on your feet again." He stepped toward me and gave me a tight hug.

I patted him on the back a couple of times. "Kick some street urchin ass," I said, stepping back.

"I will. What else you got going on this weekend?"

"Well, not a lot. Going to see my mom and probably watch some TV. Who knows, maybe I'll find a date on some online dating service."

"Online service?" Ace pointed at me saying, "No hookers."

We both laughed and I shook my head. "No. No hooker sites."

Ace waved goodbye as we parted ways.

I put my hands in my pockets and began walking back to my condo.

One of three tasks done for the weekend, I thought. It was good to catch up with Ace and to know he's doing well. He always does well. Maybe I could learn something from him. Put my fixations on the Crystal Moths behind me. Find a healthy outlet for my anger.

More sex. I smirked to myself. It was humorous because I've never done well on a date by being me. I just can't relate to the women I meet. I'm better off charming them with my police training. That aside, I'm too invested in this case. Especially now that I have a lead. The deeper I investigate, the more I uncover.

Now to get some insight from a goth kid.

Chapter 14

ALLIANCES ARE FORGED

Nightfall had passed hours ago, and the snow was falling heavily. The ground had cooled enough that the snow stayed frozen long after it hit the ground. Winter is upon the city of Edmonton, and that means the drivers are going to panic and the homeless are going to struggle to stay warm. It happens every year, and there's no reason this one should be any different.

I'm going to have to find some warmer clothing if I keep doing this. Maybe an actual weapon too, I thought as I stood in a dark corner of the downtown park. The half-block-sized Beaver Hills House Park is located dead centre of the city and provides some greenery among the concrete jungle. It's refreshing to see considering how bland the rest of the city is for art. Not that I care a lot about the arts. It's always seemed like a waste of time and resources. We have too many other issues to worry about. Maybe we should hire more police rather than create pretty public structures.

That's why I'm crazy enough to be doing this, I thought. Last night was a perfect example of where the police were nowhere to be found while the Crystal Moths struck again. Sure, I took a man's life in the process, but it had to be done. The man had stabbed a kid. He would have murdered him if I hadn't finished him first. As far as I'm concerned, the man's death isn't a loss to the city. His family will cry and sob over it, but he was shit if he was working with the Crystal Moths.

I scratched my head and glanced around the park, looking between a number of pine trees, picnic tables, and the circular central area with strange, abstract metal art. I stayed near the back, which led to a shortcut to the street on the other side of a black building that the park shared. It provided some coverage with the lack of lighting in the back.

You'd think they'd offer more light in the park this late in the evening. At night, the park is an attraction for the city's scum—maybe because it's near a strip joint. No one seems to supervise the park either, which worked in my favour.

Where's that girl? I thought, anxiously scanning the park to see it was empty apart from a man sleeping on top of a picnic table. Still, the main sidewalk was filled with people and the road was packed with cars. It was risky for me to even be there. For all I knew, the girl had changed her mind and tipped me off to the cops.

I have to risk it. Ace said she didn't have much to say to them. That's promising. Perhaps I'd spooked her and she chickened out. That would have really put a damper on my day. I would have to start going back to The Glowing Monkey in hopes of running into Alex G. again. I hate that place.

Wait, I thought, spotting a girl dressed completely in black. She was walking across the street toward the park, dressed in large multi-buckled combat boots, skinny black jeans, and several hoodies layered with the outside one having cat ears. My stance perked, still hiding in the shadows.

That might be her, I thought, watching the girl walk hastily. *Punks like her aren't exactly common.*

I scanned the area again to see if there were any police or suspicious people nearby. There were a couple of parked cars, but no one was in them. Even if the police weren't there, there was a chance she brought someone else with her. Through the busy downtown traffic, it was difficult to pinpoint who might be her backup.

The girl with the cat ears moved from the sidewalk and into the park, hands in her pockets, purse hanging over her shoulder. She glanced around a couple of times and slowed her pace. The girl stopped dead centre below a spotlight beside the abstract art. Her face was clearer: the black-and-blue-streaked hair, the bangs, and the dark makeup. It was her.

Nice to see she has the chops, I thought, stepping out from the side road and keeping my pace slow while watching the nearby streets: the usual traffic. No police units were in sight. *All appears normal. This is good.*

"You alone?" I called out from about twenty paces from the girl.

She jumped and spun around. "Shit." She exhaled heavily. "Are you the guy from last night?"

"Are you alone?" I repeated.

"Are you the guy?" she asked.

"Answer the question."

"Yes," she said, glancing around. "I got a knife on me. Are you the guy?"

"I am the guy." I stopped walking, staying in the darkest portion of the park. Moving up any further would put me under the radius of the lamplight.

"I can barely see you," she called back.

"You brought a friend, didn't you?"

The girl glanced around and laughed nervously. "No. I just want to stay in the light in case you try anything fucked up. I have no idea who you are."

"True. I don't know who you are either. You do realize I took a major risk telling you to meet me here tonight?"

The girl nodded. "Yeah, I know. So did I. For all I know, you're going to try and rape me."

I shook my head. "That's a bit excessive, don't you think?"

"Perhaps. Or snap my neck like you did that other guy's. Are you the Snapper?"

"What? No, I'm not the Snapper. Just because I broke a guy's neck?"

"I saw you last week too—killing that poor homeless guy. You beat the shit out of him and broke his neck."

What the fuck is she talking about? I shook my head. "I have no idea what you're referencing. I know you're not stupid from how you're handling this so far. I assure you that I'm not the Snapper."

The girl glanced around the park again. "Okay, let's say you're not. What do you want?"

"First, I'm going under the assumption you got someone watching. If you didn't bring someone, then you are actually stupid."

The girl shook her head. "Okay, whatever. Who are you? Why did you save my friends?"

"I'd rather keep my identity hidden," I answered.

"Because you're the Snapper?" Lola asked.

"Fuck, kid, drop it. I'm not."

"So you're that viral hashtag YEGman guy then? Randomly helping strangers being attacked?"

"Fine, we'll go with that. What's your name?"

"Lola."

"That your real name?" I asked.

"As real as yours."

I smirked. *She's got attitude.* "All right, Lola, let's get to it. You know Alex G. How?"

"I went to a party he was at to rescue my friend," Lola said.

"Rescue?"

"Okay, she wasn't in trouble at the moment. But they were Crystal Moths, and it made me nervous that she was doing coke with them. I had to get her out of there."

"So elaborate. You went to this party?"

"Yeah, at Alex's apartment. My friend gave me the address, so I went there and got her out."

"What was it like in there?"

"There were three other Crystal Moths, I think. I didn't see much else. I went straight to the living room where I found my friend with the guys and a couple of girls. They were just partying. Alex G. showed up shortly after and wanted to get to business, but the other Crystal Moths wanted to keep fooling around with the girls."

"That's it?" I asked.

"Yeah. I know where it is, though."

"What's the address?"

"I want some answers first."

I folded my arms and scanned the park to see if anything had changed. Nothing. *What could this girl possibly want?* "All right."

"Why did you save me and my friends?"

"I saw you were in trouble, so I came to help you."

"With a ski mask? I can't even see your face now. You really are this

YEGman character, aren't you?"

"Let's say I am. What's in it for you? I can tell you want something. That's why you came here tonight."

"Well, yeah. Look, whatever reason you have for taking the law into your own hands, I am all for it. If anything, I'd like to help."

"Help? Kid, this shit is too dangerous."

"I've been through enough that I can handle myself. You're not alone in this."

I squinted. "Excuse me?"

"I mean, you're not the only one who thinks the city needs help." Lola looked to the ground. "I run an online news site. A blog. It's super underground and just starting up, but I want to give people the real news. Like you want to give the city real justice. I've been doing articles on the Snapper and Crystal Moths."

"That's good kid, I can respect that. The news has never been in my good books, but I really don't need your help. It'd be putting you at risk."

"I don't mind. That's what a reporter does," Lola said.

"Can you just tell me the address?" I asked.

"Only if I go with you."

I couldn't help but laugh. "Are you serious?"

Lola stood straight up and took a deep breath.

This punk is serious, I thought as I stared at the girl. Bits of snow began to build up on both of us while we looked at one another—not losing eye contact. The girl's legs shook slightly as a brisk wind picked up. I remained motionless. Patrolling the streets made me immune to this type of weather. It was cold, but I could suck it up.

"That's the only way you get to know," Lola stated.

"You want to come so you can report it on your website?" I asked.

"Yes. That's it." Lola looked back toward the streets. "I'll be honest: I did have someone else come here too. But I can tell them to go, to show you can trust me."

"No," I said.

"What?"

"It's too risky. Just give me the address."

"No. Either I join or you don't get to know where Alex G. lives."

She isn't going to budge.

"It'll help you. What you did in that viral video was amazing. What you did for my friends was amazing." Lola's voice shook slightly from the cold, but she continued. "The people need to know what you do. You bring hope. I can be your voice online—get the real story out there. There's tons of kids my age who are online but don't read the news. Think of it, we can warn them about the Crystal Moths and other shit that the news doesn't get out quick enough."

I stroked my chin with my arms still folded. *The girl has a point.* I liked her stance on free information. It was oddly similar to the free justice I've adopted. It's not like I'm very good with the internet anyway. She could be helpful.

"I don't know who you are or why you do what you do, but if my hunch is right I can really help you out," Lola said.

"What if you get caught?" I asked.

"What do you mean?"

"With your site—your blog thing. Say we were to work together and you get some real dirt that the cops don't even get. They'll come for you, which puts me at risk."

"I've got an online alias, plus my IP bounces through Russia."

"What?"

"It means my online activity points to somewhere overseas. I can't be traced."

The two of us stood motionless for several moments. The girl kept her gaze on me, shivering but still standing straight. I could tell she wasn't going to back off. If I decided to work with her, it could really be beneficial for the city.

But for how long? I thought. My goal of busting the Crystal Moths was clear, but what then? *I suppose I'm overthinking this. Act, don't think.*

"All right," I finally said.

"Yes?" Lola asked.

"Yeah, you can come with me."

A wide smile filled Lola's face. "Okay, great. When are we going?"

"Now."

Lola swallowed and nodded. "Okay. I can do that." She pulled her hands from her pockets, bringing a cellphone out. She began to tap the screen, typing something.

"What are you doing?"

"Telling my friend I'm okay," Lola said.

I looked around again. It was hard to tell who her friend was. There was a bus stop across the street where several people stood, but they didn't pay any attention to the two of us. Now that I was working with this girl, I couldn't let her get close enough to learn my identity. Thankfully, I brought my ski mask with me.

I reached into my back pocket and grabbed the mask, quickly putting it over my head while keeping the hood over my skull as much as possible to hide my head. I pulled the mask down and adjusted the eye-slits so I could see the girl in front of me. She was still typing on her phone.

"You ready to go?" I asked.

"Yeah. Just give me a second."

"Text as we go. Where to?"

"Give me a sec," Lola repeated, sighing. Her phone buzzed a couple of times and she swiped it, bringing it to her ear. I could hear another girl yelling on the other end, but I was too far away to make out what she was saying.

Lola raised her other hand and shook her head. "No, look it's fine . . . I got this. It's fine . . . It's *fine*. Bubs, seriously . . . After. . . . Yeah, I brought that up . . . Yeah, that's why we're going. . . Yeah . . . Yeah. Check on Brian, please . . . Yeah, I will. Don't go out tonight . . . It's not safe right now . . . Yeah . . . I know what I'm doing isn't— . . . Okay . . . I love you too, Bubs." Lola hung up the phone and shook her head.

"We good?" I asked.

"Yes. So the apartment is on the west side of downtown." Lola stepped back, keeping her eyes on me.

I walked forward while placing my hands in my pockets. "All right. Lead the way."

"We're staying on Jasper Ave, though, until we have to turn."

"That's fine." I moved into the light, exposing my ski-mask-covered face.

Lola stared at me, her eyes moving back and forth trying to analyze me as I stepped to her side. She kept walking west. From that close, I could see that she's actually quite young. She can't be older than twenty-four. It was pretty ballsy for her to approach me in the park alone—or she was slightly crazy like me. Either way, it could work to my advantage.

We crossed the street and continued down Jasper Ave, taking large strides forward. We were both cold and I could tell she was still nervous—her hands were back in her pockets. She was also about a person's length away from me. Too far away for arm's reach.

Lola broke the silence and spoke. "I never said thank you."

"Sorry?"

"For saving my friends. Thank you. It could have ended horribly."

"You're welcome. I hope your friend is recovering." A part of me felt ashamed that I had to lie to the girl, especially now that she was helping me. But I knew I couldn't let her know that I used her friends as bait. I'd lose my opportunity to find Alex G.

"Thanks. He'll recover. I've been with him all day."

"He's lucky to have you," I said.

Lola sighed. "That's what I thought. But who knows."

I almost wanted to ask the girl about what she meant, but I didn't want to

YEGMAN BY KONN LAVERY

know much about her personal life. The less we got to know each other, the better. I didn't want to expose my identity and didn't want to know hers. I was there on a mission, not to talk about some kid's boy problems. The sooner we got to Alex G.'s apartment, the sooner I could move on. Who knew, maybe the girl would get freaked out and she'd back off.

"So, what are you exactly looking for at the apartment?" Lola asked.

"Answers," I replied.

"To?"

I looked over at her to see her staring right back. "To see who Alex G. is to the Crystal Moths. Who's his boss? Then I can go from there."

"Yeah, they are pretty mysterious. They just kind of showed up."

"I know. No one knows who they are. That's what I need to find out."

The two of us kept on the main drag of Jasper Ave, walking west for a good half hour. Thankfully, our power walking made the hike a lot shorter than what it would have been. We passed a number of major bars near my old patrol area. I still miss being with Ace on the town, cleaning up the nightlife, but I can't get stuck in the past. This is what I am now.

Ace has moved on. He's got a new partner. I looked down to Lola who still kept a safe distance from me as we moved past large crowds of people smoking. *As do I.*

The two of us hiked down to the far west side of Jasper Ave, to 122nd Street. Lola turned north by a donair shop. Overall, that end of downtown is clean—a lot of condos and affordable apartments for people that want to be close to the action.

"It's just up here," Lola said, pointing ahead. "Just a couple blocks."

"I'm familiar with this area."

"You live around here?"

"No, I just spent time here." *Time with Ace.*

"Great, well the place is Hillside Manor." Lola continued into the residential area. Large trees covered the majority of the sky. The streetlights covered the scene with a warm yellow hue. Most of the apartments around there are only two to three levels, all with flat roofs and complete with side panelling or stucco.

A few apartments down, Lola stopped and pointed to the complex in front of us.

"That's it. He's in 203."

I nodded and began to walk around the building. "Good."

"The front entrance is that way." Lola pointed back while following me.

"I know. I want to get a good look at this building. Do you know exactly which unit it was?"

Lola shrugged. "I don't know. I wasn't really paying attention. It's probably facing the alley."

I picked up my pace and walked down the sidewalk, taking a turn into the alley. My footprints pressed into fresh snow—we were the first ones to go down there this evening. My eyes scanned the alleyway for any activity. It was empty and dark. The apartment windows were mostly lit up from the back end. The balconies were empty, and curtains covered the windows making it impossible to see who was inside the building.

There isn't much to see here, I thought, staring at the windows. My ears rang, even through the soft whooshes of cars driving in the distance. It was a quiet street—at least at about one in the morning.

"Anything?" Lola asked, stopping beside me.

"No. We'll go through the front." There was no way I could leap up to the second-floor balcony. Maybe skilled acrobats could. Besides, once I got up there, chances were that the balcony was locked.

"You're just going to buzz him? I don't think he'll let you in."

"Neither do I." I looked down at Lola. "You said you've been here?"

"Yeah."

"Well, looks like you were right. I can use you." I turned and marched toward the front of the building.

Lola nodded, gathering what I was implying.

If Alex G. was home, he wouldn't be able to resist Lola calling. At least I knew where he lived. Even if tonight was a loss, I could come back.

Lola and I made it back around to the front of the building. I opened the front door first, allowing Lola to step into the lobby. She went up to the intercom and started pressing the metal buttons. The intercom speaker crackled before ringing. It rang for a moment, then some static noise picked up and a voice spoke.

"Hello?" a male said.

"Hey," Lola replied.

"Who the fuck is this?"

"It's Becky's friend. The girl from last weekend. Is this you, Alex?"

Becky. That name. It rang a bell. But then again, it is a common name.

Several seconds went by with no response. Lola looked up at me and bit her lip.

I glanced back outside, then to the hallway behind the door. No one was there. The last thing I wanted was one of the Crystal Moths spying on us during the silence.

The lock on the door clicked and the buzzer rang.

Lola smiled at me, her eyes filled with excitement.

"Stay behind me." I opened the door and stepped into the narrow hall. The floor creaked as my boots moved across the carpet. Slowly, I walked up the flight of stairs leading to the second level, keeping my eyes focused on the hall. All the doors were shut. Muffled voices could be heard from some of the doors.

The sounds became clearer to identify as I moved past each individual door, walking slowly through the hallway.

201, I thought, reading the black letters on the door. The sound of music could be heard. It was softened, but loud enough to make out the guitars and drums. Some people talking could also be heard chit chatting.

202. No sound came from that unit.

203. I stopped just before making it to the door to avoid the peephole. I turned and waved Lola to go ahead.

Lola paused momentarily then took a step forward, removing her hands from her pockets. This time she held a small switchblade.

She's more prepared than I am, I thought as I pressed myself against the wall.

The girl stepped toward the door and knocked. It immediately swung open and Lola stepped back, keeping her hands cupped, hiding the knife.

"Hi," she said. "Is Alex G. here?"

"Maybe. What are you offering him?" Tattoo-covered arms reached out into the doorway, the wrists resting against each side of the frame—the man was in a casual stance.

Easy to lock down.

"He wanted to see—" Before Lola could finish her sentence, I rushed forward to the face the man and grabbed hold of his left arm. With one tug, I yanked the thin man forward, head-butting him in the nose. The slam caused his nose to crinkle and blood squirted out as I turned the dazed man around with both hands, keeping a firm grip on his left arm. I continued to twist it, forcing it to move against the joint

"If you move or make any sudden noise, I break it," I growled at him, gradually pulling his arm further back.

The man grunted and closed his eyes. "What do you want?" he said.

"You alone?" I asked.

The man remained silent.

I nodded at Lola who stared incredulously. "In," I said. With a swift nudge, I forced the man inside. Lola followed behind. "Close the door. Quiet," I ordered.

Lola swung the door shut, catching it before it slammed.

The man tried to break free from my grasp, so I twisted his arm further, causing him to let out a cry of pain.

"I'm warning you!" I snarled.

"YEGman," Lola said.

"What?" I turned to face the girl to see her eyeing the man's belt. Looking down, I could see he had a gun tucked into the back of his pants. Taking a criminal's gun was high risk. Who knows what the man had done with it, and I didn't need my fingerprints on it. Then again, nothing I was doing was risk free.

"Grab it," I ordered.

Lola stepped forward cautiously and then quickly snagged the gun from his belt. She held the barrel of the gun with both hands. From what I could tell, it was only a Glock.

"Careful with it," I said before leaning to the man's ear. "I'll ask again: are you alone?"

The man exhaled heavily through his nose. It was hard to judge if he truly was alone or not. I couldn't take any chances. I'd be better off to scout the perimeter and determine what we had to deal with.

"All right, so the silent game. Down." I yanked his arm downward, forcing the man to collapse onto his knees. I pushed him closer to the wall. Letting go of him with one hand, I snagged the gun from Lola's hand.

The man attempted to squirm away from my one-handed grasp. No luck. He was much smaller and didn't quite have the upper-body strength to match me.

I tightened my grip on the handle of the gun and, with one swift blow, knocked him on the top of his noggin.

"Jesus," Lola muttered, stepping back.

The man's head wobbled a bit, and he tumbled onto the floor.

I examined the gun to see if it was cocked and to check the bullet count. *Check, check, and full.* Holding it with both hands, I kept the weapon close to my chest. My shoulder faced forward and I walked on an angle to reduce exposure of any critical parts of my torso.

"Lola, stay close. Knife out," I whispered.

Lola brought out her knife and flipped the blade open, her hands shaking. "Fuck," she muttered.

She probably isn't used to this kind of an adrenaline rush, I thought. It was no surprise. I figured she was bluffing when she said she had been through stuff—like most people you encounter. All talk and nothing to back it up.

I carefully walked inward from the entryway, keeping the gun pointed ahead and ready to shoot. I felt my muscles tense from the stress. The last time I'd held a gun, I shot Alex G. and got myself kicked off the force.

I suppose I don't have to hesitate this time. Just don't get shot, I thought, glancing down the right corner into the open hall. It split two ways: straight ahead led into the living room. The right turn led deeper into the suite. The kitchen was the first turn in the hall, to the left. At the far end on the right was a bedroom. Before that, two closed doors—presumably the bathroom and another room. The bedroom lights were off, and the door was open. There were no lights visible underneath the closed doors.

The sound of a TV came from the living room—a drama of some kind. No other voices could be heard.

Never assume, I thought. The whole apartment had to be searched.

I turned right, heading into the kitchen. Like common suite layouts, the kitchen was directly behind the living room. It would provide some shelter if anyone was to open fire.

The kitchen had white tile, dark wooden cabinets, and a white countertop with chrome trim. Dishes were in the sink with a couple of knives and over a dozen empty bottles on the counter. At the end of the kitchen was the small dining room. A black table had a chrome scale and a box of plastic bags on it along with a couple of chairs tucked in.

Mostly common things. If they were hiding anything of importance, it would be kept somewhere a little less obvious. Taking a quick glance behind me, I saw Lola was still there. She looked behind to see if there was anyone behind her. Not a trace.

The two of us continued, walking past the sink and to the edge of the wall just before the turn into the living room. Each step I took, I felt my heart pumping blood throughout my system. It was that old patrol rush again. It felt good.

Go. I took a deep breath and stepped forward. Using the wall as a shield, I pointed the gun into the living room. The TV flickered as the show switched between scenes. A part of the couch was visible. To the right was the sliding door to the balcony, curtains closed. No one was there.

I kept my shoulder to the wall as I leaned forward to peek into the rest of the room. There was a black coffee table where a plate rested with a credit card and a small pile of white powder. At the far end of the room were a couple of lounge chairs. The room was clear.

"We're good," I whispered to Lola as I stepped back into the kitchen, going back to the hall where the other rooms were.

Lola followed close beside me as I squeezed by her, returning to my cautionary stance. Turning down into the hall, I kept my pace consistent and my footsteps quiet while approaching the first door. My eyes were locked on the empty bedroom, abandoning the idea of going for the closed doors. Opening them would just give my position away.

I looked back at Lola and raised my hand at her, palm forward.

She stopped at the doorway of the kitchen. The girl peeked back into the entryway to check the unconscious Crystal Moth. From my angle, I could see his still, tattooed arms on the ground and his head facing the wall. He was out cold.

I continued down the hall leading to the bedroom, keeping close to the wall. I was using the doorway as a shield. It was difficult to see inside without lighting, but it appeared empty.

Let's do this. I inhaled again and stepped into the bedroom, quickly checking both sides of the entrance. Nothing. I spotted the light switch and I turned it on, exposing the full scene. Two glass tables lined the walls with chairs at each one. Papers littered the first table, and the second had several piles of cash, more papers, and folders. The closet to the far right was open and had some hockey bags on the ground. Nothing was on the walls and there was no other furniture.

They keep it tidy, I thought sarcastically and checked behind the open door: clear.

It was a good bet nobody was there—that was probably why the Crystal Moth was quiet to begin with. I took a step closer to the table with the most papers. There were a number of business cards scattered across the surface. Most of them were medical offices.

Nice to see they care so much about their health. There were a couple of medical illustrations of the human body, complete with arrows, legends, and descriptions of the organs. There were four posters in total, each illustration focusing on a portion of the body: the pelvis, the lower and upper ribs, and the heart. They were on tabloid-sized paper and had sticky notes attached to them with chicken-scratch handwriting. One stack of paper caught my attention: it was a spreadsheet of doctor names, phone numbers, and notes. The notes column had handwritten comments on each one such as:

Name, Phone, Notes

Dr. Lang, 780.223.4453, Lung transplants

Dr. Williams, 780.440.0032, Kidneys

"What the hell," I mumbled.

A creak from the hall broke the silence. I spun around, holding the gun up, and hurried to the doorway. Lola had opened one of the doors. The other door on the left was open: simply a storage closet filled with rugged boxes.

She looked over at me and gasped. "Christ! It's me!"

I lowered my gun and sighed. "Kid, I said stay put."

"Sorry. They're both empty, though," Lola said, taking off her hood.

I tucked the gun into the back of my pants and nodded. "Good to know."

Lola relaxed her stance when she saw the tension in my shoulders lessen. "Not bad, kid," I said.

We do make a good team, I thought. *Who knows, depending on how this Crystal Moths case goes, maybe I'll keep at this.*

Lola brushed her hair aside. "So no Alex G. What now?"

"Well, that bedroom wasn't set up for sleeping and only opened more questions."

"What's in there?"

I waved my hand for Lola to follow and she came into the room with me. She paused once we'd reached the middle of the space. She examined the tables closer to look at the medical-related papers.

"What is this?" Lola asked, pulling out her cellphone. She started the camera software and began taking pictures.

"Don't take any of me," I said, walking over to the closet.

"I won't. I just want some of this for the blog."

"Right." I leaned down to the sports bags and pulled over the closest one. It was oddly heavy for a hockey bag, and the weight seemed centralized. I unzipped the top to see there were a couple of black leather roll-up storage bags with chrome handles sticking out. These types of containers were usually used to sheath knives.

I took one out, unbuttoned the snap holding it together, and unrolled it flat on the floor. There were a range of pockets, each one fit for the size of the chrome blade it held. I took one of the blades out to examine it—it was smaller, and the blade was square. Surgical tools.

A part of me was worried about leaving fingerprints on the tools—or any of the things in the apartment. But I had a hunch that the police weren't going to have anything to do with this place. Judging from the minimal amount of furniture and documents, this was an operational base and could disappear at any moment. Who knows, now that Lola and I busted in, they might shut down the shop.

That Crystal Moth I knocked out could rat us out to Alex G.

"They have a list of doctor names," Lola said, looking over to me.

I nodded and waved the knife at her. "And surgical tools."

"This isn't for drugs, is it?"

"No." I stood, putting the knife in my back pocket. "Let's ask our friend." I marched back toward the knocked-out Crystal Moth.

Lola followed close behind me until the two of us reached the front entryway. The Crystal Moth groaned and tried to crawl forward as I approached him. He was still disoriented and there was some blood on the floor, oozing from his head.

"I've seen that guy before," Lola said, folding her arms.

"Yeah?"

"He was here last time I was at this place."

I grabbed the man by the collar of his shirt and dragged him down the hall and into the bedroom. His feet skidded along the ground. Holding him upward from the back of his neck with one hand, he was forced to stand up. I held his arm with the other hand, shaking him. "What is this?"

He groaned again, his free hand up in the air, shaking. "Look, I just watch this place, man."

"Bullshit!" I forced him toward the table and slammed his head down onto the glass. The man's face slid on the table, against some of the papers. A mixture of blood and saliva soaked into the pulp.

I leaned closer to his ear and asked in a harsh tone, "What are the Crystal Moths really doing?"

"Go," the man said, swallowing a thick lump of saliva.

I squeezed the back of his neck, pressing him further into the table.

"Go fuck yourself," he said.

I felt a surge of fury course through my body. The same rage that I would have had to suppress while on duty. Now, I didn't have to put up with that kind of shit.

"Wrong answer," I said, lifting the man back up and forcefully slamming his face down onto the glass. I let go of his arm with my other hand and clutched his skull, lifting him again.

"All right!"

Without giving him a moment to say any more, I slammed his face back down onto the table. It was probably an act of instinct—or maybe I just didn't hear him. Either way, it felt good to push him into the glass one more time. This time it caused the glass to crack.

"YEGman!" Lola called out.

I looked back at the girl who stood by the entrance, mouth wide open. "He was about to talk. We're going to make too much noise."

The man grunted and tried to get up again, his arms squirming on the table. "All right," he muttered through the pressure of my force and the glass.

I turned to face the man and spun him around, putting my forearm against his neck, holding on to the collar of his shirt. My free hand held the surgical tool in my back pocket. "Start talking."

"YEGman," Lola said softly.

The man shook his head. "Fuck, all right. Alex G. had me watch this place. Three of us usually rotate shifts while the rest go out and recruit or sell some of our supplies."

Lola walked up beside me, hugging her arms tightly. "That's why they throw parties here."

The Crystal Moth nodded. "Yeah, you were there. Come on, it's harmless. Just let me go."

I tightened my grip on his collar. "What is this place?"

"It's a base for us to operate from. I swear that's all I know."

"Really? You don't know who Alex G. works for?"

"No!"

"What about this?" I pulled the surgical tool from my pocket and brought it to his eyes, directing the blade toward him.

"Fucking Christ!" The guy tried to back up from the blade, but he was as far back as he could go.

Lola stepped back from me.

"What is this?" I asked again.

"I don't know what this shit is!"

"So you just follow Alex G. without question? No clue what he does? No idea why this room has a list of doctors or medical illustrations?"

"Yes! I mean, no! I know about the drugs and the recruiting. It's what we do."

"You don't know what this room is for?"

"It's new. Alex G. brought some of this shit in the other week. We used to use this room to package the goods—divide it up into smaller sizes. You know? Simple shit." The man exhaled nervously, sweat pouring down his face. "It's what I signed up for. I don't know anything else."

"Where is Alex G. right now?"

"Probably out selling or finding new blood."

"Where?" I brought the knife to his cheek as his head shook rapidly.

"I don't know," he whined.

"Don't test me." I lightly pressed the blade onto his skin.

"All right! They're on the north side of downtown. There's a club that opened up behind the university. The Melting Pot Lounge or something."

Lola stroked her neck, clutching the skin. "I know that place. A lot of people I know go there. The Crystal Moths have been showing up in the goth scene recently."

I nodded. "Good. What time is it? Bars are closing soon."

Lola checked her phone and shook her head. "We got under an hour. Last call is at two."

"I swear, that's all I know." The man's eyebrows were slanted, mouth open as he stared at me—he was consumed by fear. It was amusing to see how a man behaved differently when you wore the uniform and when you didn't. The Crystal Moths always acted so tough. Not now.

The freedom of not being bound by the law or the uniform makes me a wildcard. It's why this Crystal Moth was about to shit his pants. Rightfully so. He had no idea who the masked man with a blade to his face was. He had no idea what I was going to do to him. I had no idea what I was going to do with him.

Act, don't think. He's seen us, I thought.

"Let me go, man. I swear I won't tell anyone about this." The man held his hands in the air.

"YEGman, please," Lola whimpered. "We got what we needed."

"He knows your face," I said, applying slight pressure to the man's cheek, puncturing the skin.

"No! No! I don't. I've never fucking seen her in my life!"

"That's not what you said earlier."

"I was bullshitting. I swear I've never seen either of you. This never happened."

"Funny how easily you told us where Alex G. is. You know, for a Crystal Moth, you're more of a rat."

"I'm not, I didn't see nothing."

"YEGman," Lola whined again.

What the hell am I doing? I thought. This was all crazy. I used to be a police officer and now I was slicing open a man's cheek with surgical tools to interrogate him. *Isn't this why I'm doing this? Getting real answers? For the city, not for the law?*

"I didn't see nothing," the man said again.

"No." I nodded and exhaled. "Dead men don't."

"No—!" Before the man could talk, I slashed the blade down on his face, causing him to yelp. The attack was followed by a slice across his neck, splitting the skin apart. His blood seeped out from his neck and poured down his throat, staining his shirt. The surgical blade was so sharp, there were no rough edges on the entry wound and no spraying of red liquid. I removed my forearm quickly to keep the blood from seeping onto my jacket.

"Oh my God!" Lola covered her mouth and stepped further back.

The man grabbed his neck as he gurgled, sliding off the table and collapsing to the ground. He landed shoulder first and rolled onto his back, half under the table. The blood continued to pour out his wounds as he choked a couple times until his body went limp. The liquid oozed down onto the carpet and began to soak into the fabric.

I turned to Lola and pointed at her with the blade. "He saw you."

"You didn't have to fucking kill him! What type of hero does that?" Tears began to seep down her eyes.

"I'm not a hero, dammit! Just because some viral video online portrayed me as this do-gooder, doesn't make it a reality." I wiped the blade on the edge of the table and placed the blade back into my pocket. "I'm giving back to the city. Giving it justice."

"You're insane." Lola wiped her eyes.

"Killing some lowlife gang member who preys off the weak and vulnerable makes me insane?" I shook my head. "No, if anything this should be seen as

YEGMAN BY KONN LAVERY

vengeance for your friend who got stabbed. What has the law done for him?"

Lola hugged herself and exhaled heavily.

"I told you this was dangerous. You can leave now and not have to deal with this."

"No." She shook her head and looked to the ground. "I'm not leaving. I just need a smoke."

JOHN

#YEGman

Chapter 15
FAST BEAT JOINT

A cigarette lit the dim alleyway as the flame from the lighter pressed against the tip of the paper. My rough hands held the steel shaft of the lighter tightly as my fingers flicked the clamp shut, placing it back into my leather coat. Smoking is a bad habit, no ifs, ands, or buts about it. After my week, though, who really cares?

One moment you're alive and breathing then the next you're gone. At least, that's how it was for that Crystal Moth I killed. A part of me thinks I should feel bad, but I really don't. Why should I? What I did was necessary. Not only was he a sack of shit, he also knew who Lola was, and he was a snitch. Snitches never last long on the streets anyway. They'll speak to anyone to save their own skin. I couldn't trust him.

"How many have you killed?" came the soft voice of Lola who stood beside me in the snowy alleyway, arms folded against her fishnet top that was under the several layers of unzipped hoodies. Her makeup had mostly run off due to the snow and her crying. She held a cigarette in the one hand while staring at the only open light a couple of buildings down.

The subtle sound of a bass track could be heard from the direction of the light. Several people were outside having a smoke and chatting loudly. They wore leather jackets, studded denim, and combat boots. They were in all black clothing, no white—scene kids.

I shrugged, thinking about the girl's question. "Not that many. Maybe five, including the last guy." I kept the smoke pressed between my lips as I spoke, folding my arms. My eyes scanned the damp alleyway as the light snow fell into the pools of water and drizzled over the dumpster beside me.

"You seem so okay with it." Lola took a drag from her smoke.

"You know why I did it, right?" I asked.

"Yeah, I do. You were protecting me and my friend."

"Yes. He preyed off people like you and would have caused you grief."

Lola shook her head. "It's just the way you did it. It was disturbing."

I couldn't help but chuckle. "Is there a nice way to kill someone?"

"You were so . . . angry."

I paused for a moment while watching a couple of the scene kids go back through the rear entrance of the building they were beside. Lola and I had rushed over to the north side of downtown, only about a fifteen-minute walk to the club known as The Melting Pot Lounge—the club that Alex G. was supposedly at. Lola was about to go in and scout out the scene after her smoke.

We had left the corpse in the apartment. It'd be a nice message to the next Crystal Moth that walked in there. It wasn't like the gang would call the cops.

I was ready to keep pursuing the pricks, but I could tell Lola was still shaken up by the death in the apartment. Someone in shock isn't exactly useful when you need them to execute a task. If Alex G. was there, Lola could lure him out.

I turned to look at the girl, whose face was expressionless. "Anger is an emotion we all experience."

"Are you always this mad?" she asked.

"Let me tell you something, Lola. Each person has their own degree of how anger affects them. They choose how to project it. Some find it easier to bottle it all in and not express anger, while some openly release it."

Lola brushed her hair from her face. "Okay, and where do you fit into that spectrum?"

I couldn't help but smirk. Her question was one I still ask myself. "I'm not sure. I don't think there is a right way to handle your anger. Internalizing it is self-damaging, and expressing it is destructive. It's one of those funny emotions that seems to have no right answer. Yet it moves the world. It is how people change. It is how people are motivated."

Lola looked to the ground. "You really think about this a lot. What do you do when you're not being Edmonton's masked hero?"

"I don't have much else to think about or do, really. That's why I'm out here hunting down the Crystal Moths."

"What about when you're done?"

"Sorry?"

"Like, let's say you manage to shut them down. What then?"

"Well, I've been thinking about too. The Snapper is at large, and there are always more freaks out there."

Lola stroked her hair. "Yeah. Well, I'm willing to help. I can share the news on the blog—get the word out. Maybe we can cut down on all the violence."

I took the smoke from my mouth and pointed to the nearby glass skyscrapers south of us. "You and I might just be crazy enough to make a change. All the violence has turned Edmonton from a place that I once knew and loved into a scum-infested concrete jungle. The streets are littered with the poor and the street urchins while the businesses continue to capitalize on people's weaknesses, making them ignore those in need. So, to answer your original question, that is what fuels my anger."

"Street urchins?" Lola asked.

"Never mind," I said.

"Well, your method is getting the people's attention. Even if it is questionable at times."

"It sickens me. I have to go to these lengths to get any sort of real results. Trust me. I tried the legal way before."

"Were you a lawyer?"

"Not quite."

Lola smiled. "You were a cop. That actually makes a lot of sense now."

"What does?"

She looked up at me. "You. Everything about you. Not sure why I didn't see it before. Maybe I was in shock from the day before."

"What clued you in?"

"You got that cop stance and way of talking to people. It's like you're constantly interviewing them."

I shrugged. "Well, you know a bit about me now. Not all cops are like that though."

"I know, just the abusive ones."

"Well, it got me kicked off the force."

"So what, you're picking up where the law fails?" Lola squinted. "You killed those two men."

"Both were Crystal Moths, and both of the kills were to save your ass, if you recall. Personally, I've never been able to find the healthiest way to express my anger. It's always gotten the better of me. I really wish that it didn't, but there isn't anything I can do. All my life, I've had this issue, and I've never found a way to counter it. In a way, I'm part of the anger and violence that's wrong with this city."

"That's not true." Lola gently touched my arm. "You don't give into it all the time."

The sudden sense of affection startled me. The only people to show me physical touch are my mom and Ace. A gentle touch from a woman is something I hadn't felt for way too long, minus that club girl at The Glowing Monkey. But this was different. Lola was learning parts of me that I haven't talked about to anyone. She's a pretty girl too—nice smile and gentle voice.

She's twenty, I thought. *Stay focused.* I shifted my stance and shrugged her hand off. "Apparently."

"Guess that makes you a fight-fire-with-fire kind of guy." Lola began to play with her hair.

I finished the rest of my smoke and extinguished it with a press against the dumpster before dropping it into the bin. "I'll tell you how long I've had these issues. Then I need you to scope out the club before it closes."

Lola nodded. "Just let me text my friend. She's been sending me texts ever since you and I left together." She pulled out her phone and swiped the screen to start typing. "Okay, go on."

I extended my hand and looked out at the skyscrapers. "Well, I can recall the burning anger all the way back to when I was in high school."

"So what, a couple centuries ago?" Lola smirked.

"I'm not that old, smart ass. I think the anger was really ignited then because of the teenage hormones. I got to admit, seeing the freedom and the power that you can have when channelling your anger is . . . addictive."

I can clearly recall outwardly expressing my rage while I was in line at a fast food joint. It was near year-end finals and I was stressed beyond anything that I'd known before. I clenched my hands tightly, not knowing if I would even pass grade ten. It was a sickening thought, especially being at the high-standard school I was at. I was easy pickings for the jocks and the preps when they wanted a good laugh. Plus, if I didn't pass the grade, my dad would simply have another reason to beat me. It was his favourite pastime. It really didn't matter what I did. He would always smack me around. Damn drunk.

"What will be your order?" came the cashier's chirpy voice.

I looked up into her blue eyes as she smiled at me. She had to be no older than eighteen, wearing the black-and-blue fast-food uniform. I couldn't quite grasp why she was being so smiley, working at a dead-end job like a burger joint. Who was I to judge, though? I was just some crummy high school kid covered in zits from the stress over his math finals.

"I'll have a cheeseburger and a medium fries," I said, moving my hands from my backpack straps onto the counter.

At that moment, the restaurant's front door flung open with a swift boot as three teenage boys entered, laughing and joking with one another. My stomach tightened at the sight of them. I knew the three. They were the preppy pricks that got a hard-on every time they roughed me up.

Unfortunately, the burger joint was close to the school and was a quick solution when you were too lazy to make a lunch. Laziness was a common trait shared among us teenagers, so you ran into classmates in the restaurant frequently—whether you liked them or not.

"That will be seven fifty," the girl said.

I turned back to her and nodded. "Yeah." I reached into my wallet and pulled out a ten-dollar bill. Just as I extended my hand, someone bumped me from behind. The blow knocked my hand directly into the cashier's left boob.

"Watch your hands, perv," came a chuckling masculine voice from behind.

"I'm sorry," I muttered to the girl.

She smiled and shook her head while taking the cash.

I turned around to see three boys standing behind me. The one in the middle was the closest. Craig was his name. He wore a pink polo shirt and kept his short blonde hair arched to the side. He looked like he came out of a Disney movie.

"Sup, Noodle Dick?" Craig folded his arms. "Good thing you're getting something to eat—maybe put some meat on those pipe cleaners."

"Or you too much of a pussy to pump some guns?" peeped the boy to the left. He brushed his black combed-over hair out of his eyes and smirked at me.

Noodle Dick happened to be the nickname that the three boys had given me. They were in grade eleven and had been the primary bullies that I dealt with all school year. It was tough being at Landon High because all the friends I had in junior high went to other, more-promising schools like Jasper Place High School. My folks weren't exactly rich and my grades weren't the best, so we had to make do with what we had. It unfortunately left me to fend for myself. I didn't do a good job at making friends in high school. I never had much in common with the other kids who enjoyed video games, movies, and sports. I was more into history at the time.

"He probably can't even get it up," the shaggy-haired guy on the right said.

Craig shook his head. "Not like it would matter, Chris. What girl in her right mind would fuck him? He's keeping that V-card."

I felt my nostrils flare up as I turned back to the cashier, putting on a closed smile.

"Here's your change," the girl said, placing it in my hand and stepping away from the till to fill the order. She clearly couldn't care less.

"That boob shot is probably the most action he's had all semester," Chris said.

"Yo. Grab my order. I gotta take a piss," said the boy on the left. He walked over to the restrooms.

"Stand aside, Noodle Dick," Craig demanded. He pushed me to the side, looking up at the menu items.

Chris also came up beside me and nudged me out of the way.

"Cut it out," I finally said.

Craig turned over to look at me with a scowl. "What did you just say?"

I took a deep swallow, realizing I should have kept silent—be submissive and go through the rest of the day peacefully. However, all the pent-up stress from finals caused me to slip up.

Cowering back, I said, "Nothing."

Craig nodded. "That's what I thought."

Chris shook his head. "Pussy."

"Assholes," I said under my breath.

Craig slammed his hands on the counter before rushing over to me. He was a good head-and-a-half taller. "You got something you want to say?"

My heart skipped a beat. *Oh no*, I thought, backing up toward the seating area of the near-empty restaurant.

Craig pushed me with both his hands. "Huh? What you got to say?"

"Nothing," I said, stopping in my tracks to avoid tumbling over the chairs.

"You trying to mess with me? You said something. So why don't you just get it out of your system?"

Chris laughed and folded his arms while watching Craig jab me with his finger.

"No, I'm fine. Look, I just want my burger and I'll get out of here. I got a lot on my mind right now."

"Aw, poor Noodle Dick." Craig laughed and looked back at Chris. "Did you hear that? He's having a bad day." Craig's eyebrows slanted back sarcastically, and he leaned down to my level. "It must be tough having a flaccid penis all the time. Is that why your dad beats you?"

The words sparked an intense sensation of energy that flooded my entire body. Craig's statement about my father hit a nerve—like a tower of Jenga that had one too many blocks stacked. My patience had fallen. That eleventh grader was about to get a taste of the collapse.

"Shut"—I shouted, clenching my fist—"the fuck *up*!" I hurtled the fist straight into Craig's nose. His face flew back in a dazed look of shock as my knuckles collided with his cartilage, crushing it inward and causing blood to ooze down his nose. I used my other hand to grab hold of his hair. Clutching it tightly, I turned to the side and chucked his face into the metal backing of the chair behind me. His face hit it with a loud thud.

"Hey!" Chris shouted, running toward me.

I lifted Craig's head up and slammed his face into the metal again before dropping him to the floor. With one swift kick to his mouth, I turned to face Chris. Quickly, I launched my backpack from around my shoulders at him. He caught the bag instantly.

It was enough of a distraction for me to charge forward and kick his shins. The blow made him yelp, and he dropped the backpack. I coiled my hand again and swung it at his face, smashing him dead centre.

I went in for a second one. This time, Chris tried to block it, but he was dazed enough from the two previous blows to keep him from raising his arms quickly enough. My attack hit him in the face, this one throwing him to the ground.

A scream came from behind the cashier till, and I looked over to see the blue-eyed girl drop my order to the floor causing the burger and fries to splatter on the ground. She stared at me in horror.

"Someone call 911!" she called out.

The bathroom door opened, and the third boy stared at me in awe. "What the fuck?"

At that moment, I knew I was in some big trouble—and I was. The third bully didn't do shit. He was in shock at what I had done. My mother and father had to pick me up from the police station and both Craig's and Chris's parents wanted to press charges against me. Thankfully, the parents were able to talk it out and nothing came of it—minus my father giving me a swift beating that night. On the bright side, that little stunt did cause my folks to completely overlook the low grades I got on the finals. I guess you can't win everything.

Lola's jaw dropped as her eyes moved back and forth, scanning my face. "So you've always been a badass at fighting?" she asked.

I laughed. "That's the most positive response I've gotten from that story. I was quite captivated by what I was able to do with that amount of anger. It was like a corkscrew popping, and the champagne was my anger. It was addictive."

Lola took her phone from her pocket and checked the screen before putting it back into her pocket.

"What is it?" I asked.

"Normally she's quick at responding. Anyways, go on."

"That's it," I said.

"So I got a question. Is the freedom you get from releasing anger why you do what you do? Even why you became a cop? Is it more of a personal agenda than for the greater good?"

I shrugged. "Good question. I don't know. I became a cop to do what was right, but that didn't pan out. I fucked up too many times. I know in my heart I'm doing this for what is right. But I enjoyed giving Craig and Chris what they deserved. They had it coming for the way they had treated me before. It was actually the first time I was able to stand up for myself. I enjoyed making them suffer."

Lola fiddled with her hair. "Schadenfreude."

"Sorry?"

"It's the German word for enjoying the pain of others."

The two of us stood in the snow for several moments. Lola kept her gaze on me as I stared at the ground. I appreciated her questions. They were things I had thought about too.

"You know, I think you'll make a fine reporter," I said. "You have the intuition."

Lola looked to the ground. "Thank you."

"Go on into the club. They'll be closing pretty shortly here," I ordered. "We got to get moving."

"Yeah, I'll be quick." She stepped forward to leave as a buzz came from her pocket. She stopped in her tracks and pulled out her phone, reading the message. "The fuck?"

I stepped closer to look at the phone. It was open to the text messaging app, where in the last speech bubble was a map. A second text soon appeared: *Come get her*.

"Fuck. That's not Becky," Lola muttered. She looked up at me then back at the phone.

"Let me see." I snagged the phone from her hand to look at the map. There was a pin icon on a street not far from Chinatown. I didn't know you could send maps through text messages, but technology moves faster than my own ability to keep up.

"That's not Becky." Lola brought her hands to her mouth. "That's not Becky. Fuck."

"You know where this is?" I asked, handing her phone back.

"No, but it's in Chinatown somewhere. Shit." Lola pulled her hair. "Becky doesn't talk like that." Lola pressed a button on the phone. "I'll call her."

We waited a moment while the phone rang. It rang twice before a voice came on the other line. "You know where she is." The voice was raspy—male.

"Don't fucking touch her!" Lola screamed.

The phone beeped, and Lola slowly lowered it from her face.

Damn it. "Do you recognize the voice?"

"I don't know, she . . . she also has a bit of a coke problem. She knows a lot of dirtbags, but she doesn't have many enemies. Everyone loves Becky Bubs."

I folded my arms. "They might be trying to get to you."

"Who?" Lola asked.

"The Crystal Moths. Alex G. You know too much."

Lola brought the phone to her lip. "Becky had one of the Crystal Moths' number. I told her to stay with Brian!" Lola turned around to face the dumpster as she began to sob.

If it was Alex G., chances are he wants to get revenge on Lola. Or to find out who I am, since I intervened with their attempt to murder Lola's friends.

Or the apartment, I thought. One of the Crystal Moths might have tried to get in contact with the shithead I killed. But there wasn't enough time for them to do that, was there? Either way, it doesn't change the fact that Becky is in trouble.

"We'll get her," I said.

"How?" Lola cried, turning to face me. Her lips trembled. "I dragged

Becky into this. It's my fault."

I grabbed the girl by her shoulders. "Keep it together. If your friend has a drug problem, the Crystal Moths would have gotten to her either way. It's what they do."

"Fuck." Lola collapsed into my arms and began to cry.

I patted her on the back lightly, unsure how I was supposed to behave—again, inexperience with human contact makes trying to comfort a girl very difficult. I wrapped my arms around her while keeping my gaze at the club up ahead. No new people were out back. It was just the two of us.

"It's my fault. I should have been with her."

I hushed her and rubbed her back a couple of times. "We'll get to her."

"What about the cops? Should we call them?"

"That's what they'll expect you to do. We're better off taking this into our own hands. They won't see me coming." I turned back down the alley away from the nightclub, making Lola move with me. "Let's end this."

Chapter 16
A Tale of Love

The engine of the vehicle hummed as its tires splashed through the ever-increasing slush of snow that sprinkled over the downtown scenery. The windshield wipers moved against the glass at an even stride, wiping off the melting snow as it hit the windshield. The plastic shielding that divided the driver from the back seat was scratched and covered in smudges—the cabby probably didn't clean the interior much. Paper bags and candy wrappers littered the floor of the vehicle.

These were small details of a larger scenario that I was involved in. It was near impossible for me not notice these tidbits all the time. It's why I was good at my job, minus all the violence. Those details were beside the point. At the moment, I was trying to figure out how Lola and I were going to handle the hostage situation that awaited us.

Lola's friend, Becky, was most likely in heat with the Crystal Moths and was being used as bait to lure in Lola. It was an educated guess. Becky and Lola knew too much, and I had a hunch it made the gang uncomfortable. They don't like loose ends. It's why they've always been difficult for the police to track down. It is why they kill their recruits if they make a mistake.

We grabbed a cab to get to Chinatown. It was the quickest way there. I would have preferred to go on foot, but the distance was too great. Who knew how much time we had to save Becky. I moved the surgical knife I had into my front pocket so I wouldn't slice my own ass sitting down. I left the gun tucked into my belt, and it pushed into my back as I sat. My ski mask stayed over my face. I'm sure it looked suspicious to the cabby, but he's probably seen a lot of weird shit at this time of night.

Lola hugged her arms and leaned against me. I kept my arm around the girl to provide her with some form of comfort. Wrapping your arm around someone is a sign of empathy, right?

The two of us remained silent for the ride. The cabby couldn't hear what we were about to do—no one needed to hear that information. We had to use stealth if we were going to have a shot at saving the girl.

We instructed the cab driver to take us a block up from where the text message instructed. The ride was only about 10 minutes. Traffic was light, and the cabs were hungry to take people places. On foot, we probably would have been walking for a good half hour or so.

The cab took a right, turning off the avenue and down the main street of Chinatown. It was obvious from the red archway directly above the street—a signature structure in the community, complete with yellow text on green signage at the highest point of the arch. The English portion of the sign reads *Gate of Happy Arrival*.

Such a happy night, I thought as I pointed to the right side of the road. "Here's good," I said to the cabby.

The cab driver pulled over to the side of the street, just behind a parked

SUV.

"I don't have any cash," I mumbled to Lola.

"Yeah, hold on." She reached into her purse and pulled out a twenty and a five, handing them over to the cabby whose open hand peeked from behind the protective shield. "Keep the change."

The cabby nodded, not saying a word, and put the cash into his pocket.

We got out through Lola's side of the car, leading to the sidewalk. The cab turned back onto the road once the door was shut. The sidewalk was empty except for the two of us.

"Okay. What are going to do?" Lola said looking down the street. "The address is right down here."

"It's probably a restaurant. I'm familiar with the area," I said.

"So we're just going to barge into the restaurant and demand for Becky?"

I waved for Lola to follow me as I began to walk. "No. I've been thinking about this on our ride over. You'll go in alone. I'll come in from the alleyway."

"What if they kill me or take me away from here? We have no way of staying in touch."

"No. But you got a better idea?"

Lola raised her index finger. "Wait, do you have a phone? Like a normal person?"

I was hesitant to respond. I really didn't want to give her my number. It tied right back to my identity. "Why?" I asked.

"Say we go through with your plan—we can stay on call. These fuckers will assume I'm alone and you can hear what's going on."

"And where are you going to hide your phone?" I asked as we crossed the street onto the next block.

Lola brushed her hair from her face, pulling on it tightly. Her eyes closed, still walking—clearly, she was trying to think of something. "I'll stick it in my boot."

"You don't think they'll see that?" I asked, keeping my eyes on the stores up ahead. The buildings were all dark.

"On the backside of my leg. It's all black anyways. It's really all I got. How else are we going to stay in touch?"

The idea was ridiculous. It was a makeshift wiretapping concept that was too conspicuous. Lola was right, though. We didn't have a lot of options.

"You better keep it hidden from their view," I ordered.

"Obviously. I'll keep it on speakerphone. It should amplify the sound so you can hear where I am."

"Good. I'll keep mine muted," I said before stopping in my tracks. A couple of buildings ahead was a single store with its lights on. The curtains over the windows made the light subtle. The sign was off but was easy enough to read from the street lights: *Lang Chinese Cuisine*.

Lang. Either a common name or I'm connecting dots here, I thought.

Lola looked at her phone and then up at the building. "That's it. Looks like it was a restaurant after all." She looked up at me, her eyes wide and nostrils flaring—she was nervous, and rightfully so.

"What's your digits?" she asked.

"You're going to be okay to do this?" I asked.

Lola kept eye contact with me. "Yeah. I have to be."

I found it hard to believe her, considering how she reacted when I killed the Crystal Moth. How could I know she wasn't going to fuck it all up? Maybe she'd prove me wrong and keep her cool now that her friend's life was in danger.

"Okay. My cell is 780.237.5437," I said while pulling out my phone.

Lola punched in the numbers on her touch screen and hit dial.

My phone screen lit up. No buzzing. I wasn't a fool and had it on silent. I swiped it and answered. "Hey." I brought the phone down and pressed the mute button before bringing it back up to my ear.

Lola brought hers up to her ear. "Hey."

Her voice came through clearly. "Good. Let's test this."

Lola pressed her speakerphone button. She looked down at her phone and began swiping on it for several moments.

I looked up and down the street to see if anyone was nearby. All clear. Looking back at the girl, I saw she was still swiping around on her phone. "What are you doing?"

"Just checking my battery life," she said then leaned down and tucked the phone into the back of her boot. She flipped the phone upside down, screen facing outward.

Bringing the phone back up to my ear, I could hear the ruffling of the phone rubbing against her boot. "Okay, walk around a bit," I said to her. As I spoke, I heard the subtle sound of myself talking through the phone, followed by the ambiance of the wind and the downtown noise being picked up by the microphone.

Lola took a few steps backward, away from the Lang Chinese Cuisine, then walked forward.

The steps she took were far louder than hearing my own voice, as was to be expected. I pressed the side volume button, bringing it down to a bare minimum—just enough so I could hear her stepping if I brought it up to my ear.

"How's this? Can you hear me talking?" Lola said, stopping beside me.

I heard her subtly through the phone. It wasn't enough, though. I bumped up the volume a couple of notches.

"Okay, that's as good as this will get." I locked the screen and put my phone in my front pocket.

Lola let out a deep breath and closed her eyes. "Okay."

I turned to face her and put my hands on her shoulders. "Stay calm. Remember, the story is you're going in alone. You have no backup."

Lola nodded. "I am so fucking scared." She laughed nervously. "That part, I don't have to fake. Okay. Get into this, Lola. Come on."

"Remember, act naive."

"Yeah."

"You have no idea what's going on, so you're here to bargain with them. While you're playing the part, I'll go around back—find another entrance. If I can't, I'll come back around through the front. This could get messy. Stay on your guard."

"Yeah." Lola nodded several times. "Let's do this."

Without any more words, we split ways. Lola marched toward the restaurant and I hurried back to the block we came down. I figured I'd be able to circle around the alleyway. Before turning the corner, I stopped to watch Lola reach the doorway of the restaurant. She pulled on the handle of the door. It didn't move.

She tried again and then knocked on the door. A second later, it swung open and an arm wearing a white blazer appeared. A spiky-haired head peeked out, looking at Lola.

The phone, I thought, taking it out of my pocket and turning the corner so I was out of sight from the Crystal Moth. I brought the phone to my ear. The sound was still too quiet, so I turned up the volume slightly. The sound of the wind was loudest, but I could hear Lola talking.

"I got the text," she said.

"Good. Get in," said the man.

We're on, I thought as I rushed down the sidewalk. I kept the phone to my ear while hurrying down to the alleyway. My eyes scanned the streets to see if anyone was around. The side road was dead quiet. It didn't even have any lights, making it exceptionally dark.

The sound of Lola walking was nearly all I could hear from the phone, but I heard the door shut behind her followed by a click. They probably locked it.

This better get me in, I thought. If it didn't, Lola was fucked.

"This way," came the man's voice.

Lola's footsteps continued.

I turned the corner into the alleyway and slowed my pace. The restaurant wasn't that far off, and I had to be cautious in case anyone saw me. With my free hand, I took out the surgical blade. I held it lightly and tucked it into my sleeve, keeping it hidden from sight.

The alleyway was as dead as the street prior: no lights, no people, no cars.

The sound of Lola's footsteps stopped as a man's voice said, "Come . . . down . . . you . . . pretty . . . remember . . ." It was difficult to make out some of the words as Lola's boot muffled the noise. The image was a challenge to paint in my mind, but it sounded like she sat down. The sound of ruffling picked up again, drowning out all other noises for a moment.

I glanced back behind me. No one was there. Looking forward, I counted the buildings to where Lang Chinese Cuisine was. About four businesses down, I spotted the back entry—it was empty.

"You come alone?" came a man's Maritime voice, crystal clear, from the phone.

Alex G., I thought. Somehow Lola cleared the signal, making the conversation understandable. Sitting probably helped—maybe cross-legged.

"Yeah, I'm alone," Lola said, her voice noticeably louder than Alex G.'s.

"Good. So you want your friend back, huh?" Alex G. asked.

"Yeah, where is she? Is she okay?" Lola asked hastily.

Stay cool, Lola, I thought as I reached the back of the restaurant. There was a dumpster off to the far side, some graffiti on the white-painted brick walls, and a brown industrial door.

"Yeah, she's fine. Why would I drag you all the way here if she wasn't?" Alex G. asked.

"Is she here?" Lola asked.

"She is," Alex G. said.

"Please, just let her go. I'm here now," Lola begged.

Alex G. chuckled. "Can't do that, doll."

As much as I wanted to hear the conversation, I had to act. If what Alex G. was saying was true, Becky had to be somewhere in the restaurant. I put the phone in my front pocket and reached for the D-shaped door handle. I tugged on it but the door didn't move.

Shit. What do I do? I thought, taking a step back. I could try the front, but that would just draw unwanted attention to Lola. What other way could I get in?

The muffled sound of a man's voice came from inside the building, followed by the jingling of keys. The heavy sound of metal clanged—the door was unlocking.

I took a step to the side where the door swung to avoid being seen as it slowly creaked open.

This could be a lucky break.

"I'll be back in a second!" came a man's voice. He walked out into the open alleyway. The flame of a lighter lit his face as he brought the fire to a cigarette he held in his mouth.

The door slowly inched back to its closed position. As it glided, I caught the full view of the spiky-haired man sporting a white coat. He was the man from the front.

His break too. I tightened my grip on the surgical blade, waiting for the door to close. It was dumb luck that he wanted a smoke after letting Lola in.

The man stared out into the alley. The door finished sliding and clicked as it closed, leaving the two of us outside. He put his lighter into his pocket and took a puff of the smoke before grabbing it with his hand.

Now, I thought, rushing forward. I wrapped my free hand around his chest and brought the surgical blade to his neck.

"Say a word and I slice open your throat," I growled.

The man slowly raised his hands, keeping silent.

"Good," I said. "Is the door still unlocked?"

"Yeah."

"Thanks, asshole." I lashed the surgical blade away from the man's throat, tearing his neck open and letting him go.

The man gurgled as he turned around, clutching his neck in an attempt to stop the bleeding while he fell to his knees.

I put the blade back into my front pocket and pulled the gun from the back of my belt, turning to open the door. As he said, it was unlocked. I flung it open, held the gun close to my chest, and stepped into the building.

He was talking to someone. I had my guard up, ready to fire at any moment.

The hall itself was dark. At the end of the hall were the same warm lights that projected from the front of the restaurant. There were a couple of closed doors on each side of the hall. Directly to my right was an L-shaped staircase leading to the lower level. A light shined up the staircase. No one else was in the hall. Whoever the Crystal Moth was talking to had either moved downstairs or into the restaurant.

I pressed my hand to the door as it closed, aiding it to shut gracefully. Once it finished closing with a subtle click, I turned forward. My first guess was that Becky was downstairs. I had to check up on Lola first—make sure that she was still stalling Alex G.

Slowly, I pulled the phone from my pocket, keeping my gaze down the hall. Bringing the phone to my ear, I heard Lola's boots stomping and shouting.

"Please just let us go!" Lola cried.

"You'll get to see your slut," Alex G. shouted back. "Keep moving," he said.

It was odd to me that I couldn't hear them from the restaurant, considering how loud they were. Several sets of footsteps could be heard through the phone, followed by heavy echoes. It didn't sound like they were outside. There was no wind and the steps were too reverberated. They were still in the building.

Downstairs, I thought. There had to be a second stairway to the basement. *Here we go.* I took a deep breath before putting the phone into my pocket and slowly taking the first step down the stairs. I held on to my gun closely so it wouldn't stick out when I turned the corner. The stairs continued to go down for another good ten steps or so. With each step I took, I saw a little more of the empty concrete floor with bright red walls. The hall had a black door off to my left. About twenty paces down, the hallway took a sharp turn left.

That's probably where the second stairwell is.

Reaching the bottom of the staircase, I heard a girl cursing followed by footsteps echoing.

"Please!" came the girl's cry.

Lola, I thought, taking a step forward.

"Put'er in here," came Alex G.'s unforgettable accent, followed by the rattling of a knob.

They aren't hurting her—yet. I picked up my pace. As I approached the door to my left, the sound of crying came from behind the wood, followed by a groan. The sounds were too generic to know if they were a man's or a woman's, but it was clear they were in distress.

Becky?

"I'll stay with her. You check on the others," Alex G. said.

Lola is fine for the moment, I thought, reaching down for the brass knob of the door. It twisted freely, and I pushed the door open, stepping into a dark room. Only the hallway lights provided a visual of five open freezers lined against the wall. Each had a naked human body inside. Their arms were chained together and hung up from the ceiling as they sat in a pile of ice, their lower halves buried in it. Each one had a ball gag strapped to their face and a blindfold around their eyes. Some of the ice cubes in the freezers were stained red where the bodies had freshly stitched scars. Blood caked around some of the cuts.

"My God . . ." I muttered as I took a step into the room. *What is this?*

The bodies breathed, indicating that they were still alive. All of them were males except for one female off at one end.

"Becky?" I whispered, rushing over to the woman. As I got closer, I could see that the lady had to be in her late forties—unlikely it was Becky. There were stitches that spread from one end of her torso to the other just below her rib cage.

They're taking organs, I thought.

Another groan came from one of the other freezers. I turned to look at the man at the other end of the row. He was scrawny, had shaggy hair, and couldn't be older than twenty. He had tears going down his face as he sobbed quietly. A long cut on the lower left of his body was stitched shut.

No . . . I thought as I approached the kid. *Can it be?* The hair, age, and frame of the boy were identical to the punk I roughed up in the parking lot.

"Hey," I whispered. With one hand, I lifted up his blindfold.

The kid's eyes went wide and he tried to scream through the ball gag.

I hushed him and shook my head. "I'm not with them. Shut up."

The kid continued to cry.

"Shut up, I'm here to help. Promise you'll be quiet, and I'll untie you."

The kid nodded then his gaze shifted over to the entrance, and he screamed.

I turned around to see a bald, brawny man with a goatee rushing toward me. He held a knife in his hand and thrust it forward.

"Shit!" I dashed to the side as the knife plunged into my right bicep.

The man pulled the knife free from my arm and went in for a second. He aimed the blade for my heart but hit my pectoral muscle just as I pulled the trigger of the gun, shooting him in the head. The bullet went in at an angle, entering through his cheekbone and exiting out the upper back of his skull. Particles of brain matter and blood splattered against the freezer and onto the kid, who continued to scream.

The Crystal Moth's grip on his knife loosened as he collapsed sideways onto the ground. The knife had only entered about a half inch into my chest, making the wound minuscule.

Fuck. A lucky shot, I thought, pulling the knife out of my chest. I groaned in pain, using my wounded arm to do the deed. My right arm ignited with heat from the open wound. It bled rapidly but wasn't enough to immobilize me.

Pain is just the system warning the brain, I reassured myself. Taking a deep breath, I thought, *they'll have heard that shot.* I got to my feet. There was no time to lose. I had to get to Lola, who was presumably alone with Alex G.

The kid continued to scream as I hurried out of the room.

"I'll be back!" I said while exiting the room, holding my gun forward.

Footsteps echoed from the hallway up ahead, getting increasingly louder.

"Shit." I hurried back into the room with the freezers, using the doorway as a shield. I peeked out only a bit so I could see the hall ahead.

Two men in white dress shirts and slacks rushed around the corner, both with handguns drawn. I hadn't seen those two before. There was no telling how many Crystal Moths were here. The two of them ran in a hurry—they hadn't seen me yet. The distance between the three of us was closing, and I had to act.

Breathe, aim, fire. I pointed directly for the closest Crystal Moth's heart. Pulling the trigger of my Glock, I fired. The bullet roared out of the chamber, hitting him directly where I aimed. The man was thrown backward from the blast, dropping his gun as he fell.

The second Crystal Moth opened fire. His aim was wild. He was unsure where my shot had come from—an amateur.

I fired again. The bullet soared through the air and pierced into the man's gut.

He cried in pain while attempting to limp backward in fear. He continued to fire, this time locking eyes with me. The Crystal Moth raised his arm and shouted, ready to fire.

I pulled the trigger a third time, aiming for his chest. The bullet hit him in his right lung before he had a chance to shoot. The impact threw him to the ground. He dropped his gun and landed with a heavy thud.

Hastily, I got up from my shielded position and rushed down the hall, passing the two dead men. My right arm began to feel numb as the blood dripped off my elbow and onto the ground. I was clearly in rough shape, but I had to press forward. My instinct was to call for backup and have another squad show up to help take this son-of-a-bitch down. In reality, though, I had no backup.

Call Ace, I thought. *No. I can't let him know me like this.* Calling Ace seemed like the reasonable thing to do. Stall the situation so no one else ends up dead. But if I did, it would open a whole can of worms with the police. Glenn of Major Crimes would be summoned, and I'd have to face the sergeant and any other officers I recognized. Embarrassment aside, I'd be cuffed, questioned, and probably put on trial for recklessly taking the law into my own hands. A first-class ticket to jail.

You've got this. Pain is only a warning. Keep on track. Four shots made, eleven free to put into Alex G., I thought, reaching the turn in the hallway. The hallway had two doors: one to the left and the other to the right. At the end of the hall was another L-shaped stairway leading up.

"Shut the fuck up!" came a masculine easterner's shout from one of the doors, followed by two girls crying. The sounds came from behind the wall to my left, making it clear which door to take. Taking an educated guess, it was Alex G., Lola, and her friend Becky.

"You're dead, you hear me! All of you!" the man, Alex G., shouted again. "If you want these cunts to live, back the fuck off!" A gun fired from inside the room, causing the girls to scream. "I'm not fucking around, asshole!"

I stopped by the door, lowered my gun, and took a deep breath.

How do I do this? If I barged in right then, I'd be risking the girls' lives. Alex G. most likely had one of them at gunpoint. If I reasoned with him, he could still shoot the girls. If I waited too long, he could call for backup and then it'd be over. I was bleeding out. Time was not on my side.

"You hear me?" Alex G. shouted again. "Acknowledge that you understand or I will cap one of your whores."

With my gun, I tapped the door twice. I didn't want to speak in case he got the bright idea to shoot the wall. Having my exact location remain unknown was to my advantage until I could formulate a plan.

Lola's phone? No, nothing I can do with that. It wasn't like I could just shoot wildly through the wall either. I could end up hitting one of the girls.

"Okay, good," Alex G. said. "So, this is how it's going to go down. I'm gonna let the girls go. You're gonna drop your gun and keep your back to the door. Tap if you understand."

This guy must think I'm an idiot, I thought.

"Fuck you!" Lola shouted. "The cops are on their way."

"Lola, shut up!" came another girl's voice—Becky.

Footsteps echoed in the room. "Shut your lying mouth up or I'll do it for you," Alex G. said.

Lola let out a guffaw. "Shoot me? You need us alive. It's all that's keeping YEGman from busting this door down and making you his bitch."

"YEGman? The fuck is that? I'll keep your mouth shut bitch—with this."

"With your size? Come on," Lola challenged.

"Fuck you!" Alex G. shouted, followed by the sound of beating flesh.

"Lola!" Becky cried.

"Try me!" Alex G. shouted again, followed by another beating.

Lola cried, "I already called the co—"

Several more punching sounds erupted, silencing her.

I took a deep breath in and shook my head. *This is my shot.* While he was distracted, I had to act. There might not be another chance. Lola was taking a heavy hitting.

With my wounded hand, I reached out for the handle of the door. *Pain is only in the mind.* Grabbing it, I took a deep breath, twisted, and flung the door open. Stepping into the room with my gun forward, I looked to the far-left side of the room where a girl with dreadlocks was tied to a chair with zip ties. The door covered the rest of the scene as gunshots erupted, blasting the wood away. A bullet grazed my shoulder, ripping the flesh open.

Ignoring the pain, I rushed past the door, keeping my aim to where the shot came from as wood splinters flew by my face. Pulling the trigger, I opened fire, shooting through the door. Stepping fully into the room, Alex G. came into view. He shielded himself behind Lola who sat in a chair just in front of him, beside Becky. Lola's arms were tied behind her back.

I fired again as Alex G. shot openly. It worried me as I fired that I would hit Lola, but I didn't have much of a choice. She was caught in the crossfire.

Several more bullets roared from Alex G.'s handgun. This time, a bullet pierced directly into my outer thigh, causing me to fall to my knees as I pulled the trigger a third time.

This bullet hit Alex G. directly in the jaw, throwing him back as he fired again. His bullet ripped straight through my chest, tearing through my innards and out my back.

Alex G. fired his gun one more time while collapsing. The bullet hit the wall nearby, causing drywall dust to rise from the bullet hole.

Becky cried and tried to squirm from her seat. "Lola!"

My vision blurred and the sound began to muffle as I stared at the two girls at the other end of the room.

Come on, it's not over, I thought, groaning. Looking down, I could see that the chest wound was just above my heart, below my clavicles. *Come on!* I grunted again and stood up. I had to free the girls—get them out of there.

"Lola!" Becky cried again.

I blinked twice while limping forward. The thigh wound had to have hit a major artery—I was losing movement from it. Even through the fresh wounds, I proceeded to hop forward. "I'm coming. Hang on," I muttered.

My vision cleared slightly, probably from the chemical rush my body was going through to battle the extreme pain. Using what strength I had, I hobbled over to the girls, collapsing on my knees in front of Lola. I dropped the gun and reached into my pocket for the surgical blade.

Lola looked up at me with a swollen face. Her nose was broken, and blood was oozing down past her chin and into her lap. "YEGman," she said in a nasally tone.

I swayed slightly while trying to keep my balance. "Hey." I swallowed heavily, scooting over to her side. Her arms were locked together with zip ties.

Glancing behind her, I spotted Alex G., whose jaw was half-blown off. He gurgled while laying on the floor—still alive, but not a threat.

"Come on." My voice shook. "You girls have to get out of here." I groaned, carefully bringing the blade to the straps and freeing Lola.

Lola stood herself up and spat blood onto the ground, wobbling slightly. She wiped her face with her hoodie, trying to stop the fluids from pouring. "We're all getting out of here. I'm not leaving you."

"You called the cops? I can't be seen like this," I said, lifting the handle of the blade to the girl.

Lola took it gently and hurried over to Becky. She stumbled to her knees next to Becky's chair. "I didn't. It was a bluff."

Carefully, I shifted myself to lean my good arm against the chair Lola was on, breathing heavily and staring at the ground. Each breath I took, I felt weaker. The blood was leaving my body quickly. My leg was wet with blood from the wound.

"Good job," I mumbled, looking up at the girl. Lola had sliced the last few straps that constrained Becky.

The girl got up to hug Lola, and the two embraced one another tightly. Lola looked over at me, blood still dripping from her chin. "We're getting you out of here." She nodded back at Alex G. "He was on his phone—he called someone."

"Fuck," I muttered. "You girls get out of here." My arm gave out and my face collapsed onto the chair.

"YEGman, no." I heard Lola run over to me and she stroked my head. "No, no, no. This isn't happening. I'll call 911—they'll get here before the Crystal Moths do."

"Police! Stay where you are!" came a grizzled voice from the entryway.

I mustered the strength to roll my head sideways, looking back to the doorway. A red-haired man in a white shirt and wool jacket had his gun out. He walked hastily toward the girls.

"Sergeant?" I mumbled. *How?*

Robert used his other hand to show his badge. "It's okay. You're safe now," he said.

"Please help him!" Becky pointed over to me. "He's dying."

The sergeant waved his gun from Lola to the ground. "Step away from him. He's dangerous."

Lola stayed by my side and hugged my head. "He saved us! He needs an ambulance."

The sergeant was under a metre away when he put his gun back into its holster. He leaned down and grabbed my Glock then checked the chamber and the bullet cartridge. He looked into my eyes before turning to face Lola. "He saved you?"

"Yes! That's what I was trying to tell you." Lola cried. "Please, we need an ambulance."

Robert stood up and put the gun into his back belt and eyed the rest of the room, examining the bullet holes in the wall, the door, and Alex G. behind us.

Becky walked over to Lola. "Can we please get out of here?"

Lola pointed back to Alex G. "Sir, he called for backup! I saw him! We got to do something."

"Yeah." He nodded a couple of times. "I know."

"What?" Lola asked, standing up.

The sergeant darted forward, grabbing hold of Becky. The girl squealed and tried to fend off the man. He was far stronger and more tactical, easily overpowering her. He held her in a choke hold and dragged her closer to me, twisting her neck aggressively, snapping it in the process.

"Becky!" Lola shouted, holding out the surgical blade. "You mother—"

Before Lola could finish her sentence, Robert pulled out the gun from behind his back, firing it at the girl in one fluent motion. The bullet threw Lola backward as blood spewed from the open wound in her back. The impact threw her back, and she dropped the blade and slammed onto the concrete.

"Shit," I mumbled, using my left arm to get up. I was too slow to react. The loss of blood made me far too woozy to do anything. I was useless. I could only watch the horrors unfold before me. *He snapped the girl's neck,* I thought as I lifted myself up.

The sound of Becky's body tumbling to the ground echoed as Robert yelled, "Fuck!"

I looked up at the man as my body shook. *Think of something. Where's Alex's gun?* My mind was moving faster than what my body was capable of doing.

"What a mess," the sergeant said as he looked down at me, the gun still in his hand. "Whoever you are, you've made this much easier to clean up." He walked over to me. Grabbing hold of my collar, he threw me off the chair. I landed on my back with a grunt.

Robert stood off to my side. "Are you the same asshole who has been getting all that attention on the news?" He leaned down to unravel my sweat-drenched mask. "Who is this mysterious vigilante?" He rolled up my ski mask, revealing my face.

Robert let out a laugh. "Holy shit! Michael?"

I coughed while trying to use my left hand to grab him. I snagged his ankle but was too weak to do anything else. "Why?" I managed to say.

Robert stood up and shook his head, sliding his leg away from me and leaving my hand to lay open on the concrete.

"Michael, Michael. Why?" Robert paced back and forth several times. "You were a good cop. Why the fuck did you have to go and get yourself involved in all of this? You could have walked away and lived a happy life!"

"You . . . her neck." I coughed. "Snapper . . ."

Robert walked back over to me and leaned down. He shook his head. "The Snapper? No. The Snapper is a bunch of horseshit. Something we made up to keep the news occupied."

"The murders?" I squinted, unsure if what I was hearing was real. *This has to be the blood loss.*

"Yeah, there were a few cases of necks being broken—most of them staged by the Crystal Moths. But as for a serial killer who breaks necks? Get real."

"Whuh?"

"We targeted the homeless because no one cares about them. It was a good distraction and got rid of some rubbies." He pointed the gun at me. "At least, that was before you snapped a neck outside The Glowing Monkey. Not like we knew who you were at the time, but Alex G. mentioned how he and his crew got their asses handed to them by some rogue hero in a ski mask. That's when I knew we could bring the Snapper to life. We could avoid our operation being unravelled. Well, before this fiasco."

"The freezers . . . sergeant . . ."

"I'm not your sergeant, Michael. I will admit I am pissed off that we have to shut down this location. Lang isn't going to be pleased." He waved the gun, pointing at the bodies throughout the room. "We'll set up shop again. This chapter closes with you as the Snapper."

"Robert." I coughed as my eyesight blurred, the sounds softening.

"No. It's over, Michael. When Alex G. called, I knew this location would have to close up with a staged scene. Alex G. was always a loose cannon. When Major Crimes get here, they'll discover you went on a rampage and killed that poor girl in your signature Snapper style." Robert folded his arms. "Yeah, you had a shootout with the Crystal Moths. You killed that fuckwad in the alley, rescuing this girl. You were obviously fixated on her with some deranged interpretation of love. It's why you rescued her and her friends outside The Glowing Monkey. The Crystal Moths kidnapped the girls to kill them. You killed her friend first because you were jealous. You wanted her all to yourself." He paused as I heard the sound of rubber snapping. "She lives. The media loves it when a pretty girl survives a tragic event."

"The . . . sh-tation won't buy . . . Ace . . . Glenn . . ."

Robert chuckled. "Really? You think everyone is just a good-hearted cop? I own Major Crimes. And your partner? He knew you were the violent type—he won't question it." The sound of scraping metal echoed through the room.

"Lola. She'll call your shit," I hissed.

"No she won't," Robert said as he stepped directly over top of me.

"She saw it . . . she'll ex-ose you." I clenched my teeth, trying to fight the pain.

"Let her try. She was in shock. Besides, you shot her."

"No." I tried to crawl away but lacked any strength to move.

"Yeah, the gun was in your hand. You shot her because she didn't love you back. It made you very mad." Robert leaned down beside me, holding the surgical blade. He wore blue cleaning gloves. "She tried to defend herself and fatally sliced your neck, and you bled to death. It's a shame. I liked you, Michael. You're like me, doing things your way. My way doesn't get me killed, though."

"No . . . Rob—" I cried, using all my might to lift myself up just as Robert sliced the blade against my neck down to my chest in a quick slash. I gurgled as my eyes shot open, coughing. My vision blackened, and my senses numbed. Sound faded and my heartbeat lightened as all thoughts I had dissolved.

The memories, the emotions—everything led to these final thoughts.

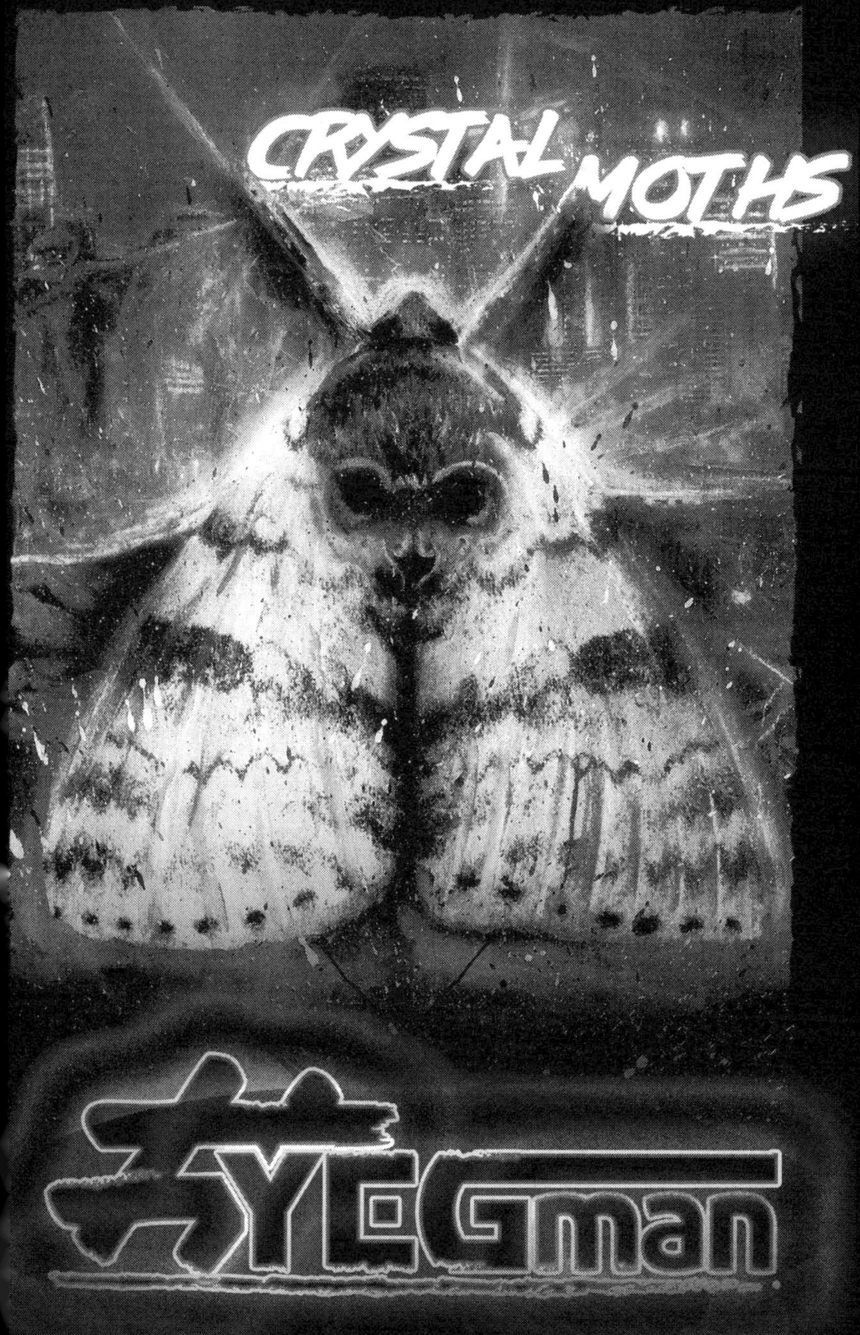
CRYSTAL MOTHS
YEGman

Chapter 17
IMMORTAL

"You sure you wanna do this?" came the nervous voice of the larger, long-haired, pale man. He sat on an old wooden chair in a small apartment bedroom. The room was covered in band posters. Black curtains covered the windows, leaving the room dark except for the slits of bright light that beamed through the edges of the curtains and the white glow from a laptop screen on a glass desk.

He looked over to the girl who sat beside him on a cheap office chair.

The girl pulled her blue-streaked hair and let out a heavy sigh as she stared at the laptop screen. She looked over at him and said, "Yeah, Donnie, I am."

He shook his head. "Lola, you're looking for serious trouble."

"I know. That is why I wanted you here." She hugged her arms and said, "You're always the voice of reason."

"Like I was about Brian?" Donnie smirked.

Lola couldn't help but return the smirk. "Yes, smartass. I'm done with him anyways. Seriously, though, there's nothing else I can do with this story. It's not like I can take it to the police."

"Take it to Mayor Chard."

Lola shook her head. "No, he might be a part of this. The sergeant is. Who else has their fingers in this operation? And I won't take it to a provincial level. I really don't trust this will go anywhere there. The fastest and most effective way to get results is to get this into the hands of the people. They'll eat this up once it's online."

"Got a point there."

Lola looked back at the screen. It had an internet browser window open, displaying her blog's back-end dashboard where she managed the website and added new posts. She had a new blog page open. Currently, the article was saved as a draft. The cursor was near the blue button that said Publish, one click away from making her story live.

Donnie pointed at the screen. "Remember, soon as you publish this, you'll be known to the whole world. The copy, the photos, and the audio say it all. You were right there when the sergeant confessed. Think about it, you've withheld evidence—for months. That isn't taken lightly."

"I know, but I needed time to process it all." Lola grabbed the white business card with the moth silhouette from the table. It was the card Donnie gave her.

"Then there's that card. Ever call the number?" Donnie asked.

"No, not yet," Lola replied.

"That's more evidence you held back."

Lola knew Donnie was right. Clicking the button on the laptop would create a whole series of problems just waiting to happen. Months. Lola clenched her fists, recalling the dreadful night like it was yesterday.

"I'm just warning you—as your friend. This is opening a can of worms that scares the shit out of me. I don't know why you want to do it this way."

Lola turned to look at him dead in the eye. "I can't just let this go untold. It's not just about busting the sergeant and that fucked-up organ-extraction operation they had. It's about justice for Becky. She got caught in the middle of all this, and I can't let my closest friend go down without even trying to do something about it." Lola's voice trembled.

Donnie looked to the ground. "Yeah."

"And Michael." She extended her hand to Donnie. "Come on, you saw how the news exploded over the scene after the police exposed YEGman to be Michael, the infamous Snapper and a former police officer. It's insane. Think of everyone who knew and looked up him. His friends, his family— they all think he was a lunatic. Yes, this is going to explode like wildfire and it might burn me with it, but this isn't about me and my safety." She swallowed heavily. "Becky needs her vengeance. They're going to pay."

Donnie nodded. "No, I get it. It's just crazy." He squinted. "How did you know to record it on your phone?"

Lola shrugged. "Michael and I decided to try and keep in contact with each other with our phones on call when I went into the restaurant. Alex G. was expecting me to be alone. I guess my reporter intuition kicked in and I set the phone to record the call. I didn't tell Michael—he was already irritated with my constant use of my phone that night."

"The police didn't confiscate your phone?"

"They did." Lola gently rubbed her arm and her shoulder flared up as she did—it was still sore from the bullet wound. "After the sergeant killed Michael, he left the room and I ended the call. I uploaded the MP3 to my cloud storage—chewed the fuck out of my mobile data, but it was worth it. After that, I deleted the recording and everything else from that night before putting the phone back into my boot. Then I waited there for the sergeant. He showed up with the police and ambulance a little later."

"You just lay there with all those bodies?"

"Yeah, I couldn't really absorb what had just happened. I needed to process it."

Donnie gently patted her back. "I'm sorry."

"It's okay, Donnie. This will make it right. Then I'll know Becky and Michael didn't die in vain."

"How'd you meet YEGman anyway?"

Lola let out a deep breath. "I only knew Michael for a day. He found me at The Glowing Monkey with Brian and Robby. He wanted to meet me to find out where Alex G. lived. When we met, I was super nervous—Becky came with me to watch if anything weird happened. When I started talking to Michael, it felt like we understood each other. You know how you meet someone and it just clicks?"

Donnie nodded. "Yeah."

"He had problems with how the justice system handled things, and I had troubles with how the media presented stories. Turns out we were both right, and he took the fall for us. His truth needs to be exposed."

Donnie folded his arms. "What you did was metal as fuck."

Lola smirked. "Thanks, Donnie."

He smiled back. "So? We doing this?"

Lola nodded and leaned closer to the laptop, bringing out her finger to press the trackpad. "Let's rain havoc on these pricks."

THANK YOU FOR READING YEGMAN, WOULD YOU CONSIDER GIVING IT A REVIEW?

Reviewing an author's book on primary book sites such as Amazon, Kobo and Goodreads drastically help authors promote their novels and it becomes a case study for them when pursuing new endeavors. A review can be as short as a couple of sentences or up to several paragraphs, it's up to you. Links to reviewing YEGman can be found below:

AMAZON
https://www.amazon.com/Konn-Lavery/e/B008VL8HQE/

KOBO
https://www.kobo.com/ca/en/search?query=Konn%20Laveryr

GOODREADS
https://www.goodreads.com/author/show/6510659.Konn_Lavery

ADDITIONAL WORK BY KONN LAVERY
MENTAL DAMNATION DARK FANTASY NOVEL SERIES
SEED ME HORROR NOVEL

S.O.S. - YEGMAN NOVEL SOUNDTRACK
WORLD MOTHER: SEED ME NOVEL SCORE.

Find the YEGman Novel Soundtrack (S.O.S), Mental Damnation series, Seed Me and the World Mother: Seed Me Novel Score at www.konnlavery.com

ABOUT THE AUTHOR

Konn Lavery is a Canadian horror, thriller and fantasy writer who is known for his Mental Damnation series. The second book, Dream, reached the Edmonton Journal's top five selling fictional books list. He started writing fantasy stories at a very young age while being home schooled. It wasn't until graduating college that he began professionally pursuing his work with his first release, Reality. Since then he has continued to write works of fiction, expanding his interest in the horror, thriller and fantasy genres.

His literary work is done in the long hours of the night. By day, Konn runs his own graphic design and website development business under the title Reveal Design (www.revealdesign.ca). These skills have been transcribed into the formatting and artwork found within his publications supporting his fascination of transmedia storytelling.

Made in the USA
Columbia, SC
11 March 2018